FIVE ACRE HILL

Also by PAUL COREY

THE RED TRACTOR

FIVE ACRE HILL

BY

PAUL COREY

ILLUSTRATED BY JAMES MACDONALD

WILLIAM MORROW & COMPANY · NEW YORK

For
Persis *and* Padraic Burns

CONTENTS

FIVE ACRE HILL

CHAPTER ONE

SPRING FEVER

WITH one quick glance back down Delaware Street Jon Woodward turned in at Number 1524, taking the four steps to the porch in a bound. Then he paused, his strap-held schoolbooks dangling from his hand.

The March wind, unseasonably mild, blew gustily along the line of squeezed-together houses and whipped Jon's unruly sandy hair. Again he glanced back across the postage-stamp lawns in front of the houses, his gray eyes anxious. His stocky, fifteen-year-old body seemed to shrink up in his tan finger-length coat, but the emptiness of the street reassured him: he wasn't being followed. He ducked quickly into the house.

"Phyllis, is that you?" came his mother's clear voice from the kitchen.

"It's me, Moms." He swung his books to the stairway step and slid out of his coat. His round face lost some of its worried expression as he walked briskly through the big living room and dining room and into the kitchen.

"You're never home before Phyllis," said his mother. "What's the matter?" She looked around from the gleaming work-space of the chromium-trimmed kitchen unit, while her slender fingers went on swiftly paring apples

I

for a fruit salad. Her red print apron over her blue
afternoon dress gave a dash of color to the immaculate
kitchen.

"Nothin's the matter, Moms." Jon didn't meet her
questioning blue eyes, but pecked a kiss at the soft round
cheek she tilted up, and snitched a slice of apple.

She slapped at his darting hand but missed. "You!"
she scolded. "You!"

"Is there anything to eat, Moms?" His strong white
teeth munched the white meat of the apple.

"You can wait until dinner."

His quick tug untied the strings of her apron.

"Jon Woodward, you're a pain!" She swung the flat
of her hand at him again, but he ducked away. "Can't
you find anything to do except torment your mother?"

Jon slouched against the edge of the kitchen sink and
made no further attempt to tease her. His eyes clouded
with worry again. The picture of a driverless ice-cream
truck starting to roll down Seneca Street had flashed
into his thoughts. In an attempt to hide this memory,
he fixed his attention upon his mother working at the
table.

She looked as if she liked to do what she was doing.
His forehead crinkled. That was something he'd noticed
recently—just since their last cook had gone to work in
a factory and they'd been unable to replace her. Moms
hadn't made a fuss about doing her own cooking the
way Mrs. Holland and Mrs. Loren and Mrs. Curtis and
the others in her set had. "Put the money in bonds for
Phyllis's and Jon's college education," she'd said to Dad.

And Jon knew that his mother disliked having Mrs.
Hannigan come to the house every Friday to clean. "I

always have to do half of the work over after she's gone," Moms complained regularly. She preferred doing her own housework.

Jon's glance shifted to his distorted reflection in a bit of curved chromium, then away to the clock, dials and buttons of the electric range. His mother enjoyed what she was doing and that seemed to annoy him. He slammed noisily out of the kitchen and down to the shop his father and he had fixed up in the basement. But once downstairs he resumed his slouching posture, this time against the bench.

The gate-legged table his father had been working on in the evenings held his attention. Dad got a kick out of making things like that. Before his eyes the unfinished table seemed to change to the driverless ice-cream truck starting down Seneca Street toward the business section of New Delphi.

He looked frantically away. To escape this nagging memory he tried to define the way he felt: like a seed or something that's all soaked up by the spring rains and all hot from the spring sun, but can't break out of its shell. It wanted to start growing and couldn't. Yes, sir, that was how he felt. Spring fever, he guessed, was what was wrong with him. He wanted something. He wanted to do something that counted.

Dreamily he gazed out of the narrow basement window across the tiny back lawn between the house and garage. There was one scrawny tree—he'd never known or cared what kind of a tree it was; it didn't seem like a natural tree out there, flanked by two lawn chairs facing a cement birdbath.

His eyelids pinched. If he could just take the ax and

cut down that tree he felt that all the knots inside him would be broken. If he could just make himself felt upon something, then he'd break the hard shell that held him. His shoulders jerked irritably. Mr. Jones, the landlord, would blow his top if he touched that tree. But what else could a fellow do around a place like this that would mean something?

The answer didn't come and he gave up the search for it. He looked up at the neat tool rack of saws, chisels, mallets, hammers, planes, bits, drills—his dad and he had a pretty complete set of tools. There was something satisfying in that thought.

His idly moving hand brushed his latest airplane model. Indifferently he picked it up and examined the wings and fuselage. Holding the model with thumb and finger, he put it through banks and dives. For just an instant he felt as if he were escaping his shell, breaking free at last. Then his glance lifted to the dozen or more plane models hanging from the ceiling—all the latest types. He sagged against the workbench—old stuff. Boredom crushed him.

The sound of footsteps on the front porch tightened him like a spring. He stared, eyes gleaming fearfully, toward the basement door; his breath remained choked in his throat. He heard the door open upstairs and realized that Phyllis, his older sister, had arrived home.

A sheepish grin spread over his face. He relaxed like a taut spring suddenly let loose. After all, he assured himself, he had nothing to be afraid of. He hadn't done anything. He'd just been loafing along with Ted Carlson behind the other fellows. It was Pickles Malone who did it. He'd seen Pickles open the truck door and release

the brake. All the fellows had scrammed out of there the instant they realized what Pickles had done. No one waited to see what happened.

The question struck Jon bluntly now: "What had happened afterwards?"

He didn't know. The fact seemed to irritate him. He poised the plane he'd been holding and hurled it with all his strength across the basement. It glided swiftly, easily, and crashed into the opposite wall, the "green-house" crumpling, one wing breaking off; then it fell to the floor, hours of patient, careful work reduced to splintered wreckage in a wink. He stared at it without a twinge of regret, and without a backward glance he climbed the stairs and entered the living room where his sister sat in their father's big chair beneath the bridge lamp reading the evening paper.

"Hi-yuh, Phil. How'd you make the hill?"

"Oh, stop that jive talk! I'm sick of hearing it all day." She didn't bother to look up from the paper.

Jon walked around the room restlessly, hands in his pockets. He wanted to blow off steam. The desire to do something grew inside him until he thought he couldn't stand the pressure an instant longer.

The dead ashes in the fireplace attracted his attention: he'd start the fire. But he dismissed the idea at once and sauntered on past the big maroon davenport facing the hearth. Swinging past the radio, he snapped it on, then snapped it off before the tubes warmed up. He ran a finger along the backs of a row of books on the corner shelves. The next time around the room his attention focused on his sister's bright red fingernails and he snatched the newspaper away from her.

"You pest!" She sprang up, her blue eyes blazing, her hands clawing at him.

He grabbed her arms. She tried to pull free and he tried to get both of her wrists in the grasp of one hand so that he could tickle her with the other. Her long, curled bob whipped along her shoulders as she struggled frantically.

"I'll kick your shins!" she panted, her round face flaming with anger and exertion.

"You do and I'll tickle you silly," he threatened. His eyes gleamed with the same reckless expression that had been in them when he flung his model plane across the workroom a few minutes ago.

Their mother came resolutely through the dining room. "Stop it! Stop it, you two! Stop it this minute!" She marched into the living room and the two youngsters separated instantly. "Jon, what's got into you lately? You're getting to be an impossible torment."

"Aw, Moms, I wasn't doing anything." His voice pleaded, but his eyes still sparkled with mischief.

"Doing nothing!" Phyllis tossed her head indignantly. "Breaking my arms is nothing, I suppose." She rubbed her strong wrists vigorously.

"I'll be glad when Van Buren High can get an athletic director who'll work off the surplus pep of you youngsters," stormed their mother. "You're enough to drive a person frantic. Jon, I'm going to report you to your father when he gets home." She walked to the wide front window of the room. "He's out talking with Patrolman O'Donnel now."

Phyllis joined her. She was almost as tall as her mother. The two looked through the tan net curtains, over the white porch railing, the postage-stamp lawn and the box hedge to the stocky man in gray topcoat and gray Homburg talking to the blue-uniformed policeman.

Mr. Woodward slowly shook his squarish head from side to side as if considering a very serious problem, while the patrolman talked, snapping his night-stick flippity-flip on the loop of its leather thong. Then Bob Woodward stopped shaking his head and said something. For a moment both were silent is if pondering, then they saluted, separated, and Bob Woodward came springily up the walk and up the steps to the front door beneath the white fanlight.

Mrs. Woodward and Phyllis turned immediately to the wide archway opening off the living room to meet him, and both noticed at once that Jon was gone. He had quietly disappeared. They heard a door close upstairs just as Bob Woodward breezed into the entrance-way of the house.

"Well, this is wonderful," he exclaimed in a ringing voice, his vigorous face shining. "Fancy being met at my door by my wife and daughter. How are you?" He kissed Jane and pinched Phyllis's cheek, then separated the two packages he carried and held one out to each. "Here you are, flowers."

"Flowers!" said Jane. "What for?"

"There you go, suspecting my motives." He popped his eyes with mock indignation. "It's spring, Moms."

Jane's fingers tugged at the string, but Phyllis already had her bouquet unwrapped.

"Violets! Oh, Dad, they're lovely." She flung her arms around his neck and gave him a loud kiss.

"Ah-hah, that's more like it," said Bob Woodward with satisfaction.

Jane's hands worked harder. "Spring," she kept repeating skeptically. "Spring. Tomorrow it'll blizzard." Then she gasped as the green tissue opened in her hands. "Roses. Oh, Bob, they're wonderful. They're beautiful, darling." She gave him an enthusiastic hug, then drew back, chewing her lip gently. "There's something behind this, Bob Woodward. I'm still suspicious."

"Why, Moms!" He gave her a look of heavy innocence and turned to the hall closet to hang up his hat and coat. "It's just spring, Moms. Honest. That's all." Then he added: "Jon home?"

"He's upstairs," replied Jane. She started briskly toward the kitchen. "Come on, Phyllis, let's get these flowers in water. And it's time to put the dinner on the table."

Up in his room Jon overheard most of the conversation. When his father asked: "Jon home?" he felt his skin creeping. Then his dad knew about the ice-cream truck. What had happened? He defended himself quickly: he'd had nothing to do with it. He hadn't even been near the truck.

When Phyllis called: "Jon! Dinner's ready," he came quietly downstairs, trying to make himself as inconspicuous as possible. His eyes searched his father's face nervously.

Mr. Woodward greeted him with a lusty "Hello, son," then the family took their places at the dinner table.

CHAPTER TWO

MAJORITY VOTE

DINNER at the Woodwards' was the big meal of the day, and Jane knew the appetites of her family. The big bowls of minestrone soup, her own special version, were thick and rich, and not a drop was returned to the kitchen. Tonight the meat course was lamb, and she set the steaming roast in front of her husband's plate with an air of "Find fault with that if you can." That was a manner she carried off grandly, because her family never had a fault to find.

Bob Woodward poised the carving knife and studied the glistening meat. He tilted his close-cropped graying head, nodded his approval, then began to slice and serve. Jon watched his father, vaguely wondering when his dad was going to mention the ice-cream truck incident; then, taking up his fork, he began eating hungrily from the food-filled plate before him.

When the meal was well along, Bob looked across the table, eyes twinkling, and asked: "Moms, what did you do today that was fun?"

The others stopped eating, their mouths forming circles of astonishment. All of them knew that "fun" had a special meaning to Bob. A game was a game to him—energy expended. You worked off your surplus energy and toned up your body playing tennis or swimming, but that was all. You agitated the air or the water with your arms, but when you quit, the air and water returned to normal and there was nothing to show for your expended energy.

Fun was different. You expended energy, you toned up your body and you built something, you created something. You were changed and the world around you was changed, and you enjoyed what you did from the top of your head to the tips of your toes. That was having fun.

Jon wasn't certain, but he suspected that his father was making a flanking approach to the ice-cream truck affair. He assured himself again that he'd had nothing to do with it; he'd just been with the fellows—nothing more. The muscles of his shoulders tightened as he put himself mentally on guard.

His mother recovered from her astonishment. "Do that was fun?" she cried. "What do you mean? What's got into you men? Jon comes home and torments everybody. You bring flowers and want to know what I did that was fun. Well, I didn't do anything that was fun. I went to Peggy Holland's bridge party this afternoon and it was a bore."

Bob clucked his tongue and shook his head, pretending elaborate sympathy, then turned to his daughter. "Phyllis, did you do anything that was fun?"

"Nothing except smell those violets you brought me."

"Ah-hah!" He seemed pleased with that answer and turned to his son. "And you, Jon? How about you?"

The boy's face reddened. He didn't meet his father's eager look. Was this a trap? Was this to find out if he'd enjoyed the trick Pickles Malone had pulled on that ice-cream truck driver? "I didn't do anything that was fun except go to school and that's old stuff."

Jane interrupted haughtily: "Well, did *you* do anything that was *fun*, Bob Woodward?"

"There you have me." He flashed a look that was almost triumphant at his family. "Now don't get me wrong. I like to do what I did today. I pushed production up a notch higher; I kept the flow of parts from our subcontractors steady and I broke a bottleneck in the magneto assembly. But that's what Universal Electric pays me for. Like the rest of you, I've got to say, 'No, I did nothing that was really fun.' "

His mention of what he'd done that day at Universal Electric reminded all of them, but Jane more than the children, that Bob's rise to a production engineer at Universal had been slow. Bob Woodward was a workers' man, not a management's man. He never courted favors and the esteem of his superiors, but ceaselessly made himself respected and liked by those who worked under him.

In the years before production became so vitally important to the country, the men who ingratiated themselves with the big shots were consistently advanced over him, but during the past few years the big shots couldn't ignore the fact that Bob Woodward could get production where others couldn't. Now he had a really important job in one of Universal's special plants.

At last Jane asked, her voice filled with suspicion: "Well, what's all this talk about fun leading up to anyway?"

"Let me put it another way," continued Bob eagerly.

"Did any of you plan to do anything in the future that you would get fun out of?"

They were silent for a moment, then Phyllis asked: "Did you, Dad?"

His blue eyes seemed to shoot sparks like a short circuit and he shook his fork at her. "I did," he said in a loud whisper. "I heard of five acres on a hill on a farm owned by a man named Joe Summers who lives three miles east of Wayne. And it can be bought cheap."

"At last it's out!" cried Jane. "Now I see what all this is about—the roses, the talk about spring, your theme song, 'Have you had any fun today?' !" She faced him across the table erect and stubborn. "Bob Woodward, the answer is, 'You're not going to buy any five acres on any hill, or in a valley either.' "

"But, Moms—"

"No, sir!" Her voice rose. "Every year your country background catches up with you. Every spring I have to keep you from returning to the land."

"Hold it, Moms!" He began flagging her down with his napkin good-naturedly. "We've never found a piece of ground that sounds as promising as this one before."

"We've obligations enough." Jane was digging in for a last-ditch stand. "By the time you take care of your insurance, bond-buying, our rent and living there isn't enough for any five acres. You'd better start right now forgetting all about it. I know how ventures like this work out. They eat up everything. Your five acres on a hill would swallow us up."

"You're forgetting, Moms, that my last advance in salary gives us an extra ten dollars a week. With that ten we could make five acres into our home eventually on a pay-as-we-go proposition without upsetting other obligations."

"If you want to buy a home, we can buy one right here in New Delphi," said Jane. "We don't need to go out to the sticks."

"Why not the sticks?" Bob's eyes narrowed a little. "I don't expect to work as hard at the plant as I'm working now the rest of my life. Someday I hope I won't have to work more than three days a week; then I'll want a place where I can occupy my spare time. I can't see myself sitting around a place like this whittling a stick three-four days a week."

"There'd be too many shavings to clean up if you did that," said Jane, and all of them laughed.

"And to buy a place here in New Delphi," Bob continued, "we should have started fifteen years ago. And you know why we didn't, Moms." His voice dropped to a gentle tone.

Jane looked away. Fifteen years ago they had to help her parents and that had kept them from buying a home at that time. She knew that Bob didn't regret the money they had given her mother and father, but she wasn't going to let him strengthen his argument with this angle now. She started to say, "What's wrong with buying here?" but he anticipated her.

"If we bought a place here today, we'd be paying as much every month as we're now paying in rent and we'd have to keep that up for twenty years or more. I can't see us getting anywhere doing that when we can do this other thing on ten dollars a week and never be out on a limb."

Jane looked him straight in the eye; he'd given her

a new weapon. "We'd better put that extra ten dollars into Phyllis and Jon's college money. You know we're going to have a hard time raising the funds to send them on to college."

They were all quiet after she said that. Jon watched his father lower his eyes and absently butter a piece of bread. College—that was the big problem facing the family. Both Phyllis and Jon assumed that they would go on to college when they finished Van Buren High School.

At last Bob said quietly: "Even with that extra ten dollars, Moms, we aren't going to have enough money to send them to college for more than a couple of years."

They returned to silence again. Phyllis eyed her father, her lips parted as if she wanted to cry out her disappointment. Jon only felt a little stunned. "But I want to go straight through," he kept thinking over and over.

Jane said: "Jon has two years and Phyllis one before they'll be ready for college. We may be able to put aside more for them than we can now."

After taking a deep breath, Bob looked around grinning. "This is what I've been figuring. With that extra ten dollars a week we can take that five acres and little by little build it into a home. It'd be something we'd all enjoy doing—even you, Moms. We'd be working in the outdoors, we'd be creating something ourselves— a family creation, not just looking after something that someone else had created for us."

He waved his hand to the front and back of the house as if to include the postage-stamp lawns as well as the building. Then he went on: "While Jon and Phyllis are still in high school they could help us and by the time they are ready to go to college we might be able to have a place out there we could move to. What we now pay out in rent added to what we've saved for their future education would be enough to see them through college. We couldn't lose, Moms."

All this time Jane was shaking her head. "Why couldn't we lose? What makes you think we could do anything with five acres with ten dollars a week?"

"If we stuck to our ten dollars a week and never went into debt, and a time came when we decided to give it up, we could always resell and get our money out again." His eyes were shining with his enthusiasm.

"It'd be fun!" said Phyllis abruptly, and her eyes reflected the shine in her father's.

The idea was slowly unfolding in Jon's mind. Gee, that would really be something to do. He glanced furtively toward his mother. She sat there stiffly. His own enthusiasm waned. Moms still wasn't sold on the idea.

"It could be our family recreation spot," Bob went on. "Our hobby that'd pay off in the end. There'd be flowers, animals, a garden, a house, landscaping. All this for us to tend and build. It'd be a never-ending picnic for our free time—a never-ending prospect of fun."

"With never-ending bugs, ants, mosquitoes, sudden rainstorms and dirty hands," Jane sniffed.

"Good clean dirt, Moms. Good clean country dirt."

"No!" Jane came back firmly. "We're not going to start any Woodwards' Folly at our age."

Bob chuckled, refusing to admit he was stopped. "Well, Moms, I've always believed in running our family democratically. We'll put it to a vote—not to buy you understand—but to go out to see this five acres on a hill come Sunday." He ducked his head a little and looked at his daughter first. "What's your vote, Phil?"

She tossed her dark curls, remembering the violets he brought home, seeing woods violets spreading among brown leaves. "I'm for going."

Jane twitched her nose. "I'd expect you to vote for your father's hare-brained scheme."

"Now Jon." Bob searched the boy's face. "How do you feel about having a look at this place we might turn into an exciting pastime spot for all of us? Something better'n hanging around New Delphi where there's nothing to do but get into mischief after school."

Jon didn't look at his father. His eyes shifted to his mother appealingly. She was expecting him to side with her—he usually did—confidently awaiting his negative reply to tie the vote. His glance lowered to his empty plate. Thoughts raced helter-skelter through his mind. His father hadn't mentioned the ice-cream truck. The white and blue truck standing on Seneca Street flashed into his mind. He remembered his dad talking to Patrolman O'Donnel. He remembered thinking about chopping down a tree. A huge stand of big trees grew in a mental picture. His plate became a large white chip.

"I—I think we might give it a look," he said. His eyes flashed swiftly to his mother, then to meet his father's pleased expression.

"Jon," he heard his mother say reproachfully.

"Ah-hah. I win, Moms." Bob rubbed his hands together gleefully. "We go to see five acres on a hill."

"I hope it snows," cried Jane petulantly, then she added: "I don't either."

They all laughed heartily.

Bob made a gesture of pulling up his sleeves. "Now, for the next two days we can have fun planning our trip."

"I'd like to know what fun I'm going to get out of it," Jane stated flatly.

"Why, Moms, you can plan and fix the biggest threshing-dinner of a picnic lunch you ever made," replied Bob.

"What fun is that for me?" She looked at him squarely, her eyes still full of resistance. "Bob Woodward, you never will forget the threshing dinners your mother used to cook in Illinois thirty years ago."

"I've seen you do almost as well, Moms."

"Oh, phoo!" She became abruptly embarrassed.

Jon had been listening to this exchange and he remembered the look of satisfaction on his mother's face while he watched her get dinner. Now he spoke up: "I think Moms was the only one of us who had real fun today. I watched her getting dinner. She was getting a big kick out of it."

"Jon, you—you traitor!" The look of indignation she gave him didn't hide the fact that she enjoyed being teased. "I hate cooking—I hate housework."

Bob threw back his head and laughed loudly. "Tell us, Moms, what *do* you get fun out of? Playing bridge?"

"You're all against me!" She sprang up from the table and fled to the kitchen to get a thick golden cake and the glass coffeepot. The laughter of the others followed her, because they all knew she was putting on an act.

After dinner it was Phyllis and Jon's chore to wash

the dishes. As they worked, Phyllis leaned back from the sink once and said: "It would be fun if we had a place where we could raise flowers and chickens, wouldn't it?"

"Maybe." He didn't want to show too much enthusiasm. Flowers and chickens, that was Phil's idea of it. He wanted a place where he could do things—build things. His hands swiped the towel over a plate. Then he remembered his father talking to Patrolman O'Donnel and frowned.

As soon as the last dish was dry he slipped quietly up to his room to do his homework. He had just started the lesson in his general science book when he heard footsteps in the hallway outside his room.

"Jon, it's Dad. May I come in?" His father entered and sat down on the edge of the bed.

The boy gripped his book tensely, hardly breathing.

"Son, O'Donnel told me that some of you fellows from Van Buren High released the brake on a double-parked ice-cream truck while the driver was in a drugstore and started it down Seneca Street. Do you know anything about it?"

The room seemed terribly still to Jon. He saw his father's eyes gleaming in the shadows thrown by the study lamp.

"Yes," he answered slowly.

"You didn't do it?"

"No." This time his reply came quickly.

"You realize what a terrible thing it was to do," said Bob gravely. "People might have been killed."

"Yes." Jon's voice was only a whisper. He faced the big question: What had happened? Had anyone been hurt?

"Fortunately," continued his father, "a jay-walker caught it." He watched his son try to hide a big sigh. "But you can realize what might have happened if that truck had plowed into the congested business section." He accepted Jon's faint nod and let the silence between them grow. Then he stood up. "What do you think about this five-acre project?"

Jon looked up with a glimmering smile. "I don't know, Dad. It'll be a lot of work, won't it?"

"A lot of sweat and stiff muscles, but fun." Then he added: "You really want to go to college?"

"I sure do." The boy met his father's gaze. "And I'm going too, Dad, even if I have to work my way like you did."

Bob's big hand slapped down on his son's shoulders, fingers squeezing affectionately. "That's something I like to hear. And maybe you could start working your way through college on this five acres. You know I believe one of the things our real pioneers enjoyed most was the clearing of a piece of ground and the building of their own homes with their own hands.

"I've never told Moms. She'd think I'm loonier than she does now." He chuckled. "But I'd like all of us to build our own home with our own hands. I think that'd be more real fun than I've ever experienced or ever could experience." He paused; his fingers tightened on his son's shoulder. "Think we could do it?"

"Maybe." Jon stared into the shadows of the room.

"A lot of responsibility for it would fall on you," said his father.

Jon looked up at him again, grinning. "Well, that's something real to think about anyhow."

"That's the way to begin it," Bob said. "But we haven't bought it yet. Maybe Moms won't let us." Again he chuckled. "Moms is a conservative, you know, when it comes to spending money. Good thing for us in a lot of ways. But it means we'll have to prove ourselves every step."

Jon heard his father go downstairs and sat staring into space. What would it be like to build his own home with his own hands? Vaguely in the corner of his mind he remembered building houses of blocks when he was younger.

Bob found Jane sitting before a crackling fire reading a book. "Darling," he said, "I think I pulled a fast one on you with that vote at dinner."

"What do you mean?" She looked up, eyes narrowed.

He recounted briefly the incident of the boys from Van Buren High and the ice-cream truck, adding: "I think Jon voted for me because he thought the results were a lot worse and I knew all about it. He didn't want to cross me."

"You're a cheat," she accused. Then she said: "But he's got enough of you in him to fall for such an idea."

He sat on the arm of the davenport above her and slid his fingers across her shoulders. "You're not sold on it at all, are you, Moms?" She didn't reply. "You're going to make us prove it's a sound investment every step of the way, or you'll have none of it."

She suddenly pinched him hard. "Oh, Bob, you and your dream of a chunk of land in the country. When am I ever going to get you civilized?"

"When I get it." He gave her a quick hug.

CHAPTER THREE

FIVE ACRE HILL

SATURDAY morning at breakfast Jane asked: "How're we going out to this five acres tomorrow?"

"In the car," Bob replied.

"What about gas?"

"Why do you think I've been walking to work every day for a month?" Bob wagged his head with self-satisfaction.

"Then you didn't just hear about that land," cried his wife. "Then you've been planning this whole thing for weeks. Bob, you big conniver, you!"

Bob Woodward opened his mouth wide, pulling his face as if he were guffawing loudly, but he didn't make a sound. Jon and Phyllis laughed.

This was the sort of half-serious, half-humorous struggle that went on regularly in the Woodward household. It was a game that kept them all mentally alert. Jon had heard his mother say to his dad often enough: "I guess that's why I married you. Every few months I find myself involved in some wild project. I'm in it before I know what I'm doing, then it takes all my wits to get out. Anyhow, it's exciting."

Every spring there was talk about buying a place in the country. They had even looked at possible places before, but there hadn't been any extra money and

21

Jane's cautious nature had won out against buying. But this year there was ten dollars a week. Jon sensed that his father's technician's mind had worked out many maneuvers which wouldn't be revealed to the family until he was ready to spring them to his advantage.

Jon felt a little sorry for his mother. Moms was going to have a hard time if she managed to win out again this year. And after breakfast he did the little things she asked him to do without grousing; he sort of felt that he was making up to her for the fact that he hoped they would get a place in the country this time.

In the afternoon he went to the movies and came out feeling bored. His body plagued him with a restless, uneasy feeling as if his clothes were too big. Ted Carlson tried to get him to come down to the park along the Iroquois River, but Jon said he had to get home. He didn't have to, but he wanted to be alone. All the way up Delaware Street he tried to stir up inside him the same enthusiasm that his father had for building a home in the country. The idea didn't strike fire in him. He just liked to think about it, that was all.

They set out about ten o'clock the next morning, Bob driving, Jon beside him and Phyllis and Jane in the back seat. Bob seemed in no hurry. He drove slowly through the Sunday-quiet streets of New Delphi and out southwest on Route 7. The air was clear and a little crisp with large grayish clouds forming in the west and floating lazily down the Iroquois Valley.

As the car topped the south ridge Jon looked back at the city bunching about a bend in the river like a swarm of bees on a crooked limb. He saw the solid mass of huge buildings to the west that was the Universal Electric Company, where his father was a production engineer.

The sight of New Delphi vanished behind a fold of ground as the car rolled down through the hills and valleys to the south. Along the road and in the fields patches of dirty snow still lay unmelted. Corners of woodland, bare-branched and gray, stood out conspicuously on the blue-tinted hills. They passed farmyards, huge barns, great rambling houses. A sign, "Cattle Xing," amused them. How did cattle X?

Phyllis asked: "Dad, does this land have a house?"

"No. It's just five acres."

"What can we do with land and no house?" complained Jane. "The whole idea is ridiculous!"

"Moms, we'll plant a house seed and let it grow." Bob chuckled. "This five acres can be our private sand pile."

Jon heard his mother's disapproving, "Sand pile! Such nonsense!" Then he remembered the sandbox he used to have in the basement at home when he was younger. He had made houses and forts and roads and tunnels in it; he had played for hours in the wet sand. That had been fun.

The car slowed for the quiet village of Wayne, passing the outer fringe of new bungalows and cottages, cutting the ring of old Dutch Colonial houses, some made of yellowish stone, and coming to a stop at the traffic light in the center of the red brick business section. They watched the villagers walking sedately to church until the light turned green, then Bob swung the car left on

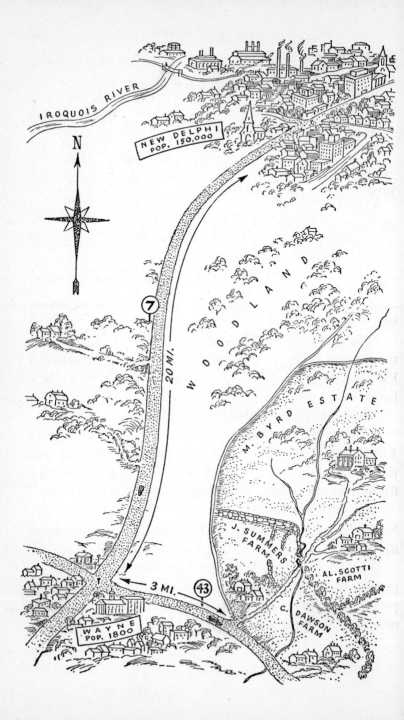

State 43 and drove out of the village on the winding, glistening black-top road.

"Three miles," Bob said as they crossed the town limits, "right at a fork in the road."

Ahead Jon saw the black-top divide suddenly and his father, peering at the mailboxes on the left, read out: "Summers." He cut the car into the drive of a neat farmyard and stopped. "This must be it."

A lanky man came out of the gray barn and crossed the yard toward them. Bob cranked down the window.

"Are you Mr. Summers?"

"That's my name. Joe Summers." He stressed the "Joe" and a smile made his reddish cheeks shine.

"I'm Bob Woodward. Al Scotti's been tellin' me about five acres you've got for sale down here."

"That's right. My boy'll show you the place." He turned and yelled: "Tom! Taw-om!" A "Yup" answered him in the barn and Summers faced the car. "You Al's boss?"

"Guess that's the way it is," replied Bob.

A string-bean of a boy, perhaps a year older than Jon, burst out of the barn, paused, shook chaff off his jacket and came toward them. He grinned, his blue eyes flashing from Phyllis to Jon, then back.

"Mr. Woodward wants to see that five acres," Joe Summers said to his son, then to Bob: "You can drive up to it."

Jon swung the car door open on his side for Tom to get in, while his father said: "We'd like to go over it pretty thoroughly; would you mind if we had a picnic on it?"

"Go right ahead," said Joe Summers.

As they drove out of the yard, Tom directed: "Take the left branch."

Jon felt the boy's strong thigh alongside of his. He wondered what Tom did to amuse himself out here; he wondered if Tom was keen about something.

"You can park right in there." Tom pointed to a spot where an old woods road broke through the stone wall.

Bob stopped the car, and they climbed out to stretch their legs.

"There's the west boundary," said Tom, indicating a flat slab wall of dark gray limestone that ran up the hill through the woods. His eyes flickered to Phyllis, standing beside her father, hands thrust deep in her coat pockets, the breeze whipping her gray slacks about her ankles.

They stared up the wooded slope. A short distance in Jon saw five large trees recently felled. His father waved toward them: "Someone start lumbering and give it up?"

"A gang cutting guard rails for the highway on the Byrd estate got in here by mistake," explained Tom. "They cut those before we chased them off."

"Well, let's see some more," said Bob.

"This west boundary runs right to the top of the hill," Tom explained, and started up the overgrown woods road.

Jon followed close on his heels, then came Phyllis and Bob. Jane brought up the rear, frowning as branches caught at her slacks. The woods road wound up to a small clearing on the eastern edge of the timber above a broken ledge of gray limestone. Ten feet below the base of the ledge ran another stone wall and beyond it was what had once been a field, which was now covered with foxgrass margined by a ragged growth of birch and maple saplings slowly edging out toward the center.

At the clearing the party stopped. Jane caught up with them, remarking: "This would be a good place for our picnic dinner. A fire on that flat stone would be safe."

Jon noticed that her face was suddenly bright and smiling as she stared off to the southeast. He followed her gaze. They were high enough to look down a long valley of farm land and woods, misty and soft and soothing in the sunlight. Jon saw a cloud shadow racing across a distant field. His eyes flickered back to his mother. She was watching him now and they both grinned.

"You can see the other boundaries from here," Tom was saying. He pointed to the north, where another stone wall ran down past the edge of the field below them to the corner of woodland on the east, then another wall ran southward toward the road. They could see now that the five acres was an irregular piece of ground with all four sides of different lengths.

Bob looked around at the stand of oaks and maples on the hills and down at the overgrown field. Jon eyed Tom, who watched Phyllis as she crouched to examine a mound of bright green moss. Suddenly he wanted to find out how Tom felt about the country. He swung his arm toward the north and east boundaries. "Let's follow them around," he suggested.

Tom started off at once, Jon following.

"I'm staying right here," Jane said. "I don't see any sense in being pulled to pieces in that brush."

Phyllis didn't seem to notice that the boys were leaving, and Bob remarked: "Guess I'll stay and start a fire for Moms."

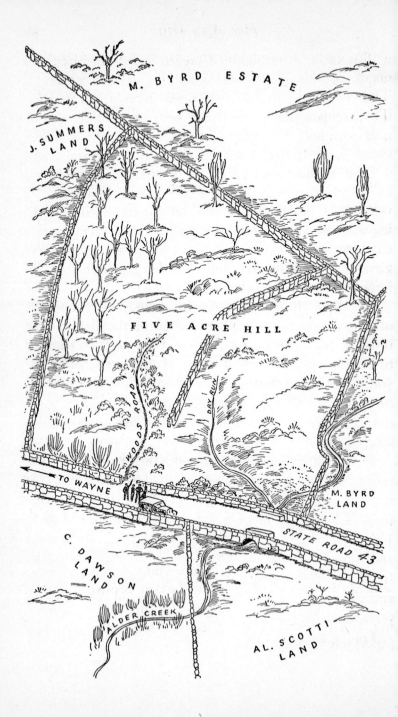

The boys plunged into the woods and Jon asked at once: "You like living in the country?" The same instant Tom asked: "You ever lived in the country before?" They both seemed embarrassed and grinned.

It was Tom who answered: "I guess I like it in the country. I've never lived in town."

"What do you do out here?" asked Jon eagerly.

"I raise chickens and ducks and look after our two cows and the pigs. We don't do much farming now that Dad's working in the foundry at Universal. I raise chickens and garden to earn money to go to college—I'm going to be a biologist." He added this last with an important air.

Jon didn't reply; he felt a little disappointed. None of these things which interested Tom interested him much. Building something, that was the way he was going to help toward his college career. And a biologist—poof! Jon had his mind set on being a construction engineer or maybe an airplane designer. He hadn't made up his mind. What annoyed him about Tom was that Tom seemed to have his mind made up.

The two continued their exploration, reached the north line and followed it down a sharp slope into the narrow valley at the top of the ragged field. As they stumbled past the north end of the broken ledge of rock, Jon saw a rough shanty built with walls of flat stone slabs and roofed over with stones and slabs covered with dirt. It caught his attention. He remembered the shanty he and the gang had built out at the edge of New Delphi years ago when he was in the sixth grade.

Tom explained: "My brother and I built that. We

used to play pioneers in there." His tone seemed to suggest that he considered it all kid nonsense now.

They plunged on toward the east boundary. But Jon suddenly recalled his dad talking about a sand pile on the ride out here—the family sand pile. He felt a little tightness between his shoulders at the brief recollection of what fun it was to make roads and houses in damp sand.

His glance shifted up to the clearing where his father and mother stood by a blazing fire. A plan began to show faint outlines in his mind: clear that woods road and build a house up there of flat stone slabs. The first vague picture of that house in his mind bore a strong resemblance to the shanty Tom had built back there by the ledge.

"This is the corner." Tom interrupted the growth of the idea in Jon's mind and the two headed down the eastern boundary toward the road. Brush and briars caught at them as they struggled along until they came out on the ice-fringed brook that cut the corner of the lower field.

"Could this be dammed up for a place to swim?" Jon asked as he jumped across it.

"If the water didn't back up on old man Byrd's land," replied Tom. "He'd raise a fuss if that happened."

They clambered over the stone wall to the road, then circled back up the hill by way of the woods road. The fire burned vigorously, snapping and cracking, filling the air with the smell of cedar. Jon sniffed deeply and he seemed to feel relaxed and suddenly pleased.

"Well, have you seen everything?" asked his mother,

smiling at Tom Summers. "You'll stay to a picnic lunch with us, won't you, Tom?"

"Thank you, Mrs. Woodward." The boy fidgeted, tempted by the smell of cooking food, and his glance shifted to Phyllis, who now had a collection of moss she was studying. "But I've got to look after my baby chicks," he added regretfully.

Phyllis's glance flashed up eagerly. "Oh, do you have baby chicks?" she cried.

"Sure." Tom blushed. "I've a hundred Plymouth Rocks."

"Could I see them?" Phyllis sprang up, her moss collection forgotten.

"Shu—sure."

"You can't go see them now, Phyllis," interrupted Jane. "We're going to eat in a few minutes."

Bob looked up from whittling the bright heart-wood of cedar. "You can see them when we stop to talk with Mr. Summers on the way back," he said. "That be all right, Tom?" The boy nodded, smiling. "And thanks for showing us the land."

Jon watched Tom swing off through the woods toward the road. His sister's eagerness to see Tom's chickens stirred up his old restlessness. He tossed a pebble at her.

"Come up and see my baby chicks sometime. Cluck," he said scornfully.

She tossed her head, made a face at him. "That to you, smarty." She returned to studying the moss samples, her fingers moving gently through the pale green furry growth.

Unable to start a squabble with his sister, Jon's attention shifted to his father, sitting on a little pile of flat stones, no longer whittling, but just staring thoughtfully down the southeast slope of the land. He thought his dad looked disappointed; maybe this place wasn't up to his expectations.

His father's precarious seat of piled-up stones brought back to Jon the vague plan he'd had earlier of building a stone cabin up here. The idea took stronger hold now and he walked around the fire excitedly. This would be a swell place for a cabin.

He became conscious of his mother crouching near the bean pot, one hand balancing the frying pan, her face pink and her blue eyes bright and eager. She certainly looked as if she was really having fun. The smell of heating baked beans and his mother's rolls toasting on a flat stone and the spicy fragrance of sputtering sausage excited him to the point of blurting out his plan right then and there.

But his mother set the frying pan off the fire, saying: "All right. I guess we can eat."

"That's the news I've been waiting for," cried Bob.

In an instant they were all heaping rich brown beans upon pasteboard plates and ringing the mound with gleaming sausage, buttering hot rolls, and filling their cups with hot chocolate. Bob threw more wood on the fire. The smell of fresh wood smoke prodded their appetites. They returned for second helpings and third helpings.

"Gee, Moms, this is good." Jon could hardly get his words of rapture above a stifled whisper.

"Wonderful, Moms, wonderful." Bob slowly shook his head. "I don't see how you do it."

"Thank you." Jane refused to let her face express the

pleasure she felt. She looked away down the valley. They didn't need to think they could sell her this wilderness by flattering her. Before she was aware, her eyes were intent upon the sweep of hills and hollows, fields and wooded lands; she could stare for hours at such a quiet, restful scene.

Finally they could eat no more. The used plates and cups were burned and the picnic hamper repacked. Bob lighted his pipe and tobacco smoke added its tang to the smell of burning cedar. The family seemed too well fed to talk.

"It's been a fine picnic," sighed Bob at last.

"Yes," Jane agreed, "but that's no reason why we should buy it. There are plenty of places where we can have picnics without having to buy them." She expected Bob to swing a host of arguments at her, but he remained silent.

It was Jon who spoke up. "But, Moms, we could do things here besides picnic. Dad and I could build a cabin and we could come out week-ends and holidays and trim up the woods and clear the field and raise a garden and—we could do lots of things. We could—maybe—could build a house . . ." His voice trailed off as if he'd become self-conscious of his long speech.

"Big talk," scoffed his mother. "Even bigger than your dad's." She was afraid to look at Bob; she felt that he was just sitting quietly, mentally rubbing his hands with satisfaction. She rushed on: "You'd get sick of it in a couple of weeks and we'd just have a white elephant on our hands."

Jon's face puckered. "No, Moms, I wouldn't get sick of it. It'd be fun to build us a stone house—honest."

"Delusions of grandeur!" scoffed his mother. "A stone house on ten dollars a week." She laughed scornfully.

Jon saw his father wink and shake his head.

Then Phyllis said: "If we could live out here during summer vacations, Mother, I could raise chickens."

"Where would we live?" cried Jane, recognizing the increasing pressure. She wondered when Bob would add his weight to the children's arguments. "You all talk so blithely about houses and living out here. Houses cost money. Don't forget all we have to spend is ten dollars a week."

"I think Jon and I can build a comfortable cabin, Moms," Bob said. "And the ten dollars a week would pay for the material." He saw his son's sudden eager look.

"But the land will have to be paid for first," cried Jane. "If you can get it for fifty dollars an acre, that'll be two hundred and fifty dollars—twenty-five weeks, six months—next September before we can touch it." She looked around at the others triumphantly, pleased by this almost miraculous demonstration of a mathematical ability which she didn't know she had. Leaning back, she waited for surrender—she had them with that argument.

"I've been saving ten dollars extra a week, Moms, for almost eight months." Bob's face was stiff, holding back a grin.

Jane sat up straight, furious. "No! You've been saving ten dollars a week all that time and haven't told me about it! Bob Woodward, you—you—" she hunted for a name, her exasperation bursting—"you—you pinch-penny!"

Bob threw back his head and his laugh rolled through

the woods. Jon and Phyllis joined in and Jane laughed with them.

Phyllis, looking toward the road, said: "Who's that?"

The others turned and saw a thick-set man on a chestnut horse jogging up toward them on the woods road. The rider pulled up and without a greeting asked belligerently: "Who gave you permission to build a fire up here on this land?" U. S. 856955

Bob stood up. "Mr. Summers gave us permission. We're thinking of buying this property." His eyes narrowed, watching the rider's heavy, stump-like jaw.

"I'm buying this property," growled the stranger, "so clear out and make sure that fire's extinguished."

"I'm sorry." Bob's eyes shifted to the glowing coals. "Mr. Summers didn't tell us he had a buyer."

"We've got too many wops and foreigners and trash from town coming out here spoiling the country," stormed the stranger, color mounting in his pale cheeks. "So clear out, all of you, do you hear!" His voice rose to a yell, then he swung his horse around with a sharp yank on the bit and cantered back down the hill.

Jane was the first to recover. "Trash!" she snorted indignantly. "Trash from town, are we? Why—"

"Joe Summers didn't act as if he had a buyer this morning." Chagrin and disappointment held Bob's voice low. "I suppose the 'wops' he was talking about is Al Scotti. He has a place out here somewhere."

Jon poked at the ground with a stick. "Aw, gee," he grumbled. The idea of doing something with this land, which had been taking root, wilted abruptly.

Phyllis complained: "Now I won't be able to raise chickens or flowers unless you find another place, Dad."

So they couldn't buy this five acres after all, but there wasn't any look of triumph on Jane's face as they put out the fire and marched glumly down the hill to the car.

"I suppose we ought to thank Summers for letting us picnic up there anyway," said Bob, and drove into the Summers' yard. They waited in the machine for someone to come out.

They hadn't long to wait. Joe Summers and Tom and three younger children burst out of the house and came down the walk. Tom looked eagerly at Phyllis and was the first to speak: "Want to see my chicks now?"

Phyllis didn't move and her father said: "Thanks for letting us picnic up there. We didn't know you had a buyer."

Summers' long neck seemed to lengthen and his chin jerked. "I haven't any buyer I'm considering selling to."

The Woodwards stared at him in astonishment.

"Some fellow rode up and told us he was buying the land," explained Bob crisply, "and ordered us off."

"What!" yelled Summers. He looked at Tom. The younger children drew together, foreheads wrinkled. At last Joe seemed to comprehend. "That must have been old Merrivale Byrd. He owns the land to the east and he's been after me to sell the whole farm to him. I won't sell. I wouldn't sell it to him at any price. All he wants to do is turn this country back into wilderness where he and his crowd can go fox hunting. No, sir, Mr. Woodward, he's no buyer for this land."

A concerted "Oooh" came from the car, then Tom looked in at Phyllis, his eyes bright. "Come see my chicks."

She was out of the car in an instant and following him across the yard to the white brooder house on the slope.

"I'm sorry that Byrd spoiled your picnic," apologized Joe. "He's the county supervisor—controls enough votes to get himself re-elected every time and thinks he runs the country around here."

"We thought maybe he did," replied Bob with a chuckle. Then he continued: "We can see a lot of possibilities in that land, but we'll have to think it over."

"Sure," agreed Summers.

"We want to all be sold on the piece we buy before we stick our necks out." Bob gave a twinkling glance toward Jane, but she was staring off across the Summers' neat lawn.

Then Phyllis and Tom returned. "They're the cutest things," cried the girl. "And Tom says they're not hard to raise. I'd like to raise chickens, Mother."

"Raise them in what? Your hat?" asked Jane.

Everyone laughed and Bob started the car, saying: "I'll let you know what we decide, Joe."

It was Jon who spoke first after they headed toward New Delphi. "Gee, maybe we could build a stone house . . ."

Bob kept his attention on the road, but his right hand dropped down on Jon's knee and squeezed it. The boy didn't continue, and his father said: "I don't know that it would be a sound move to buy land next to anyone as disagreeable as that fellow Byrd."

"Trash, he called us!" Jane snorted suddenly from the back seat. "I certainly wouldn't let anyone like him keep me from buying it."

Her outburst stunned them all into silence, then Bob

asked incredulously: "Moms, was it you who said that?"

"It certainly was!"

Their laughter filled the speeding car.

Later when Bob and Jon put the machine in the garage, Bob said: "A stone house is something we can figure on, son. I've been reading up on building with forms—it's not such a trick. But don't talk about it before Moms. We've got to convince her that we can build a cabin first."

That night Jon lay awake picturing a fine drive cut through the woods to a big stone house with turrets and battlements like a castle. It was a rosy dream. He liked it. He liked to build that castle stone by stone in his mind.

In the adjoining room he heard the murmur of his parents talking.

"Darling, I still think buying that five acres is wacky," Jane said. "But I'll go along with you. The youngsters are sold on it. Just the same, you've got to stick within the limit of the ten dollars a week extra from our income."

"That's the fun of it, Moms." Bob sat on the edge of his maple bed, massaging his scalp vigorously. "It wouldn't be any fun if we had all we wanted to spend on it. Besides, to every ten dollars we put into that place we'll add our labor, which'll just about triple the amount. We can't pick up the money for Phyllis's and Jon's college education any easier way. You don't believe me, Moms, but we'll show you. You just give us a chance." He looked at her with hard, shining eyes. "Gee, Moms, to build a home out of five acres on a hill with ten dollars a week—that'll be more fun than I've ever had."

Jane looked around from the dressing table, and said, smiling: "I thought I had only two children, but I've got three."

"That's right, Moms." He chuckled happily.

CHAPTER FOUR

TWENTIETH-CENTURY PIONEERS

AFTER that first trip to Five Acre Hill, breakfast, dinner and evenings at the Woodwards' became periods of excited planning and sober discussion. Each member of the family except Jane, who became a sort of moderator, had brought back a mental picture of the land and each built a dream from that picture.

Phyllis wrote to the Agriculture Department Extension Service for bulletins on chicken-raising, and she pestered the New Delphi librarians for books on poultry. Tom Summers and his brooder house and his chicks filled her thoughts until she talked as if she already had a flock of her own.

"But, Phyllis," said her mother, "you can't raise chickens on week-ends, and we haven't even a roof on that land."

"We're going to have a cabin soon, aren't we, Mother?"

"Soon!" Jane looked at her eager face. "If we have one by next year we'll be lucky."

To hide her crestfallen feelings, Phyllis turned to the flower sections of the seed catalogues her father had picked up, and dreamed about raising flowers.

Mention of a roof on the land broke into Jon's dream. He pictured the laying up of walls with slabs of gray limestone like the building of a house with his toy blocks, which had long ago been stored away in the attic. But he didn't talk about a stone house to his mother. He said: "Aw, Moms, we'll have a cabin before next year."

"It'll take money and time, Jon. A lot more money and time than we'll have this year."

Jon looked at his father and saw Bob slowly shaking his head, meaning, "Let the matter drop." But Jon could still build a mental castle and when he got tired of that he turned to damming up the brook in the corner of the land and making a swimming pool. He could almost feel the cool water around him.

At Van Buren High neither Jon nor Phyllis talked about their family's venture to their schoolmates. Jon didn't even tell Ted Carlson. Both were a little bit afraid of being jeered at for going to the country. And keeping it to themselves at school made them talk about it all the more at home—made them dream more about it when alone.

Their father had his dream too, but it was more down-to-earth. He talked about clearing the brush from the field and sowing oats and alfalfa and planting corn. What he pictured in his mind were bright green cocks of hay, golden shocks of grain and yellow ears of corn. "That's what I used to like best about our farm in Illinois when I was a kid," he said.

"Once a farm boy, always a farm boy," teased Jane.

"Guess you've got something there, Moms," he admitted, and went downstairs to the workroom ostensibly to sandpaper his gate-legged table, but he had signaled Jon to follow, and together they planned the cabin they hoped to build.

Not all was dreaming with the Woodwards. Bob hunted up Joe Summers in the foundry and told him they wanted to buy the five acres. The job of clearing the title, mapping the tract and drawing up a deed was begun. That took time. A week passed, then Joe Summers suggested that the Woodwards might as well start doing what they wanted to do on the land before all the details of the deal were finished. So the following Sunday the family again drove out to Five Acre Hill.

The ax, the hedge clippers, Jon's Boy Scout hatchet, and the new red-bladed brush hook Bob had bought the afternoon before were loaded into the trunk of the car along with the picnic hamper full of Jane's proud handiwork.

"The commissariat," she said. "That's all I am. The most important part of this crazy adventure."

Jon said: "The only reason we're goin' to do this work, Moms, is to get a bigger appetite for your grub."

Laughing, they climbed into the car and drove out of New Delphi through the crisp air and the frost-white countryside. Bob stopped at the Summers' to let Joe know they were out for the day.

"Don't work too hard," Joe said with a laugh.

Jon saw Tom wave from the door of the chicken house up in the orchard and he heard Phyllis cranking down her window to reply. Bob swung the car out on the road again and up the left fork to park in the entrance to the woods road. They all sprang out as if they couldn't wait to see the land again—all except Jane, who just sat in the car and watched the eagerness of the others, smiling to herself.

"Come on!" yelled Jon, and ran up through the

woods. Phyllis followed and Bob came striding behind. At the spot where they'd had their picnic two weeks ago, Jon looked for the place he'd pictured building his castle. Where was it? This couldn't be the place. His glance swung wildly as if he'd been tricked. This wasn't the land they'd seen before.

Phyllis came panting up. Her eyes searched the top of the rock ledge below—for two weeks her imagination had covered it with wild flowers. And where was that cleared, grassy spot where she'd dreamed of playing with baby chicks? Brown oak leaves, patches of unmelted snow and rocks and brush were all she saw.

Even to Bob the place seemed to have suddenly turned into a wilderness—there wasn't half as much brush and undergrowth when they were out here before. Where was the field? Brow wrinkled, perplexed by the apparent change that had taken place, he stared down into the tangle of birch and maple saplings spreading over the rank reddish-brown grass.

Not one of them spoke. They couldn't quite realize that Five Acre Hill hadn't changed but that they had so glorified it in their imaginations that it now looked different. Each sought frantically for the picture each had built so carefully during the past two weeks.

At last Jon said: "Gee, Dad, it looks like we're hooked. This is a worse mess than I thought it was."

Neither his father nor his sister had the courage to add their own disappointment to his.

Jane joined them, read their dejected expressions, and glanced over the sweep of fields to the southeast. She'd hardly thought of that view since she was here before. It was still there, unchanged, faint clouds of mist in the hollows, the early sun gleaming on the folds of the land.

"Well, that view hasn't changed," Jane said, taking a deep breath of satisfaction; then she added with a faint smile: "Looks to me like there's a lot of work to be done and it won't get done while we stand here."

Grinning a little sheepishly, Bob and Jon returned to the car for the tools and commenced clearing the woods road. They cut the brush close to the ground, careful not to leave sharp stubs that would injure the car tires. Jane and Phyllis made neat piles of the cuttings.

"We'll burn this stuff on our garden," Bob said. "Wood ashes make good fertilizer."

Snipping, chopping and hacking they progressed slowly up the hill. The sun rose higher, grew warmer. Their muscles loosened beneath the heat. They shed jackets.

As Jon flung his windbreaker down, he glanced back along the cleared lane. "Gee, that looks swell!" he exclaimed, as if the sight had surprised him.

The glow in his cheeks came from more than heat and exertion. He'd dreamed of a white gravel drive for a fortnight, but now this raw woods road, fresh-cut stubs oozing sap, seemed more perfect than his dream. They had accomplished something; they were getting somewhere; this was fun. For the first time his body seemed to share his mental enthusiasm for this project. He grabbed up the red-handled clippers, careless of the blisters rising on his soft palms, and began clipping maple shoots furiously.

The others stopped to look at the job they were doing when Jon did, and something of the same feeling which possessed him took hold of them. They worked harder than ever and by eleven o'clock they were nearing the picnic spot. Half an hour later Bob and Jon burst into the little clearing, chopping and slashing right and left almost in a frenzy. The job was done. With knotted muscles, aching backs and blistered hands the two gazed proudly down the hill to the highway.

"Looks all right," Bob remarked, taking a deep breath of satisfaction; then he added: "I could eat."

That seemed to remind Jon. "Boy, am I hungry!" He dropped down on a rock dog-tired.

"Woman's work is never done," complained Jane. "I pile brush all morning, now I've got to feed you." And she sank down on a stone to rest. "If you want to be fed —Bob, you bring up the picnic hamper, and, Jon, you start the fire."

Phyllis joined them. "Look what I found!" She held out a cluster of tiny hepatica cups and a spray of pink trailing arbutus. "Aren't they lovely?" But the others were too tired to exclaim over them, and she sat down to examine each carefully and enjoy them by herself.

When Jon began laying larger sticks on the pyramid of burning twigs he had ignited, he heard the car coming and swung around in time to see his father drive up the woods road and circle to a stop in the clearing.

"That was easier than lugging the hamper up here," yelled Bob from the car. "She came up like on pavement." He jumped out and the others gathered beside him to look back at the tire tracks in the leaves and soft dirt.

"Bet that's the first car that ever came up here," remarked Jon.

"We're twentieth-century pioneers," added his sister.

"All right, you pioneers," said their mother. "Unload that covered wagon if you want anything to eat."

While they ate and rested and looked around them at Five Acre Hill, they began to realize that their dreams were shaping to the reality of the land.

Jon gestured toward an elbow of the hill to the north which flattened out to the limestone ledge. "I think we ought to put the cabin over here."

"What's the matter with right here?" asked Jane.

"We'll want to build our stone house here." Jon looked fearfully at his father—he'd forgotten and had mentioned the stone house. But his dad was staring at the site he'd indicated.

Jane said scornfully: "A stone house—that'll be years from now, if ever."

"That's the place I had in mind for the cabin," Bob said. "This is the best building site. Just for that reason we don't want to build a cabin on it. If we ever have to resell, the land'll lose value if the building site for a house is cluttered up with a cabin." He gave Jon a wink.

Jane seemed satisfied and said no more.

Phyllis called their attention to smoke rising beyond a house a short distance down the road.

"I think that's Al Scotti's place," Bob said. "He must be burning off a field." His glance dropped to the tangle of grass and brush below them. "I don't know why we couldn't do that here," he added.

Jon stood up suddenly, excited by the idea, staring down at the field. "Gee, that'd speed up clearing that piece."

"You'd better not try it," cautioned Jane.

"Why?" came back Bob with a confident look. "There's hardly any wind. Farmers always burn off their land in the spring."

He sprang up and stood beside Jon. Phyllis joined them. All three were seeing the clean job a fire would do to that field. Together they started toward the north boundary.

"You be careful, Bob," Jane called after them. "You're not out in Illinois now." Then she began packing away the picnic equipment and what remained of the meal.

CHAPTER FIVE

THE WIND BLOWS

FIRST we'd better get some cedar branches," Bob said to Jon and Phyllis, "to control the fire with if we need to."

They stopped at the clump of cedars above the stone shanty Tom Summers had built, and Bob cut each of them a three-foot sucker shoot. Down they plunged to the narrow north end of the field. A gust of wind blew in their faces and Bob hesitated, his forehead pinching a little. But the wind slackened. He touched a lighted match to a clump of dry grass at the edge of the brush about midway along the width of the field.

Jon watched the flames leap up quickly, spreading through the layers of old leaves and dry grass. The fire ate outward in a circle, a shimmering orange wall flinging a thick blue-gray cloud of smoke high in the air. It burned up against the boundary wall and died out, while Jon and his father and Phyllis retreated slowly southward ahead of the advancing flames. The burned-over area was left black and strangely empty.

"This'll save us a lot of work," said Jon.

Bob grinned at him. "You bet; all we'll have to do now is cut the brush and the ground'll be ready for the plow."

Another gust of wind drove the flames toward them

suddenly. Sparks and bits of flaming grass jumped ahead of the orange wall, starting new fires. The three fell back from the heat, fanning the smoke away from their faces. The wind died down again, but Bob frowned and Jon's blistered hands felt sweaty on the sticky branch of cedar.

Phyllis moved away toward the hill and called: "Dad, the wind's coming up."

Her father didn't reply.

Jon saw the line of flames extending the width of the narrow valley now, leaping ten feet high where the grass stood thickest. His mouth felt dry and the smoke stung his eyes, making him squint and look away. He saw his mother going down through the trees toward the right flank of the fire.

Again the wind blew in with a sudden whoosh. The flames leaped ahead, caught in the dry grass, and blazed fiercely. The heat drove them back, lashing and whipping at them. Jon saw his father start beating at the advancing flames with his cedar branch, attacking the relentless, rushing wall, flailing away violently. Jon followed his father's example, beating at the hissing, crackling flames with all his energy. He heard his father yell: "Phyllis! Get help!"

Then Jon no longer had time to notice what his father was doing. The fury he fought took all his attention. For just an instant he saw himself a knight in armor fighting a many-headed dragon. He cut off heads, but more sprang up. The wind swept the flames around him and he had to retreat to keep from being encircled. His clothes were soon soaked with sweat; his eyelashes and hair scorched; his mouth dry as if he'd been drinking fire.

The fierce crackling grew louder and louder. Jon realized that he was losing the fight. If the wind would only drop for a little while. But the wind kept blowing in gusts. How much longer could he keep up the battle? He didn't know what else to do except beat at the flames and keep on beating. His arms ached. A stitch caught him in the side, almost doubling him up, still he fought on in the choking smoke, his eyes smarting and hardly able to see.

Back he retreated, but the fire leaped faster. The smoke rolled down, shutting him off. He thought the flames were all around him now. He was lost. He beat frantically. Terror drove him to fight more furiously than ever.

Then someone grabbed his arm and pulled him back. A voice yelled: "Let it go here! Get over on the side! It can't jump the road. Keep it from spreading on the sides!" The hand grasping his arm shoved him roughly toward the stone wall of the eastern boundary.

Jon stumbled out of the smoke, aware that it was Tom Summers who had pushed him. He looked to the west to see his father and Tom retreating to the hill and farther to the north along the flank of the fire he saw his mother beating out the flames. Down the center of the valley the fire rolled like a flood; only the highway and the brook could stop it.

At the stone wall along the Byrd Estate Jon began beating the edge of the blaze. He suddenly felt terribly weak; his heart seemed to fill his chest, leaving no room for air. But as he snuffed out the orange tongues along the line, his strength came back—he was winning a little now.

Once the flames were beaten out to the rear, he turned back to fight the east edge of the main blaze. He was surprised to see someone already there ahead of him swatting the flames with a broom. At first he thought she was Phyllis; then he saw two small boys with cedar shoots helping her.

She was a slender girl about Jon's age, wearing blue denim overalls. Her hair was black, curling back from her pale forehead, whipping about her slender neck as she worked swiftly. When Jon came up, she smiled and panted: "You take a rest. We'll look after this."

For a moment Jon was only conscious of her shining violet eyes. He couldn't say anything; he could only grin. He didn't know that his grin barely showed on his dirt-smudged face.

By this time the main wall of the fire had reached the brook. Back on the field clumps of grass still glowed red, then turned black with a puff of smoke.

Jon helped the girl and the two boys beat out the flames along the stone wall, then they started across the black field to the edge of the hill where Tom and Bob and Jane still fought to keep the fire out of the woods. Phyllis was just coming up from the direction of the Summers'; she had run all the way there for help and had to rest before she could come back. The three younger Summers children were with her.

Halfway across the burned-over field Jon found his voice. "Thanks for coming to help," he whispered hoarsely to the dark girl with him. The words tore at his parched throat. "Gee, I was scared for a while."

"The wind was tricky today," she replied. "And this field hasn't been burned for years."

By the time they reached the others the main fire had burned out along the brook and the road. It didn't take long to finish off the flames creeping up the hill. Then, trembling and panting, tired, dirty and scorched, they watched the last curls of smoke rise and the gusty wind whirl bits of burned leaves and grass and sweep them across the black ground.

"Guess the excitement's over," sighed Bob.

Tom Summers greeted the girl with Jon. "Hi, Maria." Then he introduced her and the two boys to the Woodwards—"Maria, Tony, and George Scotti."

"Well, we certainly appreciate your help," Bob said, "all of you. Guess I started something I couldn't finish."

Phyllis and Maria were eyeing each other, their lips quick to smile in friendliness.

A car stopped on the road and two troopers climbed out.

"Did you say the excitement was over?" asked Jane.

"The fire's out, isn't it?" replied Bob confidently, but he frowned, watching the officers.

Another car stopped and Mr. Byrd joined the police.

"Oh—oh!" whispered Maria suddenly.

The troopers and Mr. Byrd came toward them. "Who started that fire?" asked an officer with sergeant's stripes.

"I did," said Bob.

"Do you have a fire permit?"

Bob swallowed and looked around. "No. I . . ."

"The law requires you to have a Conservation Department permit to burn brush and grass."

"I didn't know that." Bob's face showed red through its layer of soot and grime.

Merrivale Byrd spoke up officiously: "This man is subject to arrest and fine for starting a grass fire on his land without a permit. Sergeant, do your duty. Irresponsible people like these need to be taught a lesson."

"My father has a permit for today," said Tom abruptly.

"His permit doesn't cover this man's property." Byrd actually rubbed his hands together with satisfaction.

Bob squared his shoulders. "But this isn't our land yet." He glanced quickly at Tom. "It is still Mr. Summers' property—we haven't title to it."

"Then I guess you're covered," said the trooper.

"Make them produce the permit," growled Byrd.

"I'll get it," said Tom quickly, and started for home.

The sergeant turned to Byrd. "Was there any damage done to your property?"

"I haven't investigated. I expect there is, though."

The officers and Mr. Byrd started across the black field toward the line stone wall to check up.

"It didn't get over the wall," said Jon after the three were out of earshot.

"Oh, he's just hunting something to make trouble about," said Maria Scotti haughtily. "He wanted this land. He wanted ours too, and he tries to make trouble for us."

Bob shook his head, perplexed. "I don't see how as County Supervisor he can afford to make trouble like this."

"His family have been here a hundred years," explained Maria. "His relatives elect him. He doesn't

want new people coming into the township. Dad says
that sometime there'll be enough new voters to defeat
him."

"Well, he certainly won't get our vote," snorted Jane.

Tom returned with the pink fire permit and the police
and Mr. Byrd came back across the field, the latter scowling his disappointment. The sergeant checked the permit and with a word of caution about future fires, he
returned to the road, followed by the other trooper and
the disgruntled Mr. Byrd.

Bob clapped Tom on the shoulder. "You certainly
helped us out of a bad spot. Thanks."

"Oh, that's all right, Mr. Woodward." Tom seemed
to appreciate more the smile Phyllis gave him. "We got
a permit to burn off our garden and I figured it'd cover
you here."

Bob's glance shifted back to the cars on the road. "Incidentally, what's the fine for burning without a permit?"

"Byrd got my dad fined twenty-five dollars for not
having one the first spring we were here," said Maria.

"A nice Byrd," remarked Jane, and they all laughed.
Then she added: "Well, you fire fighters, how about
going up to the car and having a lunch?"

"Swell idea, Moms!" cried Bob. "Come along, everybody."

They climbed the hill and Jane, magician of food,
made sandwiches for them all. Tom and Maria talked
about the big fires they'd seen out here. One had burned
over half the Byrd Estate. Someone had set it to get back
at Byrd for something. And two years ago hunters had
started a fire in the south woods.

"I've had enough fires this afternoon to suit me," said
on.

"When we get that field cultivated, we won't have to
urn it off again," said his father; then he turned to
om. "Who can we get to plow it for us?"

"Cal Dawson," replied Tom. "He's a relative of Mr.
yrd's. Not very dependable either—drunk most of the
me."

"Is he all we have to draw from?"

"I guess so."

All of them had stuffed themselves on Jane's sand-
iches, much to her satisfaction. The younger children,
ony and George Scotti and Phillip, Mildred and Caro-
n Summers had wandered up into the woods to play.
aria Scotti broke up the rest of the group by announc-
g: "The skunk cabbage are up."

"Where? I'd like to see them," cried Phyllis.

"By the brook," said Tom.

Jon went with the two girls and Tom. His arms were
eginning to stiffen and ache, the blisters on his palms
urned, and he felt tired out. He looked sidewise at
om Summers. It seemed to him that Tom was swagger-
ng. He didn't need to act so cocky just because he'd
elped them fight the fire and had produced the permit.
nd Phyllis seemed to think Tom was about perfect.
on's glance shifted to Maria, walking beside his sister.

In the edge of his vision he saw Tom look out over
he burned field, then back up the hill. He felt prodded
nto boasting: "We'll raise a lot on that field. And when
ad and I get our stone house built up there, we'll move
ut here and won't have to pay rent in New Delphi."

"That's a pretty big undertaking," was Tom's reply,

and Jon thought he seemed skeptical. He gritted h
teeth—well, he'd show him!

They reached the brook and with a cry, "Aren't the
beautiful," Phyllis crouched and examined the gree
speckled, dark red, hard-shelled skunk cabbage flowe
thrusting through the stony bank like cobra heads. "I
like to take one home," she said, her fingers diggin
around the base of the flower.

"You won't when you get it home," said Tom, laugh
ing.

Maria giggled.

"Why?" Phyllis looked up questioningly.

"You'll find out why it's called skunk cabbage."

"Oh." Phyllis drew back from the plant as if sh
thought it would bite, and they all laughed.

"When the first leaves come up they make goo
greens," Maria said, glancing at Jon.

A piercing whistle came from the direction of th
Summers' yard and Tom, looping an index finger in h
mouth, shrilled back. "That means I've got to go home.
He looked at Phyllis. "Come along and see how my chick
have grown."

She stood up quickly. "Jon, tell Dad to stop for m
on the way back to town, will you?" She set out wit
Tom.

Jon only grunted his reply to Phyllis and watche
them go. That guy and his chickens! He looked aroun
at Maria. She was staring up across the burned-off fiel

"That'll look nice when you get it cleared an
plowed," she said, and her dark eyes turned to search h
face.

Jon's weariness loosened his tongue; he wanted t

npress someone; he blurted out: "You bet! We're going
to raise corn and oats and alfalfa on it." He was surprised
at his sudden volubility.

"It's awfully old ground," she said. "You won't get
much the first year."

"Sure we will. And we'll build it up. We're going
to build us a house up there, all of stones." He waved
toward the clearing and the car. "We're going to do it
all ourselves—all the work. That's the way I'm going to
help get the money to go to college."

"That'll be a lot of work." Maria was smiling and Jon
read no skepticism in her reply. She continued: "Dad's
fixing up our place and I help him. It's a lot of fun."

"That's what I figure it'll be—fun. We're going to
have fun." Suddenly Jon's words dried up. He stood
tongue-tied, staring around helplessly. He saw Tony and
George Scotti coming up the road kicking small stones.

"I've got to go," Maria said, starting to join her
brothers.

"We'll be seeing you," he called after her. "Thanks
for helping us out."

He headed back up the hill toward the clearing, hardly
aware that he was tired now. He felt eager and excited.
He and his dad would raise a big garden and build a
house, first a cabin, then a stone house—that would be
something. Moms would like it and Maria . . .

His father had started cutting brush on the burned-
off field, but he gave up in a little while and joined Jon
and Jane at the car.

"Looks like my big pioneer has given up for the day,"
said Jane, smiling.

Bob chuckled. "Guess I've had enough."

"Come on, Jon," said his mother. "Help me put thi stuff back in the car. We'd better pick up Phyllis an head for town." Once she paused and looked at the dirt faces of her son and husband, then she folded in her lip and remarked: "I hope we can slip into the house with out the neighbors seeing us."

Jon and his father laughed. They all climbed into the car and started down the woods road toward the highway

CHAPTER SIX

RAIN

STIFF muscles and sharp aches reminded them all the next day of Sunday's excitement on Five Acre Hill. Jon displayed his blistered palms at school and boasted of fighting a wall of fire fifty feet high. He still didn't tell the gang that his dad was buying a place in the country; he just pretended they had happened upon this grass fire.

At dinner that evening, his mother said: "I can't get over that fellow Byrd trying to have us arrested."

"Well, if it hadn't been for Tom Summers, we'd have been pinched to the tune of twenty-five dollars," replied Bob.

"That would have been two and a half weeks of Five Acre money gone up in smoke." Jane looked grim.

"Tom's going to get a hundred more chicks," Phyllis announced, adding, "I wish we lived out there now, Mother."

"Why?"

"Then I'd get me some baby chicks."

"Cluck, cluck!" said Jon scornfully. "Tom's just an old hen. He doesn't think we can do much on that place."

"He does too," defended his sister sharply.

Jon couldn't prove his point, so to avoid an argument

59

he said: "Dad, Maria Scotti says we won't raise much
on that land the first year."

"I don't imagine we will, son. That ground was beaten
to death before it was abandoned."

The next evening they prepared an order for garden
seeds: peas, beans, lettuce, radishes, carrots, spinach,
beets, parsnips, sweet corn, squash, turnips. Phyllis insisted on flower seeds: asters, marigolds, delphiniums,
nasturtiums, zinnias. The bill came to five dollars and
forty-three cents.

"Phil's got to pay for those flowers out of her own
money," Jon said.

"I'd like to know why?" argued his sister.

Jane said: "I'll pay half on the flowers because I'm
interested in them too. But Phyllis and I are going to
set an example. There are things you men are going to
want that don't interest us any more than the flowers
interest you, and we'll see to it that you pay out of your
own money."

Bob and Jon weren't too happy about that decision.

The planning returned to the burned-over field and
how it should be planted after it was cleared and plowed.
The whole family began looking forward to Sunday and
their trip to the country. On Saturday morning, Jon
asked: "What're we going to do with the brush, Dad?"

"Burn it," replied his father.

"More fires!" Jane began to stiffen at once. "Haven't
you learned your lesson?"

"We'll get a permit this time and we'll burn the stuff
on the burned-off ground where it'll be safe."

Sunday they started early, stopped in Wayne just long
enough to get a fire permit, then drove straight up to

Five Acre Hill. Jon and his father flung off their jackets and attacked the brush on the lower field, hacking and swinging furiously. They trimmed up the bigger saplings and piled them to dry for firewood, while Jane and Phyllis threw the brush on a fire. All morning they worked hard, and by noon more than half the field was finished.

"Gee, that looks nice," Jon exclaimed, surveying the job done. He was amazed at how much bigger the field appeared after the brush had been removed.

"We'll finish it this afternoon," said his father; "then we'll look up this man Dawson and see if we can get him to plow for us."

Jon sank wearily down on a stone by the picnic fire and watched his mother heating up the beef stew.

The work seemed to go more slowly in the afternoon. Occasionally Jon paused to look down the road toward the Scottis', hoping that he might see Maria. He'd like to have her come over and see the job they were doing. Sharp-faced Tony went past on the road and waved, but he was the only Scotti they saw.

And they didn't see Tom Summers until they stopped at the Summers' place on their way home. Phyllis went to see Tom's chicks as usual. Joe Summers came down and said that the title to the five acres would be delivered this coming week.

When Bob mentioned that they were stopping at Dawson's to get Cal to plow for them, Joe said: "Make sure he plows deep. He'll only scrape the top if you don't watch him."

At first, rock-headed Cal Dawson would promise nothing about plowing—maybe he could and maybe he

couldn't. He chewed his bushy mustache, and his breath
thick with the smell of applejack, penetrated the open ca
window. Bob pressed him for a promise until he said
"Guess I can turn your ground next Saturday if it don'
rain." He turned his bloodshot eyes up to the sky as i
he hoped it would rain.

"And if it rains Saturday, will you plow the first Sat
urday it doesn't?" insisted Bob.

"I reckon I can do that," replied Dawson reluctantly

"Then Jon here'll be out the first clear Saturday and
show you what we want done."

"You don't want nothin' more'n plowin' and har
owin', do you?" Dawson's tone indicated that he felt tha
any other work would be beneath him.

"No. Only we want it plowed deep."

"That'll just dig up stones. The good ground's or
top."

"We're looking for stones," said Bob, chuckling.

Dawson didn't seem to think that was funny, and hi
look said: "Crazy town folks don't know nothin' abou
farmin'."

"Then we'll leave it like that," concluded Bob. "Th
first bright Saturday, Jon'll be out here."

"All right," grumbled the farmer, and shuffled away
across the yard.

"He's almost as pleasant as his relative, Mr. Byrd,"
remarked Jane as they started for home.

On the way Phyllis said: "Tom says that if I ge
twenty-five chicks, he'll start them with his and they'll be
big enough to do without a brooder by the time we
move out to our cabin in June."

"But will we have a cabin by June?" asked Jane.

"That's something we've got to start figuring on," said Bob, and grinned at Jon.

"And who's paying for those chicks?" Jane wanted to know.

Phyllis was thoughtful. "I've been saving money out of my allowance for a new tennis racket. I can make the old one do and use that money." Then she added: "And if I raise some and we eat them you'll have to buy them."

"Buy them!" That was an angle Jane hadn't considered.

Bob chuckled. "That'd be only fair, Moms."

"Well, we haven't a cabin," said Jane. "This is all talk, anyway."

"Dad, you and Jon have got to start building a cabin," insisted Phyllis. "I want to get some chicks."

That week Jon and his father set down their cabin plan: a building twelve-by-twenty. They listed the materials: two-by-fours, two-by-sixes, roofing boards, siding, flooring, roll roofing, windows, doors, nails and paint. It would have two rooms. A small one at the end for Phyllis and Jane, and the big one would be kitchen, dining room, living room, and have two cots in it for Jon and his father.

"We'll be packed in like sardines," complained Jane.

"That'll give us lots of room, Moms," said Bob. "When you live in the country you spend most of your time outdoors."

"Except when it rains," she answered.

On Friday it started raining. A slow, steady, drizzling rain that, after a few hours, seemed never to have started and showed no sign of ending. Bob didn't seem disappointed. "It'll make the plowing easier tomorrow," he explained, but that didn't wipe away the look of worry on Jon's face.

All week he'd dreamed of going out to Five Acre Hill alone, with full responsibility for getting the plowing done properly. He'd planned how he'd stand up to old man Dawson and make him plow deep. Sometimes he'd pictured himself driving the horses. Maybe Dawson wasn't such a grouch after all, and he'd say: "Well, lad, want to try your hand with that team?"

The rain hadn't stopped Saturday morning, so there was no going out to Five Acre Hill that day. Jon looked down-in-the-mouth and his father said: "There's a job you can do right here, son. You can take that list of materials for the cabin down to the lumberyards in New Delphi and get estimates. We'll probably get the stuff in Wayne, but we've got to see how the cost fits our ten-dollar-a-week restriction."

That brightened Jon up and he slipped into his rain coat and hurried downtown to call on the lumberyards. When he returned home at noon, his mother stared at him.

"What's the matter with you? Your face is so long you can step on your chin."

He had a hard time telling her that the estimated cost of the material for the cabin came to almost five hundred dollars. Worse than that, the roofing boards and flooring were not to be had, and the lumberyards didn't know when such material would be available.

"But we've just got to have a cabin," cried Phyllis.

Jane read the disappointment in their faces and all she said was: "We'd better not say any more about it until your father comes home. We can talk it all over then."

Bob didn't hide the fact that he was stunned and disappointed by the report. "I figured that stuff would come high, but not that high. And I didn't figure on our not being able to get some of it. A floor and a roof are fairly important," he added, trying to make a joke of the situation.

"But, Dad, we've got to have a cabin," wailed Phyllis.

Jane said: "Five hundred dollars—that would mean a year of saving ten dollars a week."

The only bright light Bob could cast on that was: "Well, we've a couple hundred of that saved already."

Sunday it rained. It was a dreary day for all the Woodwards. Jane suggested they might plan on a wigwam or a sod house, but that didn't go over very big. None of them were in the humor to be amused. Jon suggested a tent and Bob got out his catalogue on camping equipment and they looked at tents.

But the realization that depressed them all was the fact that the whole project would fail unless they could build a permanent house on their five acres. They couldn't make a home under a tent. They couldn't save the rent they were now paying and turn it toward the college education of Phyllis and Jon if they couldn't get a house built. The cabin had only been planned as a first step—a bigger and better house was to come later. And they were being blocked in their first step.

Jon recalled the stone shanty below the ledge built by Tom Summers and his brother. But that sort of thing was no solution. Kids could play in it—might even sleep in it, but Moms and Phyllis couldn't live in anything like that.

The week passed with the problem unsolved. One evening Bob said: "They've been developing some composition sheeting material for outside walls that is cheaper than lumber. It'll be worth looking into. As soon as I get the time—"

"Why couldn't I do that?" asked Jon eagerly.

"I think maybe you can," replied his father. "But the weather's cleared and the ground's drying. You've got to go out Saturday and see that Dawson does the plowing." He rubbed his bristling hair. "Anyhow, as far as I can find out from talking around the plant, none of this new stuff'll replace roofers and flooring and that's what's unavailable right now."

The problem was still unsolved. Saturday morning the sun came up bright, and Dawson was supposed to plow. But what was the use of plowing that field, Jon kept thinking, if they weren't going to be able to build even a cabin?

CHAPTER SEVEN

BREAKING GROUND

JON let his hopeless feeling slow him up so that he was forced to run the last block to the bus station to catch the Boyington bus which would let him off at Wayne. All the twenty miles of the trip he stared out of the window, watching the mist in the hollows, the cattle browsing in the spring-green pastures and the birds flying over the fields, but his mind was preoccupied with the problem of a cabin. Maybe they could cut enough trees to build a log cabin.

At Wayne he climbed off the bus and with a feeling of being already tired, he started across the village to the road to Five Acre Hill—three miles to Cal Dawson's place. He paid hardly any attention to his surroundings until suddenly he realized that he was passing the Wayne Lumber Company. His head jerked up and on an impulse he entered the office.

The manager, a middle-aged man with pepper-and-salt hair and bristling mustache, greeted him. Jon, carried on the crest of the impulse that turned him in here, blurted out: "We've bought five acres of land out by Merrivale Byrd's place and we want to build some kind of a place to live in during the summer. We don't want it to cost too much."

"How large a place?" asked the manager.

Jon looked into the man's clear blue eyes. He liked the friendliness he saw. "We were figuring on twelve-by-twenty." Then he added: "Just a cabin—a shack."

"Your worst problem is flooring and roofers," said the manager. "That stuff costs too much if you use wood even if you can get it." He ran the eraser of his pencil from his temple back over his ear, then said: "Come along." They entered the sample room, tables stacked with small squares of wallboard and the walls hung with types of shingles. The manager crossed to a full-sized piece of black material four feet long and two feet wide. "We've got plenty of this at four and a half cents a square foot. It's been used for outside walls and for roofing with a coat of tar."

Jon examined the material. One long edge was convex, the other was concave; the exposed ends showed the white gypsum of which it was made; it was about three-eighths of an inch thick. He tapped it with his knuckles.

"It's been used for roofing?" he asked.

"Yes. Double thickness with tar." The manager indicated a roof cement sample on one of the tables. "Costs less than two-thirds of lumber and shingles."

Gee, maybe this would work! Jon felt the skin across his shoulders tightening. "What would we use for flooring?"

"There's plenty of cement." replied the manager. "That'll give you a floor at about a quarter of the cost of wood."

Suddenly Jon wanted to get out of here and think about this. Maybe they could work it out. "I'll tell Dad." He edged toward the door. "We'll have to figure. Thank you."

But the manager followed him. "Did you say you'd bought five acres out near Merrivale Byrd?"

"Yes."

"How do you get along with Mr. Byrd?"

Jon saw a malicious twinkle in the manager's blue eyes. "He tried to get us pinched for burning off a field," Jon blurted out.

The manager laughed. "He won't like you folks building a cabin either."

In his eagerness to get outside and alone where he could think about this new building material, Jon couldn't find words to reply to the lumber company manager's last remark. He just grinned and ducked out the door to the street.

His legs moved faster and faster as he approached the edge of the village. Maybe they could get a cabin after all. Now there seemed to be some point in getting the ground plowed at Five Acre Hill. He remembered his father's final words: "You're foreman out there today, Jon. See that a good job's done."

He kept up a brisk pace the three miles down the valley and came swinging into the Dawson yard, his face eager, eyes darting about. There was no one in sight. Perhaps Dawson had already gone over to the field. He walked quickly up to the back door, scattering ducks and chickens as he went, and knocked. A thin dirty-faced woman opened the door just a crack.

"What do you want?"

"I'm Jon Woodward. Mr. Dawson said he'd plow for us up on that five-acre piece we just bought from Mr. Summers. Has he gone up there already?"

"I don't know nothin' about that. He's gone over to Sam Jaffee's to plow."

"But he promised to plow for us the first sunny Saturday morning."

"I don't know nothin' about it," grumbled the woman, then she slammed the door.

Jon walked slowly out of the yard. Now what was he to do? That big dope! That big rummy! He'd promised to plow. The boy hesitated a moment on the road, then swung up the fork to the Summers' place. Tom saw him coming and came out of the garden to meet him. Jon ripped out the details of Dawson and the plowing in one fierce breath.

"That's what he always does," replied Tom. "You can't depend on him for anything."

"Where's Sam Jaffee's place?"

"First past Scotti's on the right."

"Well, I'm goin' up and see that guy. He promised to plow for us." Jon set out belligerently up the road.

Unfairly, he felt sore at Tom for not coming up with a way to make Dawson keep his promise. Tom was only interested in chickens, he grumbled. As he walked past, he hardly glanced at the field his father and he had cleared the last time they were out. Striding around a curve in the road, he saw a neat white house up ahead, and where the ground sloped up sharply he saw a series of neat terraces held up by stone walls. From the road he could see that the ground on these terraces was already smoothed and squared up with small stakes sticking at even intervals along the edges.

That must be a garden, it occurred to him. His attention was so caught by the neat terrace walls and the good

rich soil that he was startled to realize that someone was
raking the yard in front of the house near the road. It
was Maria Scotti. This was the Scotti place. Jon had only
seen the rooftop from the picnic spot on Five Acre Hill.

"Hello," she said.

"Oh, hel-lo," he stammered, then he added hurriedly,
"You have a nice place here." He waved toward the terraces. "Is that your garden?"

She nodded, leaning on the rake. Her brother George
came around the house with an empty basket and began
to fill it with the leaves and grass Maria had piled up.
He didn't always see what he was doing; he was so preoccupied staring at Jon that he spilled some leaves and
his sister scolded him.

"You going to make a garden?" Maria asked across
the yard fence.

"If we can get our field plowed," said Jon, then he
sputtered out his gripe at Cal Dawson.

"You have to keep after him to get anything done,"
said Maria. "That's why Dad always spades our garden.
Then we can be sure the job gets done."

"Why do you make your garden in layers like that?"

"Those are terraces." Maria seemed surprised that he
didn't recognize them. "That keeps the ground from
washing. We build the ground up good and rich and
keep it that way."

"Gee, I think that's a swell idea." Jon added a grin to
the enthusiasm of his words, then he remembered Dawson and the plowing. "Sam Jaffee's place the next?"

"On the right."

"Come over and see our garden when we get it

started," he said optimistically, then waving "So long," he hurried up the road.

He heard old man Dawson shouting at his team before he got around the next curve in the road and could see him. For a moment he hesitated on the edge of the field, then set out resolutely across the plowed ground. The team came to a stop as he approached.

"Giddup!" shouted Dawson, but the team didn't move. He saw Jon and slapped furiously at the team. "Giddup! Cuss yuh!" he yelled. The team took two steps and stopped. It was no use and he turned to Jon. "Well, what d'you want?"

"You promised to plow for us the first sunny Saturday, Mr. Dawson," said the boy. "I'm here to show you what we want done."

The old farmer looked up at the sun as if he wanted to assert that it wasn't sunny. "I didn't promise anything," he growled.

"But you did!" Jon's voice rose full of indignation. "We all heard you."

"That's too hard plowin' over there."

"This team looks to me like it could do the job easily." Jon patted the nose of the bay horse nearest him. "They don't look like plugs to me. They look like good horses."

"They *are* good horses!" yelled Dawson.

"Then what do you mean it's too hard for them to plow our piece?"

"I didn't say it was too hard for them to plow."

"Then what do you mean it's too hard plowing over there?" Jon gave a violent wave in the direction of Five Acre Hill. "You mean it's too much for you?"

"I didn't say it was!" stormed the old man.

"Then why didn't you come over and do it like you promised?" Jon was all set to keep this nagging up until he got results.

"I didn't promise." Dawson shook both fists at the boy. "You dang-cussed kid, leave me alone. Giddup!" He slapped the lines furiously at the team.

Jon stroked the horse's nose, running his fingers under the bridle strap, and the team didn't move. The old man swore violently and wrestled the plow handles in desperation, then he yelled: "You—you! I'll come over and plow that piece of yourn when I get this done."

Instantly Jon stepped back and the team moved off. He walked grimly to the red-wheeled wagon at the edge of the field and sat down, determined to wait and see that Dawson kept his word this time.

It was ten-thirty before the plowing and harrowing was finished here. Jon helped Dawson lift the heavy plow back into the wagon and the spring-toothed harrow after it. The old man hesitated, glaring at the boy. At last, grumbling that he was supposed to go on up to the Hinkle place, he turned down the road toward Five Acre Hill.

Jon rode on the tailboard of the wagon. When they passed the Scottis', he saw Maria in the back yard and waved. She waved back and he saw her laugh. That made him feel pretty good. Maria could see that he was getting his way with the old man. When Dawson pulled to a stop on the field at Five Acre Hill, Jon jumped off the tailboard to help unload the plow. Well, he'd gotten the old guy here, anyway.

The area to be plowed was a little more than an acre, rising on the side toward the woods and picnic spot and flattening out toward the brook and the Byrd property. Dawson hitched his team to the plow, then stood to one side and looked over the field, swearing under his breath. At last he said: "Well, how you want it plowed?"

"As deep as your plow'll go," came back Jon promptly.

"There ain't more'n a couple of inches of good ground here. Shouldn't go no deeper'n that." Dawson kicked at the earth as if to prove his contention.

"We don't care. Dad says we want it plowed as deep as your plow'll go."

"Dang-cussed folks from the city. Don't know a hoot about farmin'."

Jon squared his shoulders and his voice rose. "We may be from the city, but my dad was raised on a farm in Illinois where they've forgotten more about farming than you hillbillies around here'll learn if you live to be a thousand."

"Hillbillies!" yelled Dawson; then in exasperation he slashed the reins at the team. "Giddup!" The horses moved out along the edge of the field.

The plow went into the ground about three inches. Jon scowled, following close behind in the furrow, watching the stony soil roll over and the plowshare tear out the small stumps and roots of the brush. At the first stop, he said: "That plow isn't set very deep."

"Dang-cussed cocklebur of a kid," grumbled Dawson, and reset the clevis to the plow beam. When he started up the team again the share nosed down a good six inches.

That was more like it, but Jon kept close behind the old man, flinging stones and roots out of the furrow as

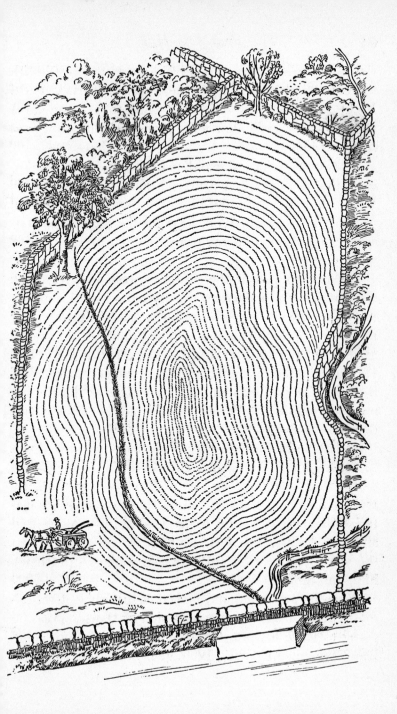

the plow turned them up. Five Acre Hill echoed with shouts: "Giddup! Get along there! Mike! Harry! Whoa! Back! Back up there! Giddup!" The turned soil lay a yellowish-gray sprinkled with shards of limestone and small cobbles.

At twelve o'clock the old man stopped, hitched his team to the wagon, and drove off home without a word. Jon looked at the strip of plowed ground with a feeling of weary satisfaction. Well, he'd got the job started. His arms ached from throwing stones. He felt pretty satisfied with himself.

He had stopped at the brook to wash up. When he straightened and looked around over the field, his glance ran along the sloping ground below the stone wall near the woods. Suddenly he remembered the Scottis' terraced garden. They could terrace that slope for their garden. He transplanted his memory of the Scotti terraces against the hill. The idea excited him. He walked to the sloping area and studied it. Yes, sir, they'd have a terraced garden too.

At last he climbed to the picnic spot and sank down to eat his lunch. His glance shifted to the elbow of hill to the north, where they planned to put the cabin. By making a cement floor and using that new sheeting material, they might be able to get a cabin for two hundred and fifty dollars. The future glowed bright again. Then the warm sun and his full stomach were too much for him, and he fell asleep.

When he awakened and looked at his watch it was almost two o'clock. There was no sign of Dawson. Was he going to leave his plow and harrow here and not come back? Jon got up grimly. Well, guess he'd have to go get the old man again and nag him back to the job. Then he heard the slow clop-clop of the team on the black-top road.

The plowing was finished by four o'clock and the harrowing started. Jon's arms were like sticks from flinging stones and dragging away the tangle of roots pulled up by the spring-tooth harrow. His back and shoulders ached.

Tom Summers came through the woods and helped him throw off stones and roots. "You got him to do a pretty good job," he praised, waving toward old man Dawson.

A feeling of pride tingled through Jon: he guessed he'd shown Tom Summers that he could get things done in the country. But Dawson had pulled up beside his wagon and stopped.

"That good enough for yuh?" he yelled.

"Yes." Jon started across the plowing, relieved that it was finished at last.

He and Tom helped load the plow and harrow on the wagon, then Jon asked: "How much do I owe you, Mr. Dawson?"

"Twenty dollars," said the farmer.

"Twenty dollars!" Jon's shoulders jerked up so straight that every ache in his body tortured him. His father had only given him ten—this was outrageous! "That's too high."

"Twenty dollars's my price," said Dawson stubbornly.

"When did you start here?" Tom broke in.

"You keep out of this, Tom Summers."

"Eleven o'clock," said Jon.

"You dang-cussed Summers kid! This ain't none of your business." The old man glared at Tom.

"The heck it isn't!" flashed Tom. "You're not goin' to take anybody while I'm around." He turned to Jon. "He charges twelve dollars a day with his team. That's his price. He didn't put in more'n two-thirds of a day, so he hasn't a right to charge you more'n eight dollars."

With tired, trembling hands Jon counted out the money and held it up to old man Dawson on the spring seat of the wagon. The farmer looked at it, swept it up in his gnarled fingers, and yelled at his tired team to get along home.

"Thanks," was all Jon could say to Tom. He felt suddenly too tired to talk. He was so tired that his mouth and throat muscles seemed numb.

"You and your folks comin' out tomorrow?" Tom asked as they walked down the road.

"Hope so." He saw Tom's grin and knew it was Phyllis Tom was looking forward to seeing. "So long," Jon added, and set out on the three miles to Wayne and the bus to New Delphi.

He had never been so tired in his life before. Yet he'd never felt so mentally at ease. His dad had said, "You're foreman out there. See that a good job's done." Well, he'd seen that a good job was done. And Tom was really a nice guy. Maybe they'd be able to get their cabin now and Phyllis could get the chicks for Tom to start. And . . . Jon slept all the way to New Delphi on the bus.

CHAPTER EIGHT

GARDEN

JON'S nap on the bus rested him enough so that he felt equal to swaggering a little when he arrived home. After all he had good news to report: the plowing was done and he'd found a cheaper building material.

"Good going," praised his father. "You're the kind of a foreman I like to have working for me."

Jane just smiled faintly, happy to see Bob so proud of Jon. Phyllis began to pester immediately: "Are we going to have a cabin now? Can I order my twenty-five baby chicks?"

"We'll settle all that when we go out to Five Acre Hill tomorrow," replied her father.

But tomorrow brought more rain. The Woodwards went to church and came home to Jane's big Sunday dinner. All of them except Jane felt cooped up and restless.

"Blast this weather!" stormed Bob. "We ought to be getting our early garden in. Now we've got to wait until next Sunday, and if it rains next Sunday . . ."

"Stop stewing," said Jane. "There isn't any use fighting the weather."

"Dad," spoke up Jon. "I think we ought to terrace our garden plot. You know, that sloping east side of the hill below the woods. The flat bottom can be used for oats and corn and alfalfa or clover, but the slope would make a fine spot for our garden if it were terraced."

"Terraced," grumped Bob. "Where'd you get that idea?"

Jon chewed his lower lip. He didn't want to say he'd gotten the idea from the Scotti garden. "Well, it'd keep that slope from washing away," he argued. "We could build the ground up richer and keep it that way if we terraced it."

"Fiddlesticks!" The weather had put Bob in a balky mood. "We're not going to fool around with any tricky sort of gardening. Back in Illinois we plowed the ground, raked it, put in the seeds and that was all there was to it."

"But the ground'll wash," insisted Jon.

"A little, maybe," scoffed his father. He glowered out of the window at the slanting rain.

"Bob, this isn't Illinois," said Jane firmly.

"What if it isn't? We've got to get our garden in and we've no time for fooling."

"It won't be fooling, Dad." Jon's face was twisted as if he had a toothache.

It was Phyllis who switched the conversation and restored good humor. "Father, what about building our cabin?"

Bob and Jon pulled chairs up to the table and began figuring the material for the building on a basis of gypsum sheeting and a cement floor. Jane protested the cement.

"But, Moms, a few rugs'll make it warm and easier on your feet. You'll be outdoors most of the time, anyhow."

Their figuring brought the cost of the building to around two hundred and fifty dollars. Bob took a deep breath, his cheeks glowing. "If it cost us no more'n that we can do it." He laid the pencil he'd been using down as if it were some delicate instrument. "One of these first week-ends we ought to leave our list of materials with the Wayne Lumber Company for their estimate." He looked at Jane sewing, at Phyllis watching him intently, at Jon studying the figures with shining eyes; then he rubbed his hands together vigorously. "Come on! Let's start the fire in the fireplace and pop some corn."

Everyone was good-humored again.

But Jon hadn't given up his idea of terracing the garden. Monday he talked to his science teacher about soil conservation. The teacher gave him several leads to follow. He found out a lot about terracing and contouring fields for farming, but little about terrace gardening. What impressed him most was the fact that all slopes cultivated should be terraced or contour-farmed to save the soil. It had been proved that such farming resulted in better crops. All week he thought about it, building garden terraces in his imagination. But how could he get around his father's opposition?

Thursday night at dinner, he remarked: "Dad, maybe we shouldn't wait until Sunday to get the garden started. Why can't Moms drive Phyllis and me out there Saturday morning and we can get the ground raked and leveled up?" He held his breath waiting his father's reaction to this suggestion; he knew his father was looking forward to planting the garden himself.

"Swell idea!" was Bob's quick reply. "And you can leave our list of materials with the Wayne Lumber Company for them to give us an estimate."

So it was settled. Saturday morning Jon put the rake,

hoe, pick and shovel into the car, and Jane drove his sister and him out to Wayne. They stopped at the lumberyard as planned.

"How long will it take you to give us an estimate on this stuff?" Jon asked, handing the list of materials for the cabin to the manager.

The man's sharp blue eyes scanned the figures. "Couple of minutes." He began setting down numbers after each item, then added up the prices set down. "Two hundred and thirty-six dollars," he said.

That was under the two hundred and fifty Jon and his father had figured. "Gee, maybe we'll be getting some of that stuff pretty soon," he said excitedly. "Week or two maybe."

"When you want it, let me know," said the manager. "We ought to get acquainted. My name's Smith; what's yours?"

"Woodward. My father's name is Robert. He's a production engineer at Universal." Jon began edging toward the door. "Thank you, Mr. Smith. We'll let you know as soon as we're ready for this material." He ran out to the car. "Two hundred and thirty-six dollars he figures it," he panted, tumbling into the seat, slamming the car door shut.

Jane was busy getting the car underway and didn't reply, but Phyllis spoke up from the back seat: "That means we can have our cabin. Dad said if it was two fifty or under." She clutched her handbag suddenly and stared out the window at the passing countryside, her eyes bright.

When they reached the fork in the road by the Summers' place, Phyllis said: "Mother, let me out here, will you? I want to see Tom's chicks. I'll walk up later."

"Don't stay too long," said her mother.

"Cluck! Cluck! Don't forget you've got a lot of scratching to do in our garden," Jon teased as she climbed out, and got himself slapped.

Jane drove up to the picnic spot. Jon unloaded the garden tools and hurried down the slope to the plowed ground. He hoped his mother wouldn't come right away. The soil was dry and crumbly—just right for working. For a moment he paused at the stone wall which ran along the upper edge of the field and angled down toward the north boundary.

His glance shifted back to the car in the woods. He could just see the gray top. His mother wasn't coming yet. He leaped over the wall and walked across the field to the dry-run at the foot of the hill; there he stopped and looked back. It was this oblong area, two hundred yards long and fifty yards wide, sloping up from the dry-run to the stone wall, that he had pictured for their terraced garden.

Suddenly he dropped all the tools but the shovel and began throwing the earth uphill on a line which followed the contour of the slope above the dry-run. He worked frantically, occasionally glancing up toward the car. After shoveling the line down to the subsoil for a distance, he ran up to the stone wall and began carrying down flat slabs, grunting with their weight.

He laid a layer along the line he had dug, then a layer on top of them. Once when he glanced up the hill he saw his mother coming down toward him. He worked harder than ever. Before she reached the plowing, he had built ten or twelve feet of wall about two feet high. The flat slabs of stone laid up easily. It was fun to work with them—like playing with huge toy blocks. He knelt and sighted across the top of his wall and his eye level carried almost fifteen feet up the slope.

His mother had been watching. She stood slender and straight on the edge of the field, the breeze blowing her denim slacks, her gloved hands resting on her hips, a bandanna scarf holding back her hair, her eyes twinkling.

"What on earth are you doing, Jon? Father didn't say to do it like that!"

"I'm going to terrace it," he said stubbornly.

"Jon, you can't do that. Dad'll be furious."

"Moms, it'll make a better garden," he pleaded. "The books say so. The ground won't wash. It'll look nice. Honest it will." He hadn't wanted to tell where he got this idea initially, but now he blurted it out. "You ought to see the Scottis' garden. Theirs is terraced. It looks swell. Honest, Moms. This is the way it should be done here where the soil is thin and washes so easily. And Dad won't be able to say anything if the job's done by the time he sees it."

Jane looked at his eager face already streaked with sweat and his sparkling eyes pleading for her support.

"I don't know." She shook her head slowly, but the corners of her mouth twitched. "I don't know much about gardens. Just the same, something tells me your father isn't going to like this." The crestfallen look that spread over Jon's face made her let loose a smile. "But let's go through with it now you've started, and see what happens. What do I do?"

"Aw, gee, Moms, you're swell." His round face cracked in a wide grin. "You can start pulling the ground down level with the top of the wall." He handed her the rake. "From this line." With his toe he marked the upper edge of this first terrace bed. Then he rushed at the job of wall-building.

The sun grew hotter and he threw off his shirt. His shoulder muscles strained and rolled beneath his winter pale skin. After a while he paused to complain: "Where's Phyllis? We didn't come out here to play with Tom Summers' chickens."

"She'll be along," replied his mother.

She raked and pulled at the soft crumbly earth. The rake tines dragged out buried sods; she shook off the dirt and threw them down against the upper side of Jon's wall. The boy's idea of terracing the garden had struck her as sensible—so why not go ahead and do it? Bob didn't need to think he was going to have his own way about everything out here.

As the garden bed began to take shape, she realized that this was really fun, this leveling of the ground, making a place for seeds to grow. She felt some of the same satisfaction in doing this job that she always got out of tidying up a disorderly room. Neither she nor Jon noticed Phyllis's approach.

"What in the world are you two doing?" cried the girl.

Jane looked up with a start. "We're terracing, that's what we're doing."

"But Dad said not to."

"Well, we're doing it," cried her mother defiantly.

"It's about time you were showing up," scolded Jon. "Get on that hoe and help Moms."

"Don't order me around." Phyllis flashed him an indignant look, but picked up the hoe and started to work. Then she said: "I paid Tom to order me twenty-five baby chicks when he gets his. Rhode Island Reds he's going to get me."

Her mother and Jon stopped work to stare at her. She flung back her curls and hoed vigorously, refusing to let their expressions intimidate her.

"Oh, well," said Jane at last. "They'll be your responsibility. Just see to it that you don't slack."

Jon recovered from his surprise. "Cluck, cluck!" he jeered, and his sister threw a clod at him.

They worked hard. By noon they'd planted two rows of peas, a row of onion sets, some lettuce and spinach. It was mid-afternoon before Jon finished the first terrace wall, curving it up at the end of the dry-run toward the base of the pig-nut tree below the angle of the original stone wall. He started the second terrace but didn't make much headway with it.

When it was time to drive back to New Delphi, they were all so tired they could hardly drag their feet. At home, Bob questioned them eagerly: "How'd you get along today?"

Jane took a deep breath: "We got the early stuff in. And after working as hard as I did, if we don't raise anything I'll feel like murdering you for getting that five acres."

Bob chuckled with satisfaction.

Nothing was said about the terracing. Even Phyllis didn't mention it. To change the subject quickly from the garden, Jon showed his father Mr. Smith's estimate on the materials for the cabin. Bob let out a whoop.

"It's a cinch," he cried. "We'll have our shack!"

Sunday morning Bob was in a rush to get out to Five Acre Hill, but the others were stiff and lame. "It's a swell day," he insisted. "We've got to finish the garden."

Jon and his mother exchanged worried glances.

Out they drove to Five Acre Hill. Bob slammed from the car and strode down the slope to the garden area. The others followed reluctantly. "Now you'll get it," whispered Phyllis. They came up with him standing above the first completed terrace, scowling, scratching his head.

"What's the meaning of this? I told you we weren't going to terrace it." He waved his arms. "Jane, you knew I was against this nonsense. Why didn't you put a stop to it?"

"Well, I thought it was a good idea," she said calmly.

"Good idea!" he yelled, then he took a deep breath and swung upon Jon. "I like a foreman I can depend on."

"We can tear it out and put it back the way it was." Jane started to pick up one of the stone slabs.

"Tear it out? With stuff already planted?" Bob threw his hat on the ground.

Jane let go the rock slab. The others remained silent. She looked at Jon's long face and winked and watched him struggle to keep his expression from growing too bright suddenly.

At last Bob said: "Well, I guess we might as well go on with it now that you've started." He picked up the shovel. "Confounded nonsense!" he complained in disgust.

They worked on, completing the second terrace in

silence. Toward noon Mr. Byrd, astride his chestnu
horse, rode up to where they were working.

"Good morning," he greeted cordially.

Bob straightened and offered a stiff "Good morning.'

"See you're making a little garden," continued Mr
Byrd affably. "Doing a little terracing like the guineas
Sort of a waste of effort."

"Maybe." Bob glanced over the finished garden.

"Thought I'd just stop in and see how you folks wer
getting along," the Supervisor went on. "Guess I ough
to apologize for the way I've acted before. But I didn'
know you were an executive up at Universal. Great com
pany. My brother-in-law, Mr. Sullivan-Schuyler, is on
of the directors."

Bob just nodded. His face grew dark.

"Just want to let you know that we don't object to th
'right' people," said Mr. Byrd. "It's the wops and for
eigners we object to squatting out here. We welcom
good hundred per cent Americans."

Jane watched Bob's chest swell with a deep breath.

"In my opinion," he said, "the wops and foreigner
you object to come a lot nearer being hundred per cen
Americans than a lot of old families who've lived her
so long they've degenerated into a bunch of backwar
hillbillies." His chest was empty of air when he finished

Merrivale Byrd laughed as if he thought Bob wer
only joking. Then he said: "Well, I won't keep you fron
your work. Gardening's important these days. Just re
member that if I can do anything for you, don't hesitat
to call on me."

He rode away to Bob's bristling "Thank you."

Jon and Phyllis resumed their work. Jane sniffed. Bol

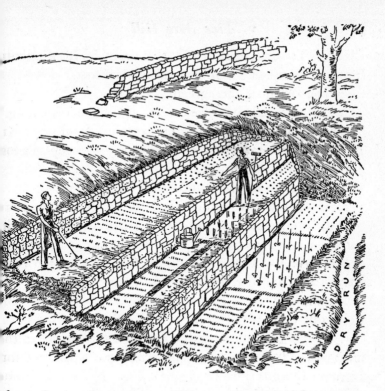

glanced over the terraces. "Waste of effort, is it?" Then
he addressed his family: "There you have a first-class
example of a cheap politician mending fences." He went
on doggedly laying up stone wall.

At lunch time Jon and his father staked off the plot
for the future cabin. They discussed details while Jane
and Phyllis prepared the meal. Both Jon and his mother
carefully kept the conversation away from the terraces.

Late in the afternoon, just as they were finishing the
last garden terrace, Maria Scotti came over with the present of a small goat's-milk cheese. Her dark eyes were
bright. She smiled at all of them but especially at Jon;
then she said to Bob: "Your terraces look awfully nice,
Mr. Woodward."

Jon saw his father stop and look around over the three levels as if he were seeing them for the first time. "Yes, they do look nice," he agreed.

And Jon's glance shifted in time to see his mother cover her mouth with her hand to hide a grin.

"My father says that's the only way to keep a good garden on this kind of land," continued Maria, "unless you make it on level ground."

"Did your father terrace his garden?" Bob asked.

"Oh, yes, right from the first. It's the way it's done in Italy." Maria spoke quickly and eagerly.

Bob gave Jon a furtive glance before he said: "We can learn a lot from the way they do things over there."

On the way back to New Delphi, Bob said: "Well, we've our early garden in." His gaze shifted to the darkening bank of clouds up the Iroquois Valley. "A good rain will start it growing and won't wash the ground away on those terraces."

Jon glanced around to his mother and Phyllis grinning in the back seat. His father was staring straight ahead now, but his lips were bent just slightly in a smile. He added: "Next week-end we've got to sow our oats and clover and we can start the cabin—maybe."

CHAPTER NINE

CABIN

NOW that the actual building of the cabin was drawing near, Jane worried aloud: "How do you know you can build it? You've never built anything like it, either of you."

"Of course we can build it," Bob replied confidently.

"Well, I don't want the roof falling in on me."

"Aw, Moms!" Bob sounded hurt.

Jon spoke up: "Moms, did anything Dad or I ever make for you fall apart? Building a cabin's no trick."

"All right, all right," Jane agreed quickly. "I'm willing to be convinced."

The following Saturday Jon left an order for eight bags of cement, one and a half tons of sand, four twenty-foot two-by-fours, twenty sixteen-foot two-by-fours and sixteen twelve-foot two-by-fours with Mr. Smith at the Wayne Lumber Company.

"We'd like to have that stuff delivered today," he said importantly, and pulled out the money his father had given him to pay for the materials.

"Sometime this afternoon," agreed the manager.

Again that morning Phyllis asked to be let off at the Summers' place to see if Tom's chicks and hers had come, and Jane and Jon drove on up to the picnic spot. This time it was Jane who headed straight down to the garden. Jon went over to have a look at the site picked out for the cabin.

Jane looked for signs of seeds growing in the terraces, but only the thin spears of onion sets showed through the soil. She felt disappointed. Her eyes lifted to the red-budded maples, the brownish green mist of elms and the golden whips of willows along the brook. Robins quarreled on the plowed field, while crows scolded in the woods across the road. A bluebird flashed to a twig on the pig-nut tree at the top of the garden and sang briefly. A bluebird meant good luck, she told herself quickly. The air was soft; a breeze blew in the faint smell of shad bushes.

Jon came down the path carrying the bags of seed oats and clover and the rakes. "We've got to get this grain in, Moms," he said, never once looking at the garden.

"Nothing's up except onions," she answered.

Even then he didn't glance at the terraces. His eyes were fixed on the field. He wanted to get the oats sowed over all but the part set off for corn, and the clover sowed on the north half of it, before the building materials came.

"Phyllis is stalling along again," he grumbled. He almost seemed indifferent to the terraced garden this morning, and it had been so important to him just a week ago. But the cabin was the important thing this week.

He strode out on the field and opened the bag of oats. After carefully determining the area to be sowed, he cuddled the bag in his left arm and scooped his right hand full of seed. His father had demonstrated in the living room at home how to broadcast grain. Grab a

handful, swing right, swing left, let the grain sift between the thumb and second finger with the index finger
acting as a spreader. It wasn't difficult. Back and forth
across the field he went.

Once his mother called: "What am I supposed to do?"

"Rake it in," he yelled, and went on sowing. When he
finished broadcasting the seed, he joined his mother at
the job of raking the loose topsoil over the scattered kernels.

At last Phyllis came along and began to help, announc-
ing: "Guess my chicks won't get here for another week
or maybe ten days, Tom says."

"Took you long enough to find that out," muttered
Jon.

By noon they had covered half the piece. But Jon was
so restless he could hardly eat; he wanted to start leveling the site for the cabin.

"Moms," he burst out, "will you and Phil finish raking in those oats while I work on the spot for the shack?"

"Slave driver," said his mother.

"I don't see why you should do all the interesting
work," complained Phyllis.

"If you can level this spot for the shack, I'll rake the
field," Jon retorted, and silenced further revolt.

With pick and shovel he graded an area twenty-five
feet long and sixteen feet wide on the elbow of ground
curving out north of the picnic spot. The long side of
the rectangle faced down the valley to the southeast.
When he heard the lumber truck laboring up the woods
road, which they now called the "drive," he went to help
unload the two-by-fours and cement.

The driver, a stocky, jug-eared chap, looked around

and remarked: "Got a nice view from up here." They began unloading the material. "Only thing wrong with this place is your neighbor over there," continued the driver, waving in the direction of the Byrd Estate. "He's one big pain."

"We certainly don't care for him," said Jon.

"He thinks he's got everything tied up around here," said the driver, grunting a bag of cement down on the other bags stacked beside the two-by-fours. "Couple of weeks ago he came down to the yard and tried to argue Mr. Holden, the big boss, into not selling you stuff to build with. The boss sure told him where he could go. The nerve! One of these days we're goin' to get enough new votes in this town to beat him."

Jon didn't know what to reply to all this. The driver added: "The sand'll be up later," and roared away in the truck.

The smell of new lumber hurried Jon back at his job of leveling. Once he glanced to the lower field to see how his mother and sister were coming with their job, then tore into his work harder than ever. He turned over in his mind what the truck driver had told him. Apparently Mr. Byrd had first tried to make it hard for them to get building material and, failing that, he had come over and tried to be friendly. Jon, remembering his father's stiff answers when Mr. Byrd called, wondered what their neighbor would try to do next.

As soon as Jon finished the leveling job, he rushed up to the car and unloaded the two sawhorses he and his father had built in the basement at home. He carried them to the cabin site and went back for his saw, square, and the red spirit level. Grunting with the effort, he lugged two twenty-footers from the pile of two-by-fours over to the sawhorses. He measured and cut each to twenty-foot length and sawed halved-joints on the ends. He laid these along the back and front sides of the leveled area. Then he cut two twelve-footers to length with halved-joints on the ends.

This was the way his father had said they would do it. He fitted the halved-joints together on the leveled site, forming a rectangle. The sound of a car door slamming made him look up: his mother and sister had finished their job in the field and were coming over to see how he was getting along.

"How do you like it?" he asked proudly.

To Jane and Phyllis, this wasn't much to see—a leveled stretch of ground with a rectangle of two-by-fours.

"Did Dad say you could cut those pieces?" asked Jane.

"No," admitted Jon. "But I did a good job. See how they fit."

"Well, you'd better wait for your father to take the lead after this," she counseled dryly.

Jon frowned. They'd never get a cabin built if they had to wait until his dad could do it on his one day off a week.

The load of sand arrived and was dumped beside the lumber and cement. After the truck had clanked and rattled away down the hill, the three Woodwards drove home to New Delphi.

Bob was already home from the plant when they got there, pacing about restlessly. He began pounding questions at them about the sowing of the oats and the arrival of the building materials. "Did you cover up the cement?" he asked.

Jon's jaw dropped. He hadn't thought of that. "No."
His voice was almost a whisper. "I didn't think—we
didn't have anything to cover it with."

"You could have taken that tarpaulin in the basement," said his father. He stepped to the living room
window. "If it rains, that cement'll be set as hard as
rock."

"Why didn't you remind us to take something along?"
asked Jane sharply.

"I can't think of everything."

They were all silent. Jon, Phyllis, and Jane were just
too tired to face this worry.

Finally Bob said: "Maybe it won't rain. It's clear out
now." He paced several times around the living room.
"If we had the extra gas I'd drive out and cover it."
Again he remarked hopefully, "Maybe it won't rain."

But that was a bad night for Jon. In spite of his fa-
tigue, he awakened several times, listening for rain.

It didn't rain. And the Woodwards were on their way
to Five Acre Hill early in the morning, the trunk of the
car loaded with short pieces of plank for a cement-mix-
ing box.

Bob examined Jon's job, testing the rectangle for
squareness and the timbers for levelness. "All right," he
admitted. "Practically perfect." Jon looked slantwise at
his mother, and Bob continued: "Guess we'd better get
to pouring cement."

At first it was fun shoveling out the mixture, four
parts sand to one part cement, and hoeing the two together, then adding water carried up from the brook
until the mix looked like thick pea soup. Batch after
batch they mixed and scooped into the rectangle of two-

by-fours. They commenced at one end and worked toward the other, using a sixteen-foot two-by-four flatwise across the width of the rectangle for a "straight edge," pulling it along to level off and smooth the wet cement.

Jane and Phyllis couldn't do much to help besides carry water and cook lunch. They enjoyed a day of comparative leisure. Phyllis discovered that the woods violets were out. Jane spent her spare time on a blanket spread out near the picnic fire gazing at the clouds floating over the valley.

By the time the last batch of cement was mixed and poured and the floor smoothed up, Bob and Jon were ready to just sit down and rest. "Some job," Jon sighed. And Bob turned to Jane, "Moms, do you want to drive us home?"

The next Saturday Jon left the order for windows, two doors, twelve hundred square feet of the gypsum sheeting, nails, roofing cement and paint at the lumberyard. This time he came out to Five Acre Hill alone on the bus. His father had given him careful instructions what to do. First he removed the two-by-four frame they had used as a form around the now hard cement floor. Then he dug a trench about six inches wide and eight inches deep around the floor and mixed cement to fill it. He set six-inch bolts in this fresh cement, two inches out from the solid floor, three bolts on each side and two on each end.

That evening as he started wearily for the bus stop in Wayne, he met Mr. Scotti driving home. The big swarthy Italian swung his car around and yelled: "Jump in, I take-a you to the bus." He didn't give Jon time to say anything. "You are Mr. Woodward's-a boy. I can see-a that. How you getta long up there? Fine? You build-a the house now. That's-a fine. Build-a the home—that's-a fine. Your dad, he's-a one fine fella. He tries-a sell every-a-body the place to live in the country like-a he does." He threw back his head and laughed loudly as if that were a great joke. "Mr. a-Byrd, he won't-a like—you see." He shook his head. "One fine fella, your dad." He reached over and touched Jon's leg lightly. "A good-a boss. That's-a him." His voice had lowered to a confidential tone.

At the bus stop, he waved away Jon's thanks grandly, "Don't-a mench," and drove off beaming.

Bob smacked his hands with pleasure when Jon reported the foundation all in and the bolts set. Tomorrow would be the big day—tomorrow they'd start putting up the frame of their cabin.

Again they arrived at Five Acre Hill early. The valley was thick with mist and a wing of mackerel sky rose in the east.

Jon and his father unloaded their tools and began work at once. They bored holes in the two-by-four frame they had used as a form for the cement floor and fitted the timbers over the bolts Jon had set in the foundation cement. Then they began cutting and toenailing up the studding.

The rear frame went up first—five feet high and two feet center-to-center for each studding. After that was plumbed and braced, they started the front frame, seven and a half feet to the plate, leaving space for windows and a door.

This was fun. They cut two-by-fours and drove nails; they squared and leveled and measured.

Even Jane came over, sniffing the smell of fresh-cut lumber. "Nice," she admitted. She looked at the frame taking shape. "It's beginning to look like something now."

But Phyllis was too excited to notice. Tom's chicks had come and hers with them. She spent most of the day in the Summers' brooder house watching the chicks. "They're the sweetest things," she said at lunch time.

"I'll tell you if you're right when they get big enough to be eaten," said Jon.

"To be eaten!" cried his sister indignantly.

"Well, what're you going to do with them if we don't eat them?" asked her brother.

That sobered her as she went back to the Summers' that afternoon. Later she returned to report that Joe Summers had several prospective buyers for his land. Bob seemed to have been expecting that news and looked pleased, and Jon remembered Al Scotti's talk the evening before: "He tries-a sell every-a-body the place to live in the country like-a he does."

By evening the sky had grayed over and it began to sprinkle. Bob and Jon gathered up their tools and reluctantly got ready to return to New Delphi, looking back at the yellowish skeleton of the new cabin standing among the trees.

Every evening the following week Bob talked to Jon about how to put on the gypsum sheeting. Jon listened carefully, because he was to start the job on Saturday.

This time Jane drove him out and Phyllis went along. The garden needed attention. The peas were showing through and some of the other vegetables, but they weren't growing well, and Bob thought a hoeing to loosen the ground might help. Jane and Phyllis were to do this.

Of course Phyllis had to stop off to see her chicks. She came along later looking tearful—one of her chicks had died and five of Tom's. Tom said that wasn't a bad record for the first week, but Phyllis mourned: "The poor little things."

Jane went on hoeing without consoling her daughter.

From the cabin came the sound of hammering as Jon nailed on the black sheeting. The most difficult part was to fit the stuff around the rafters, doors and windows. Jon was so excited by his progress that he hardly stopped to eat, and by the time they had to return to New Delphi, the walls were almost finished.

"There, Moms," he cried proudly. "How do you like that?"

"Is it going to be black?" Her voice trembled with distaste.

"We can paint it," he answered, but felt disappointed.

At home his father said: "Tomorrow we put on the roof." He looked at the clock as if trying to push morning along.

"That horrible black stuff," complained Jane.

"Won't look so bad if we give it a coat of paint. Sometime we can do that."

In the morning they started the roof, laying the black sheets on, cementing the joints with asbestos cement. Before noon they'd finished the first layer and had started the second, giving the first layer a coat of thick roof paint ahead of the new sheets, and being careful that the joints of the second layer overlapped the joints of the first.

Jon's and Bob's hands were black with tar and their clothes and faces were smeared. They didn't even try to get the stuff off before eating lunch. Jane scolded, "You're a sight, both of you," but it did no good.

"We haven't time," Bob said.

Jon's eyes kept shifting to the cabin in the trees. It really looked like something now—like a house—the walls with window openings and door openings at the end and front, and the roof on, gleaming with black roof paint. The sight of it almost pulled him up from his seat and back to the job.

Neither Jane nor Phyllis had been inside the building under construction. Jane viewed it askance, expecting any minute to hear a crash and the whole thing flatten out on the ground. She only hoped that her menfolks wouldn't be under it.

Just as the Woodwards finished lunch, Tom Summers came over with some rhubarb roots to be set out. He looked the new cabin over and, glancing sidewise at Jon, said: "I thought you were going to build a stone house."

"We will," replied Jon resolutely. "Give us time."

Jane snorted: "I might take a chance on walls like those falling on me, but I'm not taking any chance on getting crushed under a stone wall."

Tom laughed. Jon frowned: he'd show Tom Summers what they could do yet. His father sat smiling, smoking his pipe.

Phyllis found an excuse to go back with Tom to see the chicks and Jane undertook to set out the rhubarb roots. Bob said: "Guess we'd better get back on the job," and started toward the cabin.

Jon followed, grumbling: "That guy," meaning Tom, "thinks we can't build anything."

"Moms isn't very confident either," said his father, chuckling. "Guess we'll just have to show them."

They resumed fitting, nailing and tarring the sheets of gypsum. The hill echoed with the pounding of their hammers. It had to be a careful job. They finished the second layer on the front pitch of the roof and started in on the back pitch.

Jane came up and announced that some of the peas had broken the ground, but they didn't pay any attention to her. She admonished: "Now you two be careful up there."

They went on working. A dark cloud began to grow in the northwest up the Iroquois Valley. Neither Jon nor his father noticed it until a distant boom of thunder rolled in above the pounding of their hammers. They looked up then and saw the cloud, returning to the job, their movements quickening.

Faster and faster they worked. Jane came over and remarked: "It's going to rain. We'd better get ready to go back to town." They ignored her and worked on, sweating, their faces strained and weary.

The top of the pitch was almost reached. At last the final layer dropped into place. They slapped the peak with a coat of paint and nailed on the ridge boards. The cloud had rolled to the top of the sky; a cool breeze sprang up. Thunder crashed and lightning cracked the blackness, showing gilt edges.

"Bob! Jon! You'd better call a halt," ordered Jane.

They paid no attention, but went on slapping and pushing the roof paint over the black surface with their long-handled brushes. At last the final stretch was covered and the exposed edges. Bob glanced up at the advancing cloud.

"We've time to sprinkle it with sand," he said and, grabbing a pail, rushed to the sand pile. They flung the sand over the glistening tarry roof. The fine granules stuck to their fingers, but they didn't notice. Above them the sky had turned a frightening olive green.

"Bob! Jon!" Jane was pleading now, her face pale, but still they didn't seem to hear her.

Phyllis came hurrying up the drive. "It's going to be a bad storm," she panted, and stared at her father and brother frantically finishing the last of the sanding.

The wind rose, whipping the finer particles away in a cloud. A greenish darkness settled over the hill.

"Bob! We've got to start home!" cried Jane angrily.

He yelled back: "Get the tools into the cabin."

Only Jon obeyed, while Bob carried the unset window sashes and the two doors under shelter. In the northwest they heard a violent, terrifying roar.

"Come on! Get into the cabin!" shouted Bob.

Jane and Phyllis hesitated, glancing frantically from the cabin to the car, trying to decide which would be the safer.

"Will it be safe?" wailed Jane.

Bob and Jon were dragging the last of the lumber and unused sheeting inside. They didn't have time to answer. A spattering flurry of huge raindrops beat down suddenly, and Jane and Phyllis ran for the cabin. They entered wild-eyed and panting, glancing fearfully toward the roof.

Then the roar swept over them. First came a ripping, tearing wind, then a snapping, thumping and crackling din that sounded like a furious battle—hail. They heard it on the roof; they saw the round white balls bounce on the ground and ricochet off branches and tree trunks. Hail spattered in the door and window openings. Then the barrage passed. A quiet followed. The air was cold. They looked up at the twisting, tearing edge of the clouds moving down the valley. A blinding flash of lightning stunned them, followed by a jolting, ripping crash of thunder; then the rain came down in torrents.

They stood in the center of the cabin, their eyes shifting furtively to the roof. Water poured off the eaves, washing with it the sand that hadn't stuck to the fresh tar. Outside the ground turned brown in the raging swirling water. At last they began to relax. Bob stepped to the window opening and held out his hands to let the rain wash the gritty sand from them. Jon followed his example. Jane and Phyllis finally sat down on the sawhorses against the rear wall.

"Our roof's getting a good test," remarked Bob.

"And it isn't leaking either," said Jon.

"Still think it's going to fall on you, Moms?" Bob asked.

Jane didn't answer. She looked around. "These horrid black walls, inside and out."

"Sometime we can paint them."

"Sometime!" She looked at Bob fiercely. "They'll be painted before I live here."

"But, Moms, paint costs money, and they don't need

painting to weather. Remember our ten-dollar limita-tion."

"I'll buy the paint," she answered stubbornly, "out of my own money. And I'll do the painting myself."

"I'll help you, Mother," offered Phyllis.

Jon and his father looked at each other and nodded heads, grinning with satisfaction.

"Don't look so smug, you two," said Jane, and they all laughed.

CHAPTER TEN

HOUSEWARMING

BY the following Saturday it was time to plant sweet corn. All the signs were right for planting. Tom Summers said he'd heard the whippoorwill. The oak leaves were as big as a squirrel's foot; the hickory tree buds had swelled to the size of a man's thumb. Besides, it was a week later than the eighth of May, and the eighth was when folks started planting corn in Illinois, where Bob Woodward came from.

So Jon raked over the ground intended for corn and readied it for early sweet corn and four rows of popcorn. The garden was growing. Last Sunday's rain had helped it. But it was apparent to the Woodwards, although not one of them had admitted it yet, that the garden was making a mighty poor showing. Only about a third of the seeds they had planted had pushed through the ground, and these were neither vigorous nor sturdy.

But the patch sowed to oats showed green. Jon stopped planting corn a moment to look at it. Last Sunday, after the rain, Bob had stood up on the hill and remarked: "Look how green my oats are."

"My oats" were the words he used, although Jon had broadcast the seed and Jane and Phyllis had raked them in. Jane didn't remind him of that. She knew he was capturing something out of his youth when he looked down at that greening field. What she did say upset him more than if she'd reminded him that he'd had nothing to do with the oat-sowing. "I'd like to know what you're going to do with all those oats."

"Do with them?" He became defiant at once. "Why—I'm going to cut 'em and shock 'em up and—" He looked around frantically and didn't finish. "We'd better be getting along to New Delphi."

While Jon planted the corn, three kernels to a hill, his mother and Phyllis began painting the cabin. Light green on the outside and ivory on the inside—those were the colors Jane had selected and bought with her own money. And she had been anxious to get out there that Saturday morning and get the job started. She worked as if she had found something to do besides cooking that was fun.

Both Jane and Phyllis seemed to have gone back to dollhouse playing. They talked about the furniture they could bring out from the house on Delaware Street and the arrangement of that furniture in the cabin. They talked about curtains for the windows. "I suppose," Jane surmised, "that Bob and Jon'll insist that I pay for them out of my own money."

That was exactly what Bob and Jon did. "Frills," Bob snorted at the first mention of curtains. "We can't waste Five Acre money on frills." And Jon said: "We'd better spend that money for one of those wheel-plows I've been looking at in the catalogue. That'll make the care of the garden easier."

"From what I see of our garden," replied Jane with growing indignation, "a cultivator like that would be putting a gold collar on a pig."

"Well, it isn't growing too well," admitted Bob.

Jon reported what Maria Scotti had told him. "What your garden really needs, Jon, is chicken manure."

"It certainly could stand some fertilizer," Bob conceded. "Guess we should buy some commercial stuff to pep it up."

Jane reared up at once. "If I have to buy curtains and paint out of my own money, then you'll have to buy fertilizer for the garden out of your own money, Bob Woodward."

"But, Moms," he argued. "Gardens aren't frills."

"That one is," cried Jane.

They all laughed, and Bob agreed to buy the fertilizer.

After Jon finished planting the corn he went up to the cabin, which reeked with the smell of paint, and began putting in the partition, dividing the building into two rooms, one eight-by-twelve, the other twelve-by-twelve. By the time they had to return to New Delphi that evening he had finished the partition and Jane and Phyllis had given the cabin one coat of paint inside and out.

Jon, Phyllis and Jane could have slept late Sunday morning, but Bob was up, urging them to get a move on. They might have had sufficient fun out at Five Acre Hill the day before, but he hadn't, and he wasn't going to miss a minute of the fun on Sunday.

"I can see how it will be better when we are able to stay out there all night," Jane remarked, blinking sleepy eyes. "Then maybe I can get some rest Sunday mornings."

This trip out, Jane and Phyllis rode in the front seat of the car with Bob, while Jon shared the back seat with the parts of a double-decker bed, mattresses, a three-burner oilstove, old rugs, two folding chairs and a straight chair, odds and ends of still usable stuff gleaned from the attic and basement of the Delaware Street house. Immediately upon their arrival Bob and Jon began fitting the windows and hanging the doors, while Jane and Phyllis stirred up their paint and started slapping on the second coat.

By evening the shack began to look like a finished job. Bob locked the door and before they started home, all of them stared silently at the cabin in the woods. It stood there, comfortable and cozy beneath the wide-spreading branches of the elm whose new leaves matched the color of its walls.

Bob took a deep breath of satisfaction. "One more week of work and we'll be able to stay all night here."

The following Saturday another load of furniture was hauled out in the car. Jane and Phyllis finished the painting and cleaned up the rubbish around the building. Jon laid a flagstone terrace across the front. Sunday, he and his father built an outdoor fireplace by the kitchen door. That was to please Jane. She had insisted on it. She wasn't going to cook on an old oilstove except when it rained.

That day when Phyllis went over to the Summers' to see her chicks, she announced to Tom: "Next week we're going to stay all night at our cabin, and as soon as school is out we'll move out for the summer. Then I'll take my chicks over there."

Saturday, a week later, was the big day. This time the car hauled the window screens which Jon and his father had made during the week in the basement shop of the

Delaware Street house. As soon as Jane pulled the car to a stop Jon unloaded them and began fitting them to windows and doors. Jane aired the cabin thoroughly and began making the beds. The double-decker was set up in the small room for Phyllis and her mother, while two cots were put in the big room, which was also kitchen, dining room and living room.

It took most of the day just to get things put in order: curtains hung, rugs spread, food for the week-end put away. Jane drove into Wayne for ice for the small icebox which Bob and Jon had rescued from the basement of the Delaware Street house and she and Phyllis had cleaned and repainted.

In the evening she drove to Wayne again to meet Bob on the six-thirty bus from New Delphi. He climbed off, beaming, and waited for the driver to unload two huge packages.

"What on earth is in those?" Jane demanded, but he wouldn't tell.

When they reached Five Acre Hill he set the bundles out gently and announced that he was starved.

"Well, I'd like to know what you've got there," Jane insisted.

"After I'm fed," replied Bob. Phyllis tried to take a peek, but he shooed her away. Jon was smugly disinterested, because he knew what the wrappings hid.

They sat down to supper, which Jane served on a card table set up on the flagstone terrace. They listened to the wood thrushes and the catbirds singing and a veery thrush spiraling its song from the woods across the road. Phyllis said that when she was over to the Summers' earlier in the evening, Tom and the younger Summers were freezing ice cream.

Bob promised: "Before the summer's over we'll have an ice-cream freezer of our own." Then he said: "Moms, you and Phil get the dishes done and don't you dare look out the front windows." As soon as they were inside he turned to Jon, "Get me a couple of buckets of dirt, will you, son?"

He unwrapped the large oblong package first. Out came two long red enameled boxes. From the smaller of the two he removed metal brackets and screws and began fastening the brackets to the cabin wall beneath the two front windows. He screwed the boxes to these, then filled them with the dirt Jon brought up from the garden.

From the other package he unwrapped six geraniums. "Get some water, son," he ordered, and began setting out the plants, four in the big box, two in the smaller. "Now you can come out," he called to Phyllis and Jane.

They slammed out of the cabin, one from the front door, the other from the side, in a rush of curiosity.

"Oh, gee, Dad, they're lovely," cried Phyllis.

"Why, Bob, you darling!" Jane just stood back admiring.

"That's the final touch," he admitted.

No one spoke for a while; all eyes were fixed on the bright red boxes against the green walls with the red and pink flowers standing up pertly against the copper screens.

"But, Bob—" began Jane.

"Now, Moms, I paid for them out of my own money," he explained quickly, and the whole family burst out laughing.

The sound of voices startled them and, looking around, they saw the Summers and Scotti families coming into view at the top of the drive. Tom and his father carried an ice-cream freezer between them, and Maria and her father had their arms full of packages.

"We decided to give you a housewarming," explained Joe Summers as he and Tom swung the heavy, ice-packed freezer to the corner of the terrace.

"Swell of you," cried Bob in astonishment.

"This is wonderful." Jane's face glowed with surprised happiness. She hadn't counted on such friendliness.

"Ah, you fix-a the nice-a place, boss," said Al Scotti.

Lean, spare Mrs. Summers, and soft, rolling Mrs. Scotti brought up the rear, looking a little shy and uneasy.

"My husban', he say you no high-hat," said Mrs. Scotti with a nervous chuckle. "And I say that's-a what this country need—more folks who leave-a the high-hat in the attic. So we welcome you, missus."

"Thank you," replied Jane. "Bob never could keep a high hat on." Laughter whirled among them like a gusty spring wind-spinner.

Mrs. Summers came forward a little stiff and frightened. "I didn't know but maybe you folks wouldn't like homemade ice cream," she admitted diffidently.

"Not like homemade ice cream!" exclaimed Jane.

"Oh, boy!" Bob smacked his hands together. "Lady, I haven't eaten good homemade ice cream since I left the farm in Illinois. I told Phyllis tonight that before the summer was over we were going to have a freezer of our own."

Then Jane led them, all laughing and talking, for a tour of the cabin. That didn't take long. The three women remained indoors and the hum of their voices was interrupted occasionally by laughter. Jane was making them feel at ease. Finally the sound became an unbroken murmur as she began questioning her two neighbors about canning fruit and vegetables.

Outside, Bob, Al and Joe sat on the terrace talking. The younger Summers and Scotti children had marked off squares in the dirt and played hopscotch, listening to the talk of the grown-ups, patiently waiting for the serving of the ice cream.

Tom asked about the garden and Jon and Phyllis took him and Maria down to see it. "It doesn't look so good," Jon apologized. "Guess it's coming a little better since Dad put some commercial fertilizer on it last week."

"What it needs is a good covering of chicken manure next fall," said Tom. "Then you'll raise a garden."

"When Jon gets my chicken house built and I get my chickens over here we'll have some chicken manure to put on the garden," spoke up Phyllis optimistically.

"Who said I was going to build you a chicken house?" Jon wanted to know.

"That's right," put in Tom. "Jon's going to build a stone house."

Jon's face darkened. Tom Summers didn't need to needle him all the time about building a stone house; he'd show him.

Maria interrupted: "It'll be fun building a stone house—like playing with blocks." She smiled at Jon. "Dad says not to be surprised at what the Woodwards do. They just do things, my dad says."

That made Jon glance triumphantly at Tom, but Tom was grinning. "I won't be surprised if Jon builds a stone house."

They climbed back up the hill and sprawled out at the edge of the terrace, talking about high school. Next year Phyllis would be a senior, and Tom, Maria and Jon would be juniors. Tom and Maria talked about school in Wayne; Phyllis and Jon about school in New Delphi. There wasn't much difference, they agreed, only maybe in Wayne you got better acquainted with your class.

They talked about what they would do this summer— was there a place to swim near here? Phyllis and Jon wanted to know. There wasn't. Jon suggested damming up the brook, but Tom shook his head—old man Byrd would raise a rumpus.

Their conversation drifted on to the future—college. Tom hoped he might be able to study medicine, any-how, he was going to start out with biology. Phyllis said she thought biology or botany would be lots of fun. Jon curled his lips: he wanted more action—a construction engineer for him. Maria wanted to study art—she said she wished women could be architects.

Dusk settled down; the moon grew brighter; the younger children stopped their hopscotch game. All the time Jon had an ear cocked to the talk of the men. He heard Joe Summers say: "This land'll never be put back into production commercially. Dairy maybe, but I doubt if even that. That's why I'm selling my farm down to the twenty acres around my buildings."

"Our real farm land is out in the Middle West," said Bob. "This is mostly sub-marginal and should be re-claimed by people working in plants and factories for homes. They can fix them up to produce half their liv-ing and have fun doing it."

"That's-a right, Boss," agreed Al Scotti. "Joe, you should-a hear Boss sell country to the fellas at da plant. The work get behind. Foreman, he yell and cuss—it-a do no good. Then Boss come—slap this one, that one on the back. Say to Mike Brogan, 'Mike, what you need is-a home in the country, then you work better.' Zingo, we're right up to top again." And Al laughed loudly.

"I'm sellin' a piece of my farm to Mike and a couple of other fellows from Universal, thanks to Bob," said Joe.

"That's-a swell." Al blew a cloud of smoke from his black twisted cheroot. "A great-a fella, the Boss here."

"Don't lay it on too thick, Al," cautioned Bob, glad that his crimson face wasn't apparent in the dusk. "I'll have your foreman put you to pushing a broom. Besides" —he turned to Joe—"Al's always dishing out the glories of living in the country to his fellow workers. He's better at it than I am."

Al laughed, his big body shaking with good humor. "He put-a me to push-a da broom." He laughed again.

"In a couple of weeks," Joe said, "you'll hear more pounding out here like Bob and Jon have been doin'."

"That'll be good to hear," exclaimed Bob.

The women had come out of the cabin.

"Mr. Byrd won't like the sound of it," remarked Mrs. Summers. "We'd better watch out for more of his tricks."

"Byrd! He's-a no good!" snorted Al fiercely. "Next-a year we vote him out. *Abaso* that guy Byrd!"

The men sprang up to give the womenfolks their chairs, but Jane said that it was time to serve the ice cream because the younger children had to go home to bed. Every available saucer in the Woodward cupboard was brought out heaped with melting ice cream. And plates of rich Italian pastry made by Mrs. Scotti followed. Jane supplied coffee for the grown-ups.

"Wonderful," praised Bob. "I haven't tasted anything so good since I left the farm." He held up a bit of pastry to Mrs. Scotti. "This is why America is great. Here the best cakes ever invented and the best ice cream ever made get together."

"Don't-a lay it on so thick, Boss," said Al Scotti, "or you-sa be push-a da broom." And they all laughed heartily.

The last blob of ice cream was eaten and the last crumb of cake. Maria Scotti and Tom Summers set out to shepherd their respective younger brothers and sisters home. Phyllis and Jon walked with them down the long drive to the highway.

Last year's leaves rustled with scurrying bugs as they passed; peepers tinkled from the brook in the valley; a loon yammered from some place farther downstream; then a whippoorwill began whipping so close at hand that they could hear the grunting intake of his breath after each whip. The younger children didn't stray far ahead and the four older ones seemed to have little to talk about.

On the way back up the hill Jon looked at the moon glowing high in its first quarter and whispered suddenly: "Gee, Phil, hasn't it been a swell evening?"

Phyllis had been thinking of what she'd be doing now if they were in New Delphi instead of here: Peggy and Mary and she would be coming home from the movies. The roar of traffic would be thick around them. Maybe a bunch of boys would whistle at them. Mary would jive the latest hot tunes; they'd talk about the show, or maybe they'd talk about this or that boy.

Her brother's question startled her. "You're hep," she said. "This is on the beam." Then she laughed merrily; what she had been thinking and what she had answered seemed so unreal in all this pleasant reality.

Jon snorted in disgust, then he laughed too, understanding a little that she was mocking the empty life in town.

CHAPTER ELEVEN

MR. BYRD'S NEPHEW

As soon as Van Buren High School closed, the Woodwards moved out to Five Acre Hill for the summer. Bob joined Joe Summers and Al Scotti in sharing the car ride to the bus stop in Wayne. By the end of the first week the family had settled down to a comfortable routine life.

But it was a routine devoid of all town conveniences. Once when Jon expressed a wish for a place to swim, his father said: "At least we can have a showerbath." The next night he brought home a large sprinkling can. They screened off a six-foot circle behind the cabin, hung the can from the branch of a tree, and enjoyed the luxury of a daily shower. Bob was the first to try the device and he sang "Sweet Adeline" lustily and off-key, much to the amusement of the family.

All the water they used had to be carried up from the brook or the spring which gurgled just a few feet back from the stream's edge. Carrying the water was one of the chores that had been given to Jon. He grew tired of it in a short time.

"Someday we'll get water pumped up here," Bob promised.

"Someday my prince will come," sang Jane to tease him.

"Well, we will, Moms. Anyhow, this is better than living in town all summer, isn't it, Moms?"

She didn't answer. She wouldn't give Bob or Jon the satisfaction of admitting that she enjoyed it out here. They all knew that she did anyhow, so it didn't matter. She sewed, she read, she called on Mrs. Summers and Mrs. Scotti, and they called on her. Then on a shopping trip to New Delphi she returned with a set of water colors.

The next evening Phyllis went to meet her father. "Dad, Mother painted a picture this afternoon. A water color."

He set his mouth in a circle of astonishment, then whispered, eyes twinkling, "Phil, I think the country's getting Moms down."

At supper he remarked casually: "Well, Moms, how'd you bore yourself today?" He gave Jon a heavy wink.

"Doing nothing," replied Jane firmly. "Absolutely nothing at all." But her eyes were shining.

"Don't you believe her, Dad." Jon's expression became painfully solemn. "I had to carry water all afternoon for her to paint a water-color picture."

"Why, Jon Woodward, you big fibber!" cried his mother, choking abruptly with laughter.

Phyllis found plenty to occupy her time. Jon had made a coop for her twenty-four chicks and Tom had brought them over for her. She fed them and babied them until all she had to do was sit on the grassy slope below the cabin and they'd flock around her, perching on her shoulders, quarreling to sit on her head, singing in shrill piping voices. The young cockerels strutted arrogantly, looking for a fight, ruffling neck feathers at a pointed finger, while the pullets sidled up docilely, eager to be petted.

She helped Jon and Jane hoe and weed the garden; she haunted the woods and field margins looking for strange plants. Jack-in-the-pulpits were abundant along the brook; once she found moccasin flowers. When she discovered plants she didn't know, she took them to Tom Summers for him to tell her their names.

Sometimes when Tom could get away from his garden and chickens they looked for flowers and plants together. One late afternoon they came upon a luna moth drying its pale green wings on the trunk of a black birch. It was so beautiful a sight that Phyllis had to whisper past a lump in her throat, "Oh, Tom, that's the loveliest thing I've ever seen." She looked around into his lean, strong face.

He wasn't even seeing the moth; his eyes were fixed on her. Suddenly he began talking about other moths— the big ones, *Samia cecropia* and *Telea polyphemus.* He talked rapidly, repeating himself often.

At supper Phyllis reported the finding of the luna to the family, and her face glowed when she described it.

In her field searches she discovered a patch of wild strawberries in the triangular corner of their land across the brook. Jon and Jane helped her pick enough fruit for a shortcake and two jars of jam. The flavor of the berries, so rich and sweet, so strawberry, made her mother complain: "We'll never be able to eat store strawberries again as long as we live."

"We'll raise our own and won't have to," said Bob.

It was Jon who began to get bored at Five Acre Hill. There wasn't enough to do. The garden didn't take up much of his time. His father worked in it after supper just for the exercise. Besides, the ground was so poor that even weeds didn't grow with enthusiasm and it took pounds of commercial fertilizer to make the vegetables develop as they should.

Just the same the Woodwards had spinach, scallions, lettuce and endive to eat. In a couple of weeks they would have peas. The Summers let them have all the rhubarb they wanted.

Then Jon helped Maria Scotti and her brothers pick the Scotti cherries. That was fun while it lasted. Mrs. Scotti shook her apron at him and said to her daughter: "Maria, shoo-a da big robin before he eats-a alla cherry!"

Maria laughed. "Jon's a good cherry-picker, Momma."

They stripped the three big Montmorency trees and when the job was finished Mrs. Scotti pushed a heaping half-bushel of fruit toward Jon. "That's-a for you waurk."

"I don't want to be paid," protested the boy. "I was just having fun. Besides, I did eat an awful lot."

But Maria and her mother insisted that Jon take the half-bushel over to Five Acre Hill. The Woodwards ate cherry pie, cherry sauce, cherry jam and Jane canned a dozen pints. A special trip was made to New Delphi to leave the canned fruit in the basement of the Delaware Street house. "The first fruit I ever canned," said Jane proudly. "I hope it keeps."

"I don't think it'll keep long after we get back to town," predicted Bob, laughing.

To Jon there seemed to be a long time in between

exciting things to do. He studied the end of the brook near the road, figuring how he could build a dam and a swimming pool. But he remembered Tom's warning about old man Byrd. He talked to his father about starting the big house.

Bob frowned. The subject seemed to stir up worries. He put Jon off with a shake of the head. "We've got to accumulate a little more money first," he explained.

One day, to work off his surplus energy, Jon took the ax and saw and began trimming one of the five big trees felled by the guard-rail cutters down near the road. He had worked an hour or so when he heard Phyllis scream. Dropping the ax, he raced up the hill. His sister's screaming stopped, but he could still hear the shrill cries of her chickens. He reached the picnic spot and saw his mother and sister, one with a stick, the other with the broom, swinging at a small, dust-colored animal which tried to get past them at the scurrying, terrified chickens.

Jon dashed up and, without thinking exactly what he was doing, snatched a rock and flung it at the bobbing animal. The stone knocked the beast rolling and it finally lay on its back, kicking its short legs at its greenish white belly. A little blood bubbled on the end of its pointed nose, smearing the edge of snarling lips, which were drawn back over a set of yellowish, vicious teeth.

The three were staring at the twitching animal, when Tom Summers, who had also heard Phyllis's screams, came panting over the hill. "Huh, a weasel," he exclaimed with an outrush of breath. "You're lucky you got him."

"He was after my chickens," cried Phyllis. "The poor things. He chased them . . ."

"I never saw such a beast." Jane leaned trembling on the handle of the broom. "Why, he came right at us."

"Oh, a weasel'll stop at nothing, once his blood's up," explained Tom. "How'd you manage to kill him?"

"Jon hit him with a stone." Phyllis shuddered at the memory.

"Hit him with a stone!" Tom stared at Jon with admiration. "You ought to be a baseball pitcher."

"Couldn't do it again if I tried," Jon admitted, feeling weak and astonished at his own feat.

It took some time to round up the terrified chickens and quiet them down.

That evening at supper they told Bob the story.

"What we need is a dog," said Jon. "I wish we were living out here all year around, then I'd get a dog."

Bob said the chickens ought to be put in a pen. They were getting to be a nuisance running around loose. Jon recalled seeing some rolls of wire in a brush-hidden rubbish dump across and down the road. Maybe they could get enough to make a fence.

"I don't know why anyone would throw away good wire," replied Bob skeptically, but the two of them went down to have a look. It didn't take long for them to discover that the lower half of each roll was rusted and rotted away. They left the dump and Bob said he'd have to bring home some wire with him one evening soon.

On the way back up the drive, Jon pointed out the work he'd started, trimming up the felled trees. Bob examined the long straight trunks. "Shame they can't be used for something besides firewood," he remarked.

"Couldn't we use them somehow in our big house?" asked Jon, but his father didn't reply.

When they topped the hill again and could look down over the garden, the calf-tall corn and the silvering oats, Bob nodded his head approvingly. "We're going to get a crop of oats." The field looked better in the dusk than at any time during the day—that was when Bob liked best to look at it.

"What're we going to do with them?" asked Jon.

"Cut and shock 'em." That was as far as Bob ever got on the subject of intentions for his crop. He pictured a field of golden shocks like the oat fields he'd known in Illinois. The picture relaxed and rested him after a hard, harassing day at the plant.

But Jon was feeling cocky from his exploit of killing the weasel. The picture of the oat field didn't mean as much to him as it did to his father. He was looking ahead to something bigger—the house.

"Dad, let's start the big house this week-end." He felt full of determination, ready to insist.

Bob pulled himself away from his memory of shocked oats. The frown-lines that had vanished as he looked down on the field returned. "We've got to save more money first," he said, repeating his old argument.

"We don't need much to start, Dad," the boy argued. "We can start planning. We can dig the foundation. That won't cost money."

Bob jerked his shoulders irritably at this insistence. For just a moment he seemed about to explain something, instead he said: "We can't start it now and that's all there is to it!" He stalked across the hill to the cabin.

The week-end came and the sound of hammering rose over the hill from the direction of the Summers place. Three families had bought land from Joe Summers and were beginning to build cabins. The pounding continued Monday. In the afternoon, Jon's curiosity got the better of him; he stuck his ax in a tree stump and walked down the road to see those new places.

First came Mike Brogan's—Mike was a thin little man with a baby face; then came Hank Hartzinger's—Hank was so tall it seemed to make his shoulders stoop; and last was Dave Walsh. They had bought three, three and five acres, respectively. All three of them had taken their vacations from Universal at the same time and were helping each other build their cabins.

Jon watched the building, sniffed the new lumber, noticed the intent looks on the men's faces as they worked. They took time out to josh him a little, but they were too busy and earnest to give much time to fooling, and after a while Jon returned to trimming the five felled trees. He chopped and sawed, feeling relaxed inside now. Once he stopped and studied the long straight trunks: if they were squared up a little they'd make good beams for a house. He pulled away the loose brown bark. Yes, sir, those logs would make fine beams.

A solemn voice startled him: "Greetings, woodsman."

He swung around to face a boy of his own age, or a year older, taller by a couple of inches, with wavy blond hair and a long face. He wore tan, neatly pressed slacks, a light tweed sports coat and two-toned sports shoes.

" 'lo," grunted Jon.

"Your name is Jon Woodward, I presume," said the stranger with an arrogant, affected tone. "Mine is Tod Sullivan-Schuyler. Changes have taken place since I was around here a year ago. Come, my lad, show me about." As his words spilled forth, his arms made languid gestures, while his close-set blue eyes watched for the effect he was making upon Jon.

An intaking of breath swelled Jon's chest to bursting. "We don't have sight-seeing tours here," he retorted flatly.

"Of course not." Tod Sullivan-Schuyler tossed his head. "But I'm your neighbor, you see, making a call. I've a natural interest in all you're doing, old boy."

Jon pinched his lips. For two cents he'd shorten that guy's long jaw with a good right hook.

"Be a good fellow," continued Tod Sullivan-Schuyler. "Show me about."

He started up the drive and Jon followed, more like a watchdog protecting his home than someone showing off his place.

Young Sullivan-Schuyler continued: "This, I take it, is the drive—so woodsy." When they reached the crest of the hill and could look down on the garden, he waved a limp hand. "You've been terracing, I see. How continental!" Then his glance shifted to the cabin. "And what is that quaint structure?"

"That's our cabin," Jon explained shortly.

"My word, no bigger than a room in my uncle's country house. Built it yourself, I understand."

"Yes."

"Mmmmh, interesting." He laid an index finger along his jaw. "Must be frightfully crowded living in there."

"We expect to build a larger house eventually."

"Oh, of course." They had reached the terrace in front of the cabin and Jane looked up from the magazine she was reading. Young Sullivan-Schuyler introduced himself at once. "You are Mrs. Woodward, I believe."

Jane stared in astonishment. Then she saw the black fury in Jon's face and could hardly keep from laughing. "Yes," she said, holding her lips stiff.

"I was just remarking upon your cramped quarters here," Tod Sullivan-Schuyler went on. He seemed a little ill-at-ease now, but determined to carry through his act. "Your son tells me you intend to construct a more comfortable dwelling at some later date. It will be of this—this material?" He leaned over and rapped the gypsum board wall of the cabin with his knuckles disdainfully.

"No. Stone." Jon's teeth came together with a snap.

"My word! Stone? And you fancy building it yourself? But that's joking! Mr. Woodward might reasonably design his own house, but certainly he wouldn't build it himself."

"And why not?" Jane squeezed a wild giggle.

At that moment Phyllis came around the house, her dark hair blowing, and Jane introduced her. Phyllis nodded.

"Charmed," said Tod Sullivan-Schuyler, bowing.

"Did you say you lived close by?" queried Jane, deciding that she had better control the conversation.

"Yes. I reside with my uncle, the Squire Byrd." He waved a languid hand to the east, then turned to Phyllis. "May I invite you and your—ah—morose brother over to swim in my uncle's pool?"

"Thank you," murmured Phyllis. She was completely baffled by this fancy language, by the murderous look on Jon's face, and by her mother's obvious efforts to suppress her amusement.

"We're going to have a pool of our own," blurted out Jon.

"Indeed! And you'll build it yourself, no doubt?"

Jon grunted. The knuckles in his fists were white.

"How proletarian!"

Jane decided that she'd better take over the conversation again. "You must be one of Mr. Byrd's many relatives who don't live in Wayne Township."

"Obviously. My uncle has many family connections. They're a political necessity but definitely low-class. I just come here for the summer. Pater and Mater live in New York City when they're not at our manor in Florida."

"Do you find life here interesting?"

"A little dull." He shrugged gracefully. "In a few years I imagine it will be impossibly depressing." He gestured toward the sound of hammering over the hill. "There'll soon be no place for gentlemen."

"That'll be rather a good thing, don't you think?" Jane's seriousness was just a thin layer over her explosive mirth.

For the first time Tod Sullivan-Schuyler's elaborate affectation cracked. He flushed slightly. Deep in his eyes Jane saw a glimmer of hurt, loneliness, and unhappiness.

"Perhaps," was all he could answer. Then he recovered himself: "Must buzz along. Nice to've made your acquaintance." Bowing, he added: "Good afternoon," and strode stiffly up over the hill, disappearing down the drive toward the highway.

Phyllis was the first to speak. "He dresses well, doesn't he?"

"Why, that cheap jerk!" Jon picked up a stone and

slammed it down, giving vent to all his fury. "I'd like to get some dirt on his get-up. If he ever shows up around here again I'll fix his high-hat talk and his snazzy clothes."

Jane leaned back in the deck chair and laughed until tears showed in her eyes. "I haven't seen or heard anything like it outside of a comic strip," she managed to whisper. Then she sobered, adding: "I don't think he has a very good time out of life."

CHAPTER TWELVE

SWIMMING POOL

JON was like a cat thoroughly angered; it took him a long time to return to normal. Just the thought of Tod Sullivan-Schuyler would make his hair bristle and his fists clench. The trouble was that he couldn't see any way to even the score with that smarty-pants.

When Tom Summers heard about the Woodwards' afternoon caller he laughed uproariously. "So Tessy stooped to visit you? You should be flattered." Tod Sullivan-Schuyler's name had suffered from evolution in Tom's usage. First he had referred to him as "T.S.S.," then as "Tess" and now "Tessy." "We have been honored for several summers by his shining light in the neighborhood," Tom explained, mimicking Tod's talk.

"Tessy." Jon thought that was good.

But Phyllis didn't seem to appreciate this ridiculing of young Sullivan-Schuyler. "He dresses nicely," she said in his support. And Jane remarked: "Poor boy, I really feel sorry for him. He was trying so desperately to make an impression."

At supper they told Bob about the visitor, but he didn't even smile. "Yes," he said, "he's the son of Richard Sullivan-Schuyler, one of Universal's directors."

Jane laughed. "I suppose if we're not nice to the boy, his father'll try to get you removed from your job."

"He's already trying it."

The others stared at him in amazement.

"Why, Bob!" cried Jane indignantly. "They wouldn't do a thing like that. It's so petty."

"Oh, yes, they would!" Bob's lips were drawn thin. "Apparently Byrd asked his brother-in-law's help a couple of months ago to try to stop our coming here. Since Brogan, Hartzinger and Walsh have bought land, they've been trying even harder. You don't know management, Moms. There are certain elements in big companies which think that industry is run to give them special privileges. Sullivan-Schuyler is apparently one of that ilk."

"You'd think they'd fire such workers as Brogan and Walsh and Hartzinger, then, for moving out here," said Jane.

"Oh, no," Bob snorted. "They'd run smack up against the union. I belong to no union. Byrd, through his brother-in-law, can work his revenge on me."

They were all sober and silent. At last Jon said: "You've still got your job, haven't you, Dad?"

"Yes, but they're after me." Bob ate for a while angrily, then continued. "I had a talk with Hardy, the divisional superintendent, yesterday, and he tells me they still want my scalp. I'm not competent, I'm spending too much time out here and not enough on production. I'm too easy with the workers. Hardy told me there's just one thing they can't get around: production in my section is the highest in Universal. Even that wouldn't stop them from ousting me, except that production is very important these days."

"What are we going to do?" asked Jane anxiously.

"Nothing. Just sit tight. Hardy's on my side, and all the workers and foremen in my section are." Bob looked at Jon. "But this situation is the real reason I've not considered starting our house. This cabin is all right as it stands. It's an asset to our land. But if we start a house and I lose my job and can't go on with the building, the thing, partly completed, will hurt the value of the place." Then he added confidently: "But we haven't anything to worry about—we've just got to have patience, that's all."

So they couldn't plan the big house or start breaking ground for it. Jon was in the doldrums; there was nothing exciting to do.

The weather grew hot, ripening the oats. One afternoon Jon thought: if a fellow only had some place to swim and cool off. He went down along the edge of the silvering oats to the brook near the road.

He studied the possibilities of damming the stream: put a big tile in the channel and make a wooden cap for it, then build a barrier of rocks and dirt. If he kept the top low enough the water wouldn't back up on old man Byrd's place and give him a chance to squawk. He explained his plan to his father in the evening. "Well, why not try it?" said Bob. "If you'll buy the tile."

"I'll buy it," said Jon.

The next day he talked his mother into driving him down to the lumberyard in Wayne. He bought an eight-inch sewer tile and Mr. Smith knocked off ten cents from the price.

"Your father's been getting us a lot of business lately, inducing those new people to come out to the Summers' place." Then Mr. Smith chuckled. "But Supervisor Byrd doesn't like it."

"Yes, and he's trying to get my dad fired up at Universal so that we'll have to give up our place out here." Then Jon bit his tongue; he shouldn't have blurted out anything as personal as that to a stranger.

Mr. Smith grew serious at once and his eyes narrowed. "That'll interest Mr. Holden, who owns this company. He has some interest in Universal, you know."

Jon lugged his tile out, perked up by the news that Mr. Holden might be able to help his father, but afraid to tell his father what he'd said to Mr. Smith. His dad was dead set against airing family problems in public.

The next day Jon started building the dam. He put on his bathing suit and worked all morning. In the afternoon Phyllis put on her bathing suit and helped. Later, Tom Summers and his brother and two sisters came to help. Then Maria Scotti and Tony and George pitched in and gave them a hand.

The dam was a sandwich of rock wall, dirt and another rock wall. Just as they were finishing it on the second afternoon, Tod Sullivan-Schuyler came sauntering along and sat on the cement balustrate of the bridge to watch.

"Such enterprise," he remarked.

"Want to help, Tessy?" invited Tom.

"I relinquish such filthy endeavor to the hoi polloi like yourself," replied Tod sarcastically.

This crack was greeted by jeering laughter from the dam-builders, except Phyllis.

Tod Sullivan-Schuyler gave rein to his lingo: "Ditch-digging, working in muck, and all such work is quite in character with you of the lower classes—poor whites and dagoes."

Jon saw Maria wince at the word "dago" and her face turned white. He grabbed up a handful of muck and tossed it directly at Tod Sullivan-Schuyler. "Here, Tessy, catch!"

Instinctively young Sullivan-Schuyler held his hands to catch the object and the black ooze splattered his neat slacks, sports coat and two-toned shoes. He scrambled off the bridge balustrade, all dignity gone. "You'll hear about this!" he yelled and walked off up the road.

"Jon!" scolded Phyllis. "You shouldn't have done that!"

But the others laughed jeeringly after the departing Tod. Guess that paid him off.

The dam was finished, the cap fitted in the bell-top of the tile and the basin left to fill. Later all of them went for a swim in the clear cold water. They splashed and swam and dove from the dam. This was something like it—a swimming pool of their own.

But the next day the sheriff came and ordered this obstacle in the brook removed; it stopped the movement of brook trout to Mr. Byrd's property. Jane talked with the sheriff, then called Jon.

"You'll have to let the water out," she said.

Jon went down to the dam and while the others stood on the bank and Tod Sullivan-Schuyler and the sheriff watched from the road he dove in and pulled the cap from the tile. They stared at the water gurgling and whirling down through the tile and their swimming pool vanished with a sucking, angry rush. When the brook returned to normal Tod Sullivan-Schuyler and the sheriff drove off haughtily.

"Well, it was nice while it lasted," remarked Tom Summers.

"That rat, I'll fix him!" threatened Jon.

But Jon couldn't figure any way of making good his threat. He brooded and sulked. If he were only somewhere near as big as Tessy he'd fight him. Sometimes he went down to the empty dam and watched the water gurgling through the tile. He could only shake his head in despair.

The oats were ripe and ready for cutting. Sunday, his father said, they'd cut them. And Bob looked as happy as a kid. He and Jon worked with hand sickles, making little neat piles which they tied into bundles, then shocked up according to Bob's formula: two bundles leaning together, two set up against each end of these, two in the hollows on either side and one crushed down on the top for a cap.

Bob looked at the first one set up as if he were an artist viewing his canvas. But in his mind were pictures of huge fields of shocks like this one which he had known in his youth. At lunch time he talked enthusiastically about grain-cutting out in Illinois. A binder, he told the family, would lay that fly-speck of a piece down in a jiffy.

Jane asked: "What're you going to do with them when you get them cut?"

"Well—" he began, then looked down, confused and red. He didn't know what he could do with them.

At first, cutting the oats was fun for Jon, but with the hand sickle it was back-breaking, and the July sun burned down. Oh, for a place to swim! The rust on the grain made his skin itch.

When they'd cut the grain up to the jog in the east boundary wall, where the brook dipped back into their land, Jon paused to rest. He looked over the wall at the cool, swirling brook racing among the mossy stones. Then for some reason he glanced back across the field to the terraced garden.

Suddenly the idea struck him like a blow. If there was some way to divert part of the stream across the field from this jog to the dry-run that angled down to the bridge from below the garden and dam up the dry-run, they could have a swimming pool without backing the water up on Byrd's land or shutting off the trout from running.

"Dad!" he yelled frantically. "Dad, come here!"

His father came at a run. "What's the matter?"

Jon blurted out the idea. Bob pushed away his picture of acres of shocked oats for a moment and considered it seriously. At last he said: "All you'd need to do is tap the brook here with a four-inch tile and lead it across the field."

Jon went back to cutting oats, his whole body singing. He'd get around Byrd and his snooty nephew Tessy. And they'd have a swimming pool.

The next morning he began moving the dam from across the brook where it now stood to across the dry-run. Again Tom and Phyllis and Maria helped and the younger children added their efforts. Tod Sullivan-Schuyler sauntered along the road and paused to remark: "Upon my word! Such optimism! These strange specimens of *Homo sapiens* are building a dry pool to bathe

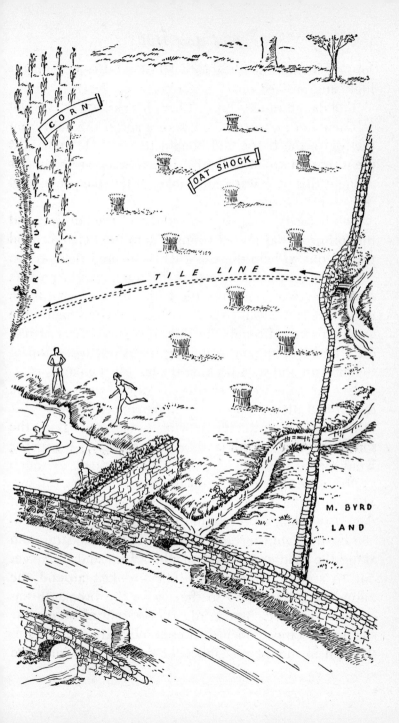

in. Oh, illusion of illusions!" He shook his head mock-
ingly and ambled on.

The dam-builders ignored his remarks.

Then Jon measured the distance across the field from
the jog in the brook and bought the tile. He explained
the situation to Mr. Smith. The lumberyard manager
thought this trick was a huge joke. "I'll make you a good
price on those tile," he offered.

Bob helped Jon lay out the course of the tap line, and
the following day all the youngsters in the neighborhood
turned out to help dig the ditch. Jon used the level to
get just a gentle pitch so that the water would flow. It
took three days to get the tile laid, then they had to go
under the stone wall to tap the brook. When finally the
water gurgled through the line, they stood back, tired,
dirty and triumphant, watching it rush into the top of
the dry-run and start backing up against the dam.

"By the time we cover this tile ditch," Jon said, "the
dam'll be full enough for a dip. Whoopee!"

They rushed at the job, pawing, hoeing and raking the
soil down over the tiles. "There goes Tessy," whispered
Tony Scotti, and they stopped long enough to watch
Sullivan-Schuyler go past on the road.

They finished the job and took a well-deserved dip in
their new pool. Later, while they were drinking lemonade on the cabin terrace, they saw the sheriff's car stop
along the road and Mr. Byrd, the sheriff and Tessy get
out to study the situation. They walked around the
boundary line and up to the jog in the brook. It was
obvious that Mr. Byrd could do nothing about it: the
stream was tapped on Woodward land and enough water
still ran in the main channel for the fish to swim up to

the Byrd Estate. The Woodwards, Scottis and Summers heard not another word of complaint about the new swimming pool from Supervisor Byrd.

Then one evening Bob came home smiling broadly. "I guess I'm saved for another year," he announced. "A big order has just come in to Universal and although some of the big shots in the corporation would like to do Mr. Sullivan-Schuyler and, incidentally, Mr. Byrd, a favor and oust me, they know darned well I'm the man to meet the new production schedules."

"Gee, Dad, that's swell," whooped Jon. "Now we can talk about the big house."

"I think we'd better continue to wait," cautioned Jane. "A year isn't long. Lose your job next year and we'll be in the soup too."

"Well, Moms," said Bob thoughtfully. "I believe we can take a chance. Superintendent Hardy told me today that support for me inside Universal has developed from right here in Wayne Township. It seems that Mr. Holden, who owns the lumberyard, is a heavy stockholder in the corporation. Things don't look so bad, Moms."

"Oh, boy!" yelled Jon. Then he hesitated, remembering his blurting out his father's situation to Mr. Smith at the lumberyard. He guessed maybe he'd better not tell his dad even now. His eagerness rolled back: "When can we start the house, Dad?"

"Don't get in a rush," cautioned Bob, but his face was crinkled with an eager look. "That house won't get built in a day."

CHAPTER THIRTEEN

PLANS

THE first problem Bob and Jon had to face in planning the stone house was to work out a design that didn't require the whole building to be built at the same time. "We've got to divide it into units—units of a size we can save the money for and build in one year's time," Bob explained.

They went over the tentative site selected for the house. The ground sloped upward gradually across the picnic spot to a knoll which rose sharply about six feet, then continued to slant upward on the hill.

"Now, this is what I've been figuring." Bob took a deep breath. "We'll start right at the base of this bank. We'll square it up and build our living room right against it. That'll be our first unit. If we have luck we can get that done during my vacation and the rest of the fall."

It was clear to Jon that his father had been working on the idea for this house a long time. He listened carefully, trying to follow the rapid unfolding of ideas that had long been growing in his dad's mind, but were just now allowed to come forth. Bob sighted, paced off areas, gestured and walked about excitedly. He pointed to the top of the knoll.

"We'll build on two levels. Our living room will be

the lower level, and the top of that bank will be the upper level." He pointed to the ground dipping away from the knoll on the right. "There we'll dig down for our basement." His hand swung across to the dip of the ground on the left. "There we'll put our garage. On the upper level which will be the top of the basement, top of the knoll and top of the garage, we'll put our kitchen, eating unit, bedrooms and bathroom."

Jon's mouth twisted in perplexity, trying to follow this rapid-fire explanation. Finally he asked: "What are we goin' to have over the living room, Dad?"

"Nothing," came the prompt reply. "We'll put on a flat roof with a natural wood railing and use it for a huge sun-deck." He pointed to the right side of what would be the rear wall of the living room. "There's where we'll put the fireplace. The chimney will carry the fireplace flue and the flue for the furnace." He paused, his eyes narrowed, then his face seemed to burst with light. He smacked fist into palm. "We'll have another fireplace opening right out on the sun-deck—an open-air fireplace on the sun-deck."

All this was too much for Jon to follow and grasp so quickly. He'd have to see plans on paper and gradually absorb the idea. Jane and Phyllis joined them and Bob repeated the description of the house plan on the ground.

"I don't get it," said Jane stiffly. "Anyhow, I don't think you'd better build a stone house. It'll fall in on us."

"It will not!" Bob's voice was sharp with anger.

Jon felt a violent, unswerving drive let loose in his father and it awed him. He was seeing Bob Woodward the production engineer in action. Here was a force turned loose that nothing could stop—an almost fanatical, fierce determination. This house could be built, it would be built and he, Bob Woodward, would do it. And Jon felt the same way the workers at the plant felt toward Bob: a love for him, a respect for his unbending determination, a deep sureness that if he said it could be done, then they would do it.

But Jane didn't feel that power in Bob. Jon looked into her troubled eyes, saw her face darkening with anxiety.

"How do you know you can build a wall that won't fall down?" she asked pointedly.

There was a sharp silence, a momentary clash of wills, then quite abruptly Bob laughed. "Well, Moms, we'll appoint you building inspector. When Jon and I get a wall finished you can give it a push and see if you can shove it over." Chuckling, he turned to Jon. "Come on, let's go over and see if we can put these plans down on paper."

They sat at the card table on the terrace in front of the cabin until dark, Bob with ruler and pencil, drawing the plans to scale. The living room was plotted first, twenty-by-thirty, then he drew the upper floor, sixteen-by-fifty, indicating rooms, windows, doors, stairways and halls.

Phyllis sat across the table watching, trying to follow the growing plans and understand them, but Jane sat in her deck chair at one side, forcing her attention on a book, refusing to fall in with this planning.

The next evening Bob came hurrying home, eager to stake out the living room on the ground and start excavating the necessary earth. Jon and he worked until dark, then went for a swim. When they came back up the hill, Bob said: "You can go on with the grading tomorrow, Jon. If we get the digging done by this week-end, we can pour the floor."

Jane didn't mention the house that evening and she hadn't been near the building site since the night before. But the next afternoon while Jon was digging, wearily swinging the pick and scooping and raking back the loosened dirt, she went over to see how he was getting along.

He stopped work and leaned on his shovel. "Moms, don't you think this'll make a nice house?"

"No," she answered flatly.

"Why, Moms?"

"Just because I don't think so." Jane recognized that most of her attitude was pique. Bob and Jon had gone right ahead without deferring to her opinions or inviting her participation.

Jon persisted: "But why, Moms? What do you want instead of this layout?"

She had no alternative plan. "We shouldn't start building as long as your father isn't sure of his job."

"He's sure of it for another year, Moms," Jon argued. "And if we don't get our house started it'll throw our whole program to have the money for Phyllis and me to go to college on out of step. Besides, if Dad should lose his job, we could live out here and not have to pay any rent, providing we have part of our house built."

"Oh, you talk just like your father!"

She looked away down the valley to the southeast. This place where she stood was to be the living room and she realized that from here she got a full view of that sweep of rolling hills and fields. Jon didn't say any more, and she stood with her back to him looking at the view, then she walked over to the cabin and got her water colors to do another painting.

Jon went on with the grading, disappointment making heavier his weariness; Moms was being difficult about this building. He wished she'd co-operate.

That week-end Jon and Bob poured the floor of the living room. All around the outside edge of the floor at three-foot intervals they set two-by-four blocks on end in the cement. Bob explained: "We'll remove these and have places to stick the bottom ends of the upright two-by-fours we use for the inside supports for our wall forms."

Once while they rested, Bob rubbed his chin thoughtfully and let out a problem that had been worrying him. "On stone walls like these we're going to put up, it's necessary to have what is called a dead-air space on the inside. Otherwise a bit of humid weather in the summer will make them sweat like a jug."

Bob lighted his pipe before continuing. "Now the way that's usually taken care of is to put heavy firring strips edgewise in the wall and after the wall is up, nail thin firring strips flatwise to these and your inside wall over the thin firring strips, which leaves about an inch space between your inner wall and the stone wall. But firring strips are practically impossible to get and they'd be ridiculously expensive even if we could get them."

They resumed mixing cement and Bob went on explaining: "Now what I'd figured was something like this: if we could get chicken wire and roll it into two-inch tubes and cover these with paper, we could insert them on the inner side of the wall at about one-foot intervals. These hollow tubes in the cement would give the necessary dead-air space. That's been done successfully. And it would be much cheaper, even if firring strips were available at a reasonable figure. Only"—he leaned on the hoe wearily—"trouble is that chicken wire is hard to get for anything but raising chickens."

Jon had no suggestion to offer and his father added: "We've got to figure out something, or we're stymied."

They went on to finish the job of pouring the floor.

The next day Jon started digging for the foundation around the edge of the floor slab. It had to be two feet deep along the front and the two ends; the inner side didn't have to be dug because that space would be protected from the frost. As he worked he pondered the problem of tubes for the inner side of the stone walls. He couldn't seem to find any answer. Maybe his dad would come up with an idea.

About four o'clock his mother called him over to the cabin for lemonade. "Tired?" she asked.

"Yeah, kind of," he replied moodily.

"You've been glum all day, Jon. What's worrying you?"

He didn't answer immediately. There was no use telling her; she was against the project anyway. And if they didn't solve this difficulty, she'd win out. Finally he decided that it wouldn't make any difference if she did know, and told her.

Jane obviously didn't understand the structural problems involved, but she smiled. "Just keep at it, son," she reassured. "You and Dad'll work it out somehow."

He looked up at her, his eyes shining, his spirits lifted by her words.

Phyllis came around the cabin, carrying a red cockerel under her arm. "This is the one who's been crowing. Rusty. I caught him at it," she said proudly. "Isn't he big?"

"Big enough to eat," said her mother.

"To eat!" cried Phyllis, horrified.

"Certainly! What have you been raising them for?"

"But I can't eat Rusty!" wailed the girl.

"That's silly." Jane looked annoyed. "What *are* you going to do with him then?"

Phyllis was silent. Her fingers stroked the dark red feathers on the cockerel's neck. At last she whispered tearfully: "I don't know."

Jon remarked: "Why don't you trade him to Tom for one of his and we'll eat it?"

"Then they'll eat Rusty!" cried his sister indignantly.

"But you won't have to eat him," said her mother. "That's a good suggestion."

"Well—" Without finishing her reply Phyllis carried the rooster back to the pen.

Jon returned to his job. His mother's evident interest in the problems of the house pepped him up, and the solution he'd offered Phyllis on the subject of her cockerels made him feel good. Then he suddenly remembered killing the weasel a month ago and his father talking about a pen for the chickens. . . . He stopped work. Those rolls of old chicken wire down in the dump heap in the brush across the road.

He dropped the shovel and grabbed the handles of the wheelbarrow and started trundling it down the drive toward the highway. He crashed through the brush to the dump and wrestled one of the fence rolls over to the barrow, then, grunting and straining, he shoved it up the hill to the house site where he tipped it to the ground and began unrolling it. Yes, the top half was solid enough to make into tubes.

To make a sample he cut a two-inch sassafras pole, then with the tin-snips he cut a length of wire netting and rolled it up on the pole. After fastening the loose ends of the wire to keep it from unrolling, he removed the pole.

"Moms!" he shouted. "This is it! This'll do it!"

She came to see. He explained eagerly where he'd found the wire—there were three more rolls.

"I knew you'd work it out, son," she said proudly, and she told Bob about the wire the first thing after he got home.

"Fine!" He nodded his satisfaction. "That eliminates one headache!" He was pleased, and Jane's show of interest in the job made him as happy as it had Jon.

Now in the evenings Bob and Jon poured the foundation. It looked as if they'd be ready to begin the walls when Bob got his vacation a week later. But as the foundation job drew to a close, it became obvious that Bob was stewing over a new problem.

One evening after Jane had been canning beans all afternoon, she remarked: "Bob, whatever are you going to do with those oats of yours? Let them rot out there in the field?"

"I don't know," he answered glumly, harassed by his other problem. He didn't want to think about what was to be done with something he'd raised just to satisfy a whim. "If we had a goat we could feed them to it."

"Well, we haven't a goat," said Jane flatly. "What's more, we're not going to have one."

To escape further talk on this subject, Bob blurted out the problem facing him: "I haven't been able to figure out what we're going to use for form boards to put up the walls of our house. We need shiplap or tongue-and-groove roofers, but they can't be bought at any price."

The others were silent, the oats forgotten. Jon's face grew sober—without boards for forms, they couldn't start the walls, and his dad's vacation commenced this weekend.

"If I could just pick up some second-hand lumber cheap—" began Bob speculatively.

"Here comes Tom," interrupted Phyllis.

The boy came striding up, swinging a headless rooster. "Here's your trade, Phil," he announced.

"Ah-hah," exclaimed Bob, rubbing his hands together, the problem dismissed for the moment. "So we begin to eat chicken."

Phyllis didn't say anything. She got up quickly and went down to the chicken coop for Rusty.

"I'll trade you again any time you want to," offered Tom when she returned.

Phyllis just mumbled "All right" and looked away.

"Don't take it so hard, Phil," soothed Bob, seeing her bright eyes. "That's the end of every good chicken."

"But—" She choked up and ran around the cabin.

Tom's face grew as red as the rooster he held. "I've got

to be getting back," he faltered, and walked quickly away, carrying Rusty gently under his arm.

Later when Phyllis returned, dry-eyed and sober, her mother lifted the headless gray chicken, hefting it for weight. "Looks like he'll be worth about a dollar, Phyllis," she said.

Her daughter looked astonished. "A dollar?"

"Certainly. I'd have to pay as much for a bird like this at the market."

Phyllis brightened up after that.

The next afternoon Maria Scotti came up to have a look at the beginnings of the new house after the youngsters had their swim. Jon explained the plans to her eagerly and her attention flattered him.

"When are you going to start the walls?" she asked.

"I don't know," he admitted soberly. "We'd figured on starting them next week when Dad's on vacation, but we can't figure out anything to use for form boards."

Maria didn't seem to have any answer for that, and they walked over to the cabin for the afternoon lemonade.

Jane waved her hand toward the lower field. "Maria, could your father use those oats?"

"Dad said a few nights ago that he was going to speak to Mr. Woodward about buying them," answered the girl.

"They aren't worth anything to us," said Jane.

"But they *are* worth something," replied Maria quickly. Her dark eyes were intent upon Jane. "Straw's expensive. We could use them for our goats. Dad's on vacation and hasn't seen Mr. Woodward recently and he's been so busy repairing our barn that he hasn't had time to come over."

"Oh, your father can have them," offered Jane. "I'm tired of looking at Bob's oat shocks."

Jon walked home with Maria, feeling tongue-tied, until she said: "Don't you have fun building your house?"

Then he opened up: "Yeah, it's fun. A fella gets tired, but, gee, if something didn't come up like this board business to stop us, we'd sail right along. We'd get it done before I have to go back to school."

"You going to be glad to go back to school?"

"Sure. Only we'll have to go back to New Delphi and I like it out here."

When they arrived at Maria's gate, her father was in the yard raking up the dry grass for bedding the goats.

"How goes-a?" Al Scotti grinned broadly. "You juss-a the fella I want-a see. I buy your oats. Hows-a much?"

"You can have them, Mr. Scotti," said Jon.

"Naw! Naw!" roared the big Italian. "I no take."

"But they aren't worth anything to us, Mr. Scotti," insisted the boy.

"Naw! They worth-a something!"

Jon didn't know what to say, then he grinned. "You don't happen to have some old lumber that isn't in too bad shape that you'd consider trading for them?" he asked.

"Trade?" Al Scotti laughed loudly. "You got your dad beat. What's-a ol' lumber I got?" He gestured toward the barn. "Some, yes, but I wanta keep."

Maria's face began to glow. "Dad, that old shanty up in the woods. That shanty those people who used to own this place used for raising pheasants. You don't need it."

Al Scotti struck his forehead. "I trade you. You bring-a

the oats and take da shanty back. How's-a that?" He thrust his pitchfork into the ground. "Want to go see?"

Jon followed Mr. Scotti and Maria up into the woods to an eight-by-twelve shack. It was old, the boards were rotting around the bottom, but the upper parts seemed solid. After examining it, Jon said importantly: "It's a deal."

Maria beamed while Jon and her father shook hands.

"That's-a fine!" said Al Scotti with satisfaction.

Jon ran almost all the way home to tell his mother. They kept the deal a secret from Bob and the next day they borrowed the Summers' two-wheeled trailer, hooked it to the car, backed it down to the edge of the oat field, loaded up and hauled the oats over to Scotti's barn. It took several trips, but even Jane got fun out of the job. Phyllis and Maria and Tom Summers all helped. In the afternoon Jon started tearing down the shanty and by evening they had hauled one load of boards home.

Bob saw them the first thing when he came up the drive.

"Where'd you get those?" he yelled.

Jane explained the deal while Jon looked on, glowing with pride. Bob swung around to stare down at the empty oat field a little startled.

"Can we use them for forms?" Jon asked anxiously.

Bob's glance came back to the lumber. "They'll be okay. Guess those oats were worth raising after all."

"Now he admits it," said Jane, laughing. "We'll get this house of yours going in spite of everything."

"House of ours," corrected Bob. "You're swell, Moms! Let's go eat so's I can get to work."

They walked across to the cabin arm-in-arm.

CHAPTER FOURTEEN

ROOF-RAISING

JON and his mother finished hauling the lumber from the shanty over to Five Acre Hill the following day then Jon began removing the nails and sawing away the rotten portions of the boards until just the best of the wood remained.

"Plenty for the forms," Bob announced after examining the pile. "We're all set for tomorrow morning."

That night Jon had a hard time sleeping. The fun was really going to begin on the big house the next day. He lay awake for a long time picturing the laying up of the walls, and when he finally fell asleep, he dreamed of a wall that grew like Jack's beanstalk. A giant hand shook that wall and he heard a voice say, "Come on, Jon, time to get up!" Then he felt his father's fingers clutching his shoulder.

The sun was barely up. Jane complained: "Your vacation is certainly going to be no vacation for me."

"Food, Moms, lots of food," Bob greeted such grumbling. "We've got to have strength."

Jon plunged his face into cold water to get thoroughly awake, then joined his father on the terrace to breakfast on golden pancakes, eggs, crisp bacon and coffee. Neither he nor his father said much but they stared across at the site of the new house as if trying to build it with their

152

eyes. Bob's face was alert and Jon's eager. They got up from the table together, and Bob said, "Let's go."

First they wheeled up slabs of stone from the ledge and broken areas of stone wall in the barrow until they had a huge pile on the cement floor of the living room. They wheeled up another pile of shards and cobbles and large pebbles to use to fill niches between the larger stones. To rest from this hard work they made chicken-wire cubes and wrapped and tied them with thick layers of paper.

A little after eleven o'clock the two-by-fours for the forms and the two-by-eights for the window and door frames were delivered by the lumberyard. They began at once to set the upright timbers for the forms, brace them, make sure they were plumb and put the first row of boards around the bottom. "We'll only do the front wall and the two front corners to begin with," Bob said. "No use trying to tackle it all at once."

By evening the forms were ready for the cement and stone. When they walked across to the cabin for supper, both Bob and Jon kept turning and looking back at the bristling timbers.

"Do you want me to serve your meals up there where you're working?" Jane asked sarcastically.

"That's a good idea," said Bob.

"Sure, Moms, save us a lot of time," added Jon.

"Well, I'm not going to."

That night Jon slept without tossing or dreaming. And he and his father were back to work early again the next morning. Now the wall would really begin. They mixed a batch of sand and cement. Bob spread a layer of the greenish paste on top of the foundation between the form boards. Then he set a row of flat slabs on edge, snug against the outside boards, from the front door frame to the corner of the building. In the space between these slabs and the inner board of the forms he laid one of the chicken-wire rolls, allowing for a half inch of cement between it and the inner wall. He filled this space with cement and small stones level with the top of the outside row of rock slabs.

Jon kept the mixed cement soft and scooped it into the forms. He watched his father to learn how the job was done. This first day they made slow progress because Bob was learning too. By nightfall they had only laid up one board-width across the front of the room and halfway across the ends.

"Tomorrow it'll go faster," predicted Bob.

"Do you think I can lay stones tomorrow?" Jon asked

"We'll see. Maybe you can."

The second day the wall really began to grow. They slid another row of boards on top of the first stand. Then Jon got ready to lay his first stone. He scooped fresh cement in on top of the stones already laid, smoothed it around with his trowel, and lifted a slab to set on edge in the green mortar.

Bob watched critically. "Slide it this way a little," he advised. "One of the things you've got to be careful about is crossing the joints of the stones below." He showed Jon how the new stone set across the joint line in the first layer.

"Yeah, I see," said Jon, chewing his lip thoughtfully

"That's to keep the wall from cracking," Bob explained.

He kept a critical eye on Jon's work, but with the two

of them laying up wall, they succeeded in completing one board-width by lunch time. They rushed down to the cabin to eat.

"It's really going up now," said Bob.

The two stood on the terrace staring at the rows of two-by-fours sprouting on the new house site. Their eyes were seeing a completed wall, not the bare skeleton before them.

"We'll finish that in a week, won't we, Dad?"

Bob shook his head. "I hardly think so." A frown grew on his face as if he'd suddenly confronted another problem.

"Will you two forget that job long enough to eat," scolded Jane. She couldn't understand how they could get as wrapped up in anything as they were in that new house.

But that afternoon she went over to see how they were progressing. She couldn't make sense out of the confusion of stones, boards, oozing cement, upright two-by-fours and braces.

"Look, Moms," cried Jon, "we're going to get more'n two board-widths done today."

She didn't reply. Her forehead wrinkled as she watched them working as if they had to finish the whole job before night. They almost seemed to ignore her. Their arms and bodies moved swiftly. The look in their eyes was hard and determined. The scraping of trowels on raw stone made her shiver.

"Why don't you take it easier?" she asked sharply. "You can't do it all in one day."

Bob began piling stones closer to his reach at the wall.

"We're not working hard," he replied without slowing up.

"Both of you'll be dog-tired again by night."

Still they paid no attention to her. Bob resumed laying stones in the forms. Suddenly Jane recognized that the fierce concentration they fixed on their work was the same that she felt when she painted a water color.

She noticed that Jon had almost used up the pile of stones near him and she began to replenish that pile. The rough limestone tore at her fingers. As soon as she found the opportunity she walked over to the cabin for a pair of gloves. She returned to take over the job of keeping both Bob and Jon supplied with small stones. Then she began carrying larger stones until Bob cautioned her not to try to lift too much.

Phyllis stopped to see how the job was going after her four o'clock swim and soon she was piling stones too. Jane tried her hand at mixing cement, pulling the hoe through the soft mortar. "Like stirring up a cake," she remarked. She found it hard to leave the job to get supper when five-thirty came.

That evening when Jon and his father went for a swim, Bob revealed the problem that had been confronting him lately. "We're all set to do the walls," he said, "but it's the flat cement roof that has me stumped. It'll need some sort of reinforcing, and steel for that can't be had."

They splashed in the cool water, pondering this problem.

"Could we use some of that old chicken wire?" asked Jon.

"Not heavy enough. Besides, it'll take all of that for the rolls."

They could figure nothing to use. Well, the walls could be built anyway.

The next day both Jane and Phyllis spent considerable time helping. In the afternoon Tom Summers stopped to have a look at the job and pitched in to help; later Maria Scotti joined them. She began carrying stones for Jon immediately as if she'd come over for that purpose alone. Her strong arms strained at the slabs, tipping them closer to his reach.

"Don't try to lift too much, Maria," cautioned Jane.

"Oh, I do this for Dad," explained the girl, her dark eyes bright.

Jon couldn't keep from showing off a little. He was laying up wall right along with his father and it made him feel cocky. "Be sure you mix that sand and cement good before you wet it down," he told Tom, who was pawing the dry stuff up in a pile.

"Now don't you start criticizing your help," said Jane. "Or we'll walk off the job."

Bob laughed. "What are you, Moms—shop steward?"

By the end of the fourth day the full length of the front wall and half the end walls were laid up four feet, the window frame set in, and half of the building wall was ready to be continued from staging. But they started the rear wall and corners next. The fireplace took longer. Bob followed the directions and specifications from the government bulletin on fireplace-building carefully.

"We want a fireplace that'll work," he said.

It took a lot of stones for the chimney, because that

chimney had to hold two eight-by-twelve rectangular flues and one eight-inch round flue. Bob and Jon spent two entire mornings wheeling stones in the barrow up to the job.

At the end of the first week they stripped the form boards from the finished lower half of the front wall. It was in the late afternoon and Tom and Maria were there; they stood back with Jane and Phyllis, while Bob and Jon did the unveiling.

"Looks terribly rough," said Jane as soon as the unfilled cracks were revealed.

Jon's face clouded with disappointment. It did look rough and ragged. He'd expected it to appear trim and neat like the stone houses in Wayne.

"It doesn't look so good," said Tom, glancing at Jon.

"But it isn't finished yet," cried Maria Scotti.

"Sure, it has to be pointed up," Bob explained. Then for the sake of family morale, he mixed a batch of fine sand and cement, proportions one-to-one, and pointed up a section, carefully filling the seams of the exposed surface. "See," he said, standing back. "That's how it'll look when it's finished."

"Oh, that's much better," admitted Jane.

Jon's face brightened and Maria smiled triumphantly. Phyllis looked pleased, and Tom said: "Gee, that looks all right now. It isn't such a trick to build a stone wall."

"Sure," said Jon boastfully. "It's not so hard."

Over the week-end the neighbors dropped in to have a look: the Scottis, Brogans, Hartzingers, Summers and Walshes. "It's going to look right nice," said Mrs. Summers.

Mike Brogan studied it carefully and applauded: "I'll

be darned. There ain't much Bob can't do when he puts his mind to it."

"I had lots of help," said Bob, laughing. "And Jon's turning into a first-class stone mason."

That made Jon glow all over.

Down on the road they saw Tod Sullivan-Schuyler ambling along, trying desperately not to show his curiosity about the activity on Five Acre Hill.

The last corner was built up to the four-foot height by Tuesday night of the next week, then Bob and Jon built a strong scaffold out of two-by-fours, braced well to support their weight and the weight of cement and stone they'd be using to lay up the additional four feet of wall. The wall-building took longer now because all the material had first to be lifted to the staging level. The continuous climbing up and down made the job more tiring. But with spaces out for windows and doors there was less wall to be laid up.

By the end of Bob's vacation the walls were all up except the fireplace corner. Work on the chimney had been held up by the difficulty Bob had in getting the blacksmith in Wayne to contrive a damper for the fireplace.

There was still three weeks before school would start and the Woodwards would have to move back to New Delphi. Bob studied the unfinished job. "With luck," he said, "we might be able to finish it up to the roof by then."

He and Jon had worked so hard that they'd almost forgotten the problem of reinforcing the cement roof. But now they had to face it and no solution was in sight. Still the work went on. During the day, after Bob returned to the plant, Jon hewed at the logs of the five trees down near the road. Bob had bought an adze and showed him how to use it; they were going to use those logs for ceiling beams. Toward evening, Jon mixed a bag of cement and four times that amount of sand, and had it ready for the addition of water, and piled stones close to the wall area being worked on. As soon as supper was over he and Bob put up as much wall as the batch of cement would build.

By Sunday they were ready to raise the roof beams. That only meant they were nearer pouring the cement roof and still hadn't solved the problem of reinforcing. "Can't figure a thing," Bob admitted to Jon. "There's no reinforcing steel available to us."

"Won't those beams hold the weight?" asked Jon.

"With cross-joists, they will. But we need to reinforce the cement to keep it from cracking." They stared up at the top of the wall around them, and Bob added: "Anyhow, we can get those beams up here."

They borrowed Joe Summers' trailer and hauled the oak logs up to the building site. This was an exciting change from wall-building. They propped each beam on the sturdy sawhorses and finished squaring it to approximately ten-by-ten. The logs showed the marks of ax and adze—they were rough-hewn, but "That's what we want, isn't it?" Bob said.

After sawing the beams to length they rolled and lifted and struggled to get them to the top of the wall. They didn't get the job finished that day and it took three nights of the following week to get them into place and to shape them into a roof bed with a two-inch pitch to the front. Then the wall level had to be built up to the top edge of the beams.

Time seemed to work against them. One more week until Labor Day and the end of the season, and they'd have to go back to New Delphi.

"Gee," Jon complained to Maria one afternoon. "We wanted to get the roof on before we went back to town, then when we came out for week-ends this fall, Dad and I could put in the windows and hang the doors and finish it off inside. But I don't see how we're going to make it."

"I hope you can get it done," she answered. She could offer no way to help solve their problem. "It's going to be an awfully nice big room," she added.

Jon was cleaning up the debris about the building, piling up the form boards and sweeping the floor. For the first time he really began to see it as a room. It was going to look swell when they got it finished. But his glance drifted to the beams overhead and the blue sky above them.

That evening after supper, Bob and Jon began laying the two-by-four cross-joists sixteen inches center to center. The next day Jon finished that job and in the evening he and his father added the crown to the wall, bringing it up even with the top of the two-by-fours.

Both Bob and Jon grew silent as the week approached its end. When they ate their meals in front of the cabin, they spent most of the time staring across to the unfinished room as if looking hard would somehow complete the job.

At last Jane demanded: "What's worrying you two? You're both being as glum as turtles."

"We're sort of stuck, Moms," Bob admitted. "I'd hoped we could get the job along to the point of pouring the cement roof slab on the Labor Day holiday, but even if we do get it ready, I still haven't doped out anything we can use for reinforcement."

Jane could offer no solution for this construction problem. "It doesn't matter so much if you don't get it finished, does it?"

"We ought to get it done," Jon said doggedly.

He and his father went over to the building and worked again until dark. When they quit, Bob shrugged: "Well, if we don't get it done, we don't get it done, that's all."

Saturday morning Jane drove to Wayne to order the gypsum board for sheeting the roof and the roll roofing Bob planned to cement over the sheeting before pouring the cement. "We can at least get the sheeting and the roofing paper on," Bob said.

Jon stayed home to work at pointing up the outside wall. It was a tedious job and he couldn't stay at it steadily; it bored him more than usual this morning. He wished the gypsum board was here so that he could start putting it on. And the problem of reinforcing the cement for the roof slab still nagged at him. Gee, if he could only come across some old steel cable or pipe or iron in a dump heap!

He stopped pointing up the wall and wandered down to the dump across the road. Leaves and brush had almost hidden the old cans and bottles. He kicked about in the covering. His toe unearthed the curved top of an iron bed. He began struggling frantically to uncover it. Part after part of the bed he freed from the rubbish and laid on the grass along the road. They could use that to reinforce the cement. He studied the rusted pieces of iron, then shook his head. It'd take a lot of such beds for the job, and this was all there was here.

His mother came speeding up the road. She didn't see him in the brush as the car flashed past, going faster than she usually drove. He saw her swing up the drive and step on the gas going up the hill to the picnic spot. What was she in such a rush about? He heard her calling him and, picking up a couple of pieces of the rusted bed, he started up the hill.

She was standing by the car. "Hurry up, Jon!" she called when she saw him.

"What's the matter, Moms?" He flung the bed pieces clanking on the ground and faced her, looking worried.

She gave a little embarrassed laugh. "It's nothing serious. Mr. Smith at the lumberyard says that we can have a roll of heavy screen fence. He ordered it for Mr. Byrd and when it came Byrd refused to take it because he said they were charging him too much. He said we could have it at cost and could use it to strengthen the cement. Do you know anything about it? I didn't want to have him send it out on my own say-so."

"Sure we can use it," said Jon.

Jane climbed back into the car and drove off to place the order at the lumberyard.

But maybe they couldn't use it, Jon thought afterwards. His father had said the chicken wire would be too light. He returned to pointing up the cracks in the wall, telling himself that they could return the fence to the lumberyard if it wouldn't work for reinforcing.

Right after lunch the gypsum board, roll roofing and

fence came. A little later the truck brought two tons of sand and fifteen bags of cement. Jon began nailing on the sheeting, but he was worried: What would they do with that sand and cement if they couldn't use that screen wire for reinforcing?

His father saw the roll of fence the first thing on arriving home. "Sure we can use it," he replied to Jon's worried question. "It's just the sort of thing I've been looking for. Mr. Byrd's done us a favor without knowing it."

They crossed to the cabin and Jane wanted to know: "Can you finish it now?"

Bob's eagerness faded. "It'll take us all of tomorrow to get the roof ready to pour the cement and we'll need more than a day for that."

All of them were silent; they were going to fail in spite of everything.

At last Phyllis remarked: "If Mother and I helped you mix cement, couldn't you get it done?"

"It'd take more than your help, I'm afraid," replied her father.

In the morning Jon and Bob went fiercely to work finishing the sheeting of the roof and tarring down the roll roofing, nailing it through the gypsum boards to the two-by-four joists underneath. Late in the afternoon, Jon looked down the hill and saw Maria and her brothers and the younger Summers children swimming in the pool. He waved and she waved back.

Phyllis stopped on the way down for a dip and asked: "How're you getting along?"

"If we only had another day beside tomorrow," Bob

groaned, and went on feverishly tarring the roofing seams.

"You could pour the cement tomorrow, if you had enough help, couldn't you?" Phyllis asked.

Bob didn't answer, and Jon replied sharply, "Sure, if we had enough help."

Phyllis walked on down the path to the pool, her red bathing suit bright against the green of the brush. She didn't swim as long as usual and Maria Scotti came up with her. Maria just smiled at Jon as she went past with his sister to the cabin. Later the two went back down the drive, Phyllis now dressed in slacks, and headed toward the Scotti place.

Phyllis wasn't home by dusk. "Where's Phil?" Bob wanted to know.

"She went over to the Scottis' for supper," Jane said.

Both he and Jon were too tired to inquire further about Phyllis's gadding. She came home about nine o'clock, but didn't say much. A little later, when Bob and Jon went into the cabin to go to bed, they interrupted Jane and Phyllis in a low-voiced conversation.

The next morning Bob said they had better figure on pouring just a part of the roof. That much they could get done. They unrolled the screen fence across the roof, cut it to length and anchored the ends to the bolts set in the top of the wall.

Tom Summers and his father came up the drive. "Need some help?" asked Joe. Tom grinned and winked at Jon.

Bob looked over the edge of the roof. "Well—" he began. Tom had already trundled the wheelbarrow over to the sand pile and his father followed him with the shovel. Bob saw Al Scotti and Hank Hartzinger coming up the drive. Behind them came Mike Brogan and Dave Walsh.

"Turn in your brass with the timekeeper," Joe Summers yelled to them.

Bob and Jon just stared.

"Well—hey—gee, it's mighty nice." Bob's words stammered to a halt. He tried again. "I really didn't expect . . ."

"Okay, Boss," yelled up Al Scotti. "You give-a da orders, we do-a da job."

The work began in earnest now and with laughing and kidding. The neighbors were having a fine time.

Phyllis came over and called Tom aside. Jon saw him follow his sister over to the cabin and in a little while there came a squawking of chickens and Tom was heading over the hill home with his hands full of the last of Phyllis's red cockerels. A short time later he came back with gray cockerels minus heads.

The commotion at the new house seemed to grow in volume as the men mixed cement in teams and carried it up to the roof where Joe Summers and Bob spread it over the screen fence with a straight-edge. A little after midday Jon saw Mrs. Summers and Mrs. Brogan coming up the drive, followed in a few minutes by Mrs. Hartzinger and Mrs. Walsh, and later by Mrs. Scotti. All carried baskets or bundles. Then a commotion rose in the cabin to equal the commotion at the new house.

By one o'clock, Bob called down to the men mixing cement: "That's the last batch." The job was finished.

"No job at all," pronounced Mike Brogan.

"That's-a way to getta job done," said Al Scotti.

"Well, it looks like we can eat now," said Bob.

They all looked across to the cabin and saw the terrace lined with all available tables filled with food.

It was hard for Jon to pull away from the house. The roof was on. Now when they got the windows in and the doors hung and the railing around the top it would begin to really look like something. He was the last to leave the building.

Maria Scotti came up, and the younger children of the neighborhood, whom she had been looking after while the grown-ups poured the roof and prepared the dinner, raced on ahead of her to the cabin.

"You got it finished," she said happily.

"We sure did. We did that job fast." Jon's voice was a little thick. He added: "Whose idea was it, getting all the neighbors to help us?"

Maria flushed. "Phil's. She came up with it while we were swimming yesterday afternoon."

"It was a swell idea," said Jon and they went on to join the others at the cabin.

That evening after the neighbors had been fed and thanked, and all had admitted it had been a fine holiday, the Woodwards sat on the terrace. They all seemed to have their eyes fixed on the new house. Finally Bob looked around: "Say, whose idea was it, getting everybody to help us pour that roof?"

"Phil's," spoke up Jon. "Maria told me."

"It wasn't," cried Phyllis quickly. "It was Maria who remembered reading about roof-raising bees."

Jane interrupted: "We have a caller."

They looked up to see Tod Sullivan-Schuyler coming past the new house trying to pretend indifference to it.

"Greetings," he said as he drew near. "What a quaint structure you have over there. Is that what is called functional architecture?"

"If it must have a name," replied Bob, chuckling.

Jon's face had darkened but Jane was smiling and Phyllis had flushed slightly as if Tod's affected language made her feel ashamed.

Young Sullivan-Schuyler brushed at a speck of dust on his tan slacks. "Just dropped in to say good-by," he said. "I'm off to V.M.I. tomorrow." He glanced haughtily at Jon. "Virginia Military Institute to the unenlightened."

"It was nice of you to stop in, Tod," said Jane, hoping that Jon wouldn't explode.

"Au revoir," said the youth. His glance lingered for

an instant upon Phyllis, and Jane saw the unhappy look in his eyes she'd seen the first time he came up here. Then he bowed slightly. "See you all next summer," adding, with thinning lips, "If you're still here."

"We'll be here, Tessy," said Jon grimly.

They watched him go back up over the hill toward the road, walking briskly, jauntily. Bob chuckled, Jane just continued to smile, Jon glowered, but Phyllis got up quickly and went into the cabin.

CHAPTER FIFTEEN

AUTUMN

THE rest of the Labor Day week was spent getting ready to move back to New Delphi. It was too dark by the time Bob got home from work and had his supper for him to do anything about the place. Jon gave the new roof a first coat of green roof paint, Jane and Phyllis canned up tomatoes and took a load of canned stuff in to the Delaware Street house.

Sunday night they locked the cabin and Bob headed the loaded car toward New Delphi. No one said anything about "returning home"; they felt as if they were going on a trip and would be staying in a strange place. They were even too tired to think much about it when they entered the big house in town; they were just glad to go to bed and sleep.

By Monday night they had begun to slip back into old ways. At dinner Jane remarked: "Well, it was nice cooking on the electric range again."

But Jon said: "I wish we were back home."

"This is home," insisted his mother.

"Well, I mean out in the country." His sun-browned face twisted with an unhappy look. All day he'd felt uncomfortable in his school clothes.

"I wonder if my pullets have laid any eggs yet," remarked Phyllis. She had left her dozen Rhode Island

Red pullets with Tom, who was to feed and house them for the winter in return for the eggs they laid, and return them to Phyllis when the Woodwards moved out to the country next spring.

"What makes you think they began laying within twenty-four hours after you left?" asked her mother.

Phyllis gave a little laugh. "It seems like we've been away so much longer than that."

When dinner came to an end, Bob slipped a notebook out of his pocket. He cleared his throat, twitched his shoulders, and his eyes sparkled.

"I did a little figuring today," he said, sweeping the family with a triumphant glance. "It cost us no more to live out there this past summer than if we'd lived right here in New Delphi. I sent off a final check to the Wayne Lumber Company to square our account and we still have twenty-five dollars of our ten-dollar-a-week accumulation. We don't owe a cent on Five Acre Hill as it stands. We've put seven hundred and thirty-five dollars into it, and I figure the place is now worth two thousand."

"Two thousand!" cried Jane skeptically.

"Sure. Why not?" Bob was ready to defend his stand. "Five acres, a field cleared and cultivated. A cabin—two rooms." He ticked these items off on his fingers. "A swimming pool. A big house started with living room and fireplace complete, all but windows and doors . . ."

Jane interrupted: "And finishing off on the inside."

"We'll get that done," said Bob quickly. "That place is worth a lot more than we put into it and we don't owe anything on it, which is the important thing."

This was the first time they had actually examined the

financial angle of Five Acre Hill. Jon's face began to shine. If it was worth two thousand and they sold it for that, that'd mean two thousand dollars for Phyllis and him to go to college on. The expression on his face froze. But they couldn't sell it. Five Acre Hill was home.

"Your figures sound fine," said Jane, "but you're forgetting something." She paused and, half smiling, watched their faces darken. "You're forgetting what we have down in the basement." Imitating Bob, she began ticking off on her fingers: "Thirty quarts of beans, forty-five quarts of tomatoes, a hundred bottles of tomato juice and twenty-five pints of corn, besides cherries, strawberries, rhubarb and pickles." When she ticked off the last item, all faces were bright again.

The first year at Five Acre Hill had been a success.

Then Jon spoke up: "We haven't harvested our carrots or cabbage yet either."

That reminded them that they hadn't really left the country for good. Next Saturday they'd be driving out as they had in the spring, with Bob coming down on the bus after work, and Sunday they'd do more work on the new house. All of them, even Jane, began living for the coming week-end.

Jon had his work cut out for him that Saturday: he had to order the windows and doors for the new house, and the hardware to go with them; and he had to give the roof its second coat of paint. It was dark by the time Bob got out there in the evening and he couldn't do anything until the next day. But Sunday morning they began fitting the casement windows. Both of them worked like fury, as if the whole job had to be finished in a day.

Jane stopped to see how they were progressing and remarked: "What's your hurry? There'll be more week-ends."

"I'd like to get this living room finished by Thanksgiving," explained Bob.

"We can have Thanksgiving dinner in it," cried Jon.

"Nonsense!" snapped his mother. "How would I cook a turkey out here?"

Bob frowned at Jon, and Jon knew by that frown that he'd spoken out of turn. Such ideas as having Thanksgiving dinner in the new house shouldn't be sprung on Moms so suddenly.

The work progressed.

But Jon decided to go out for football that season at Van Buren High. His summer work at Five Acre Hill, gardening, mixing cement, and lugging stones, had made him tough and hard. He had grown several inches and added pounds.

At the end of the first week of football practice he was playing tackle on the first team. He played in every game of the season; he was a star tackle. But the games were played on Saturday afternoons and that kept him away from Five Acre Hill. That was the only thing he didn't like about playing football—the fact that he missed Saturday in the country.

Jane and Phyllis continued to go out to Five Acre Hill Saturday mornings as usual, except when the football games were played in New Delphi; then they stayed in town for the game. Afterwards they picked up Jon and Bob and drove out to the country in the evening.

The nights grew chilly and Bob found a pot-bellied stove for the cabin; the year moved into October and the family got up Sunday mornings to look out the cabin windows at a world of brilliant colors sharpened with a rime of frost. Breakfasts were like feasts; the same food cooked on the electric range at the Delaware Street house could never have tasted half so good. The menu seldom varied: tomato juice, golden pancakes, eggs or sausage and coffee or chocolate.

"I never saw such appetites," complained Jane.

It seemed that the whole family lived six days a week just for this one day. And once in a while Jon paused in his work on the new house and wondered: What if Byrd managed to make them give up Five Acre Hill? That was a thought he flung aside quickly; that was an idea he hadn't the courage to face.

The doors and windows were hung at the new house and Jane and Phyllis painted the frames and sash on the outside, while Bob and Jon nailed a ceiling of Sheet Rock to the cross-joists between the big oak beams. Sometimes they stopped their work just to look at the country, at the flaming yellow, orange and red of sassafras leaves, the reds and yellows of maples, and the mahogany color creeping over the oaks. The sight was breath-taking.

One October afternoon at the height of the carnival of color, neither Jane nor Phyllis showed up after lunch to work on the new house. They had said nothing about not working; they just didn't appear.

"What's the matter with those women?" Bob grumbled.

"Looks like they've run out on us, Dad," Jon replied.

They went on working, but their hearts weren't in it. The autumn air coming through the flung-back windows seemed to melt their spirit. At last the trim was finished and the joints of the Sheet Rock boards cemented. The living room was ready for painting on the inside. Bob began packing up the tools.

"What do we do now, Dad?" asked Jon.

"Nothing!" said his father as if he were angry. "Nothing! If those women can take a powder on us, I don't see why we should continue to work and slave."

They walked out on the slope in front of the new house and stared at the brilliant, unspeakably blue sky, and the colors of the trees which were beyond all description. Their foreheads were pinched as if the sight were painful. Then down at the end of the terrace garden they saw Jane sitting on a stool, painting a water color. They ambled down the slope toward her, but she seemed oblivious to their approach. Her fingers moved swiftly, laying on the colors with her brush: a flaming maple against the broken ledge of gray limestone.

Jon eyed the work critically. "Pretty good, Moms."

His mother didn't answer.

"Looks like a tree." Bob's lips twitched, but his remark was met by stony silence and fierce activity. He added: "Artists are unsociable people."

The two strolled on down around the swimming pool, across the end of the field and up the far side. Once they paused to gaze at the gray front of the new house above them.

"It'll look pretty good when we get the log railing around the edge of the sun-deck," Bob remarked.

This was the first time Jon had had a good look at the

new house from a distance. He caught his breath. The sight seemed to startle him. It really looked like something. He pictured the rest of the house rising behind the finished part. It would look like a real country place when they got it completed. A house to be proud of, and they were building it themselves. He swung his glance around swiftly over the hill and field. What a change in just a year! In less than a year!

They crossed the north end of the field, the part seeded to clover. "Got a pretty good stand," Bob said.

"Need a goat next year to feed it," replied Jon.

"Over Moms' dead body."

Both of them laughed heartily.

As they wandered up the back slope past the stone-wall shanty built by Tom Summers and his brother, Jon grinned to himself, remembering how his first picture of the new house had grown from this stone shanty. Finally they reached the terrace in front of the cabin and sat down, stretching wearily as if they'd walked miles. For a long time they sat in silence, staring down the valley, occasionally breaking their fixed glance for a swift look at the square, rough, unfinished house.

At last Bob remarked: "We made mighty good headway this year." His head nodded slightly with satisfaction.

"We sure got more done than I figured we would last spring," replied Jon.

Again the peaceful silence grew between them, while they thoroughly enjoyed the calm, brilliant afternoon, slowly coming to an end. For a moment, Jon remembered the flying tackle he'd made in yesterday's game;

that tackle kept the opposing team from scoring at a critical moment.

"Woodward," said the coach afterwards. "That tackle of yours saved the game for us."

Jon's breath felt tight and full in his chest.

"If we can make as much progress next year," Bob said thoughtfully, "we'll be all set for Phyllis and you to go to college when you've finished high school."

As if Jon's prideful memories were something he shouldn't have entertained, he spoke up quickly: "We ought to get even farther next year, Dad. We can concentrate on the new house right from the beginning."

"Yes, if nothing happens." Bob's face had darkened.

Jon saw the dark look. The thought of Merrivale Byrd and the threat to his father's job at Universal confronted him. They might even be forced to give up Five Acre Hill. Jon felt his muscles tightening as they always did before a game.

"I may be looking for another job and there may not be any ten dollars a week for this." Bob gestured toward the unfinished house up the slope. His shifting eyes saw Jon hunched down dejectedly, and he regretted the black cloud he'd conjured up. "But there's no use being down-in-the-mouth about it now. We'll figure out a way to beat Merrivale Byrd and his brother-in-law if that should be necessary. Right now let's enjoy what we've accomplished—what we've got." He leaned over and slapped his hand down on his son's knee.

Jon grinned: yes, no use crepe-hanging.

They saw Phyllis hurrying through the woods from the direction of the Summers'. Jon's thoughts shifted to his sister. Might have known she was over talking with

Tom. He wondered suddenly: how was Maria Scotti? He ought to go over and say "Hello." But Phyllis didn't allow him to continue pondering.

"Look!" she cried. "My chickens laid their first egg today." She held out the small brown egg in the palm of her hand.

"I thought Tom was to get all the eggs until spring," said her father, eyes twinkling.

"Oh, he gave me this first one." Then she asked: "What's the matter? Why aren't you working on the house?"

"Why should *we* work?" Bob pulled a long face. "You and Moms ran out on us. Why should we work and slave?"

Phyllis looked suddenly confused. "Well, it was so nice out—"

"And you hadn't seen Tom for a week." Jon smirked. She slapped at him and he caught her arm.

"Don't. You'll break my egg."

They stopped scuffling.

Jane came up with her water colors and pad of paper. "The moment I leave the job," she said, "all work stops. If I'm not around to keep you at work, nothing gets done."

"She admits she ran out on us," Bob said.

"Moms, how do you expect us to work without your expert advice?" asked Jon.

Jane laughed and sat down on the terrace with them. Their bantering stopped and silence took over, while they gazed dreamily into the brilliant blue sky and the many-colored hills splashed with sunlight from the low-swinging sun behind them.

The next two week-ends were wet. Rain dripped in a steady drizzle, and the leaves, heavy with rain, spilled down noisily, glistening on the ground. But the Woodwards came out to Five Acre Hill as usual. All the outside work was done. They painted the big living room, the ceiling and walls with cold water paint and the floor with red cement paint.

"Someday we can put down a wood floor or a composition floor," Bob explained, to take the frown off Jane's face when she looked down at it. "This'll have to do for the time being."

Jane accepted the situation. She made curtains for the windows and hung them the week-end before Thanksgiving. That Sunday Bob and Jon cut wood for the fireplace and moved some of the extra furniture from the cabin over to make the big living room seem less bare.

"If we brought the table over," said Bob, looking slantwise at Jane, "we could eat our Thanksgiving dinner right here in front of the fireplace."

"Let's do," cried Phyllis.

Jon didn't say anything.

"Too much trouble," said Jane. But Thanksgiving morning they loaded the roasted turkey and the rest of the dinner into the car and headed for Five Acre Hill. "This is silly," she said. "We could just as well eat here in town." But she was smiling.

All of them wanted to make this Thanksgiving dinner their first meal in the first finished unit of their new house. Jon and Bob built a roaring fire and moved the table and chairs over from the cabin. Jane and Phyllis heated up the meal on the oilstove in the cabin and in the edge of the fireplace.

They didn't eat until three o'clock. It was a confused, disorganized meal that under any other circumstances would have made Jane frantic and furious. But they all laughed and kidded and made a joke of the confusion. The carving set had been forgotten in New Delphi, so Bob strapped Jon's Boy Scout knife at his belt and cut up the bird with it. They sang and whooped like children.

"If I had ever thought I'd live to serve a dinner like this one," said Jane, shaking her head, "I'd have died of shame long ago."

But they ate everything. The family-sized turkey was stripped to its bones and every bowl was emptied. When they had finished the last crumbs of plum pudding with lemon sauce, they leaned back in their chairs, too full for any more laughter.

After a long silence Phyllis remarked dreamily: "Next year I'll be at college. I wonder if I can come home for Thanksgiving."

Jon and Bob exchanged glances.

"Maybe," said her father.

"Don't go planning too far ahead," counseled Jane. "There's no telling what next year will bring us."

"But, Mother, I am going to college next fall." Phyllis's eyes were large and dark and questioning.

"If plans work out," said Bob.

Jon felt suddenly restless. He'd eaten too much, he needed to walk it off. Getting up from the table, he flung his jacket around his shoulders and slid his arms in the sleeves. "Guess I'll take a walk."

"We'll be going back to town in an hour," said Jane.

He stepped out into the crisp November air, his

father's words, "If plans work out," revolving slowly in his thoughts. Yes, if plans work out. But there was his dad's precarious job at Universal, and there was Merrivale Byrd and Mr. Sullivan-Schuyler. He sauntered down the drive, chin on his chest. The only thing to do was forge ahead and meet the circumstances that arose.

At the highway he turned toward Scotti's, his steps quickening. His face grew brighter as he walked. He found all of the Scottis except Mrs. Scotti out in the yard doing chores. Tony and George were carrying wood into the house. Al waved the pitchfork at him from the haystack above the barn and shouted a greeting. He met Maria at the barn door just as she had finished milking the goats.

She set the pail of milk on the ground.

"Just ran over to say hello," explained Jon. "We're going back to town in a little while."

Maria leaned back against the closed bottom half of the barn door, her hands in the pockets of her blue denim dungarees, her jacket open, the blue scarf tied around her head making her dark eyes darker.

"Have a good Thanksgiving?" she asked.

"Yeah. It was wild, but we had a lot of fun."

A couple of young goats loose in the barn stood up on the inside of the door; their sharp noses pecked at Maria's scarf. She turned to scratch their jaws. Jon leaned over the door beside her, playfully pulling a long, soft, tan ear.

"Friendly, aren't they?" he said.

"They're awful pests, but they're fun."

Jon stared into the bulging yellow eyes of the young

goat nearest him. The wild, devilish look made him laugh.

Then he asked: "How's school?" to make talk.

"Fine."

"I wish we were living out here," he added.

She hesitated before she said: "Last week, on the school bus, Harry Dawson was bragging that his Uncle Merrivale was going to break your dad at Universal."

"Let him try it!" replied Jon with more bluff than confidence.

"Dad says the workers are all for your father a hundred per cent," Maria added.

Jon didn't want to talk any more. "Guess we'll just have to wait and see what Byrd tries to pull." Then he said: "I've got to be getting back. See you the next time we're out. So long, Maria."

"So long, Jon." She waved to him when he looked back from the road.

Head down, he retraced his steps toward Five Acre Hill. Yes, they'd have to wait and see what tricks Byrd tried next.

CHAPTER SIXTEEN

BLIZZARD

EVEN before the end of the year Jon saw the pinch of worry showing around his father's eyes. Jane noticed it too, but Bob brushed aside inquiries with, "It's nothing. Production schedules are heavy and take a lot of attention."

They continued to go out to Five Acre Hill for weekends. Jon and Bob cut wood, trimming the dead limbs from the trees in their wood lot and sawing the branches into lengths for the cabin stove and the new living room fireplace.

Snow came in December and Jon and Phyllis skied. They coasted on the hill behind the Summers' place with Tom and his brother and sister and Maria Scotti and Tony and George. The swimming pool froze over and they skated.

With the exception of Christmas Day, which the family spent at the Delaware Street house, Jon, Phyllis, and Jane stayed the ten-day school holiday out at the cabin. They dressed warmly and kept the pot-bellied stove glowing.

Jon and Phyllis gave a night skating party on the pool for Tom and Maria and some of their friends from Wayne. Jane chaperoned and presided over the fire and the picnic of frankfurters and marshmallows. The valley echoed with shouts and laughter and the click and hiss of steel blades on the ice.

Maria Scotti was sober that night. Once when she and Jon skated up to the inland end of the pool and turned to watch the others sliding and clowning on the ice near the fire she said: "Byrd's hired a couple of fellows to go down to the plant and stir up trouble among the workers."

Her breath clouded up in the steel white light of the huge round moon, hiding her face. Jon no longer heard the shrill gaiety of the party.

"What do you mean?"

"They're trying to get the union to pull a wildcat strike. Dad says he's sure they aren't even union members, but they've got papers."

Now Jon understood his father's look of worry. It wasn't just the heavy production schedules. A wildcat strike would break his dad's production record and discredit him.

"How do you know Byrd has anything to do with it?" Jon's question was sharp, almost as if he were defending Byrd.

"Dad picked up one of those fellows who've been hanging around the plant, talking to the men, out at the bus stop in Wayne night before last. He told Dad he wanted to get out to Mr. Byrd's place. Dad recognized the man, but he doesn't think the man recognized him as one of the workers at the plant."

Jon couldn't find any reply. They skated back to the party.

Before going to bed that night, Jon considered passing along to his mother what Maria had told him, but decided against it. However, when his father came out that week-end and they were cutting wood alone, he mentioned it.

"Yes," Bob said, "they're trying to make trouble. They've been using every excuse possible to stir up the workers. And somebody's started a backfire among the men to the effect that Sullivan-Schuyler's hired those agitators to make trouble for me."

Bob chuckled a little. "I didn't suspect Al Scotti's fine Italian hand in that counter-agitation. You see, bringing Sullivan-Schuyler into the picture makes it look as if I were responsible for this counter-line. Superintendent Hardy pointed that out to me yesterday. I really think Byrd is working on his own this time, trying to get me, but his name wouldn't mean anything at the plant, so apparently Al's blaming Sullivan-Schuyler, whose name does mean something."

"Is there any danger of a strike?" asked Jon anxiously.

Sudden wrinkles on Bob's forehead made the bill of his ski cap jerk. "No. The workers haven't much to kick about. But gossip and rumors and this constant agitation make the less dependable workers slow up, and that slows up everything."

He went on chopping wood for a while before continuing: "But Al Scotti ought to be careful. Those two guys are out-and-out thugs. And if they find that he's discovered their connections with Byrd, they're likely to make trouble for him."

Jon wondered if he ought to warn Maria to warn her father, but he concluded that Al probably realized the danger.

The holiday ended and the Woodwards returned to New Delphi, and Jon and Phyllis to school. Nothing serious happened to Bob at Universal. Toward the end of January Bob had to go to Buffalo to straighten out a production snarl in a parts plant there. Jon wondered if Byrd might not have pulled some strings to make that trouble too, but Bob indicated no such suspicions. On Friday Jane received a wire from him: "Won't be home for week-end. Enjoy the country."

Jane, Phyllis and Jon drove out to Five Acre Hill Saturday morning as usual. The snow on the drive was melted enough for Jane to run the car right up to the picnic spot. But when they climbed out and looked up at the turtledove gray sky, Jane frowned: "I don't know, maybe we ought to go back."

"Oh, Mother, what if it does snow a little," cried Phyllis. "I'd like to be out here for a good snow once."

"Snow, maybe," said her mother, "but not a blizzard."

Jon's face brightened at the idea of being out here in a snowstorm. "Aw, Moms, it won't blizzard."

They stayed and started the fire in the cabin stove. Jon cut a supply of wood and heaped it close to the back door. By lunch time it was snowing hard—great fluffy flakes that piled up on tree branches.

"Isn't it beautiful?" cried Phyllis.

But as soon as lunch was over, Jane said: "I think we'd better start back to town."

"In this snow, Mother?" Phyllis looked worried. "You won't be able to see to drive."

That was perfectly true. Jon's face was serious.

"Well," said Jane, "the moment it lets up, we'll start."

They waited and the snow came down in a soundless, endless cloud. All afternoon the fall continued.

"We'll have to have chains on," Jane remarked. "Can you put them on, Jon?" Then she added: "We should have gone back this morning."

"Sure, I can put them on," Jon said confidently.

They waited for the storm to slacken, but the white world seemed to grow thicker. By four-thirty it was growing dark. At five o'clock Jon decided that he'd better go out and put the chains on, snow or no snow. Perhaps when it turned colder after dark the snow would let up and they could get back to New Delphi.

He pulled on his ski-suit and his thick sheepskin jacket and went out to the car. With the broom he swept the light snow away from the rear wheels. He was surprised at the depth—almost a foot. They'd never get the car through it and out to the highway.

The sooner he got the chains on, the better. He spread them out behind the rear wheels and tried to back the car onto them, but the wheels spun. Then he got the jack out of the trunk and tried to raise the car. The jack slipped on the wet ground, slipped on the cold bumper. His hands grew cold in his soaked gloves. He realized that it was getting colder, the snow finer. The wind came up and whipped the dry whiteness through the trees and around the white mound of the car.

At last he got one of the chains on. It was dark now, but in the whiteness of the snow he could see faintly and he could feel his way with the other chain. He tried turning on the car lights, but the brightness was all up in front and only hindered his work on the chain. When he went to turn them off, he heard the snowplow going past in the direction of Wayne. It had evidently gone up the road once and was coming back. If they could get out of here the highway would be passable, then.

Once his mother called: "How're you making out?"

"All right. Pretty soon now."

He went back to work on the second chain and after a struggle got it on. As he stood up and beat the snow from his clothes he thought he heard a dull crash down on the highway. The sound seemed to cushion against the snow. He took a couple of steps up the slope until he was able to look over the crest. In the road, almost at the end of the drive, he saw the dim shaft of a car's lights slanting up to the south at a crazy angle. Then the lights went out. He heard the faint chucking sound of a car door slamming.

Somebody must have gone into the ditch. He began running down the drive through the drifting snow; he reached the highway out of breath and plunged through the high bank of snow pushed up by the plow. Across the road he saw the bulky shape of a car lying on its side in the ditch, rapidly growing invisible beneath the thickening blanket of snow.

An inexplicable feeling of fear stopped him in the middle of the road. Perhaps it was the unnatural position of the machine, its ghostly appearance in the darkness and falling snow. Then he remembered the car door slamming. Probably the driver had realized that nothing could be done about it tonight and had just climbed out and walked away. Yes, there were the half-hidden footprints in the snow heading up the road.

His courage revived and he plowed through the snow to the edge of the overturned machine. Yes, whoever had

had this accident had just walked off and left the car here, he assured himself. Then he might as well go back up the hill and help his mother try to get their car down to the road.

The continuous rushing of the wind died down a moment. He had become so used to the sound that it had to die down before he realized that he'd been hearing it all the time. Then he thought he heard another sound. Something in the wind, he told himself. He remained uncertainly by the overturned car. The wind lulled again, and again he thought he heard a heavier sound coming from the machine. Now he waited and listened carefully. His heart pounded so furiously he felt sure he wouldn't be able to hear anything; his breath seemed frozen in his throat. Another lull of the wind—this time he heard it distinctly, a moan. There was someone in the car.

The same pattern of impulses which had brought him running down the drive, now sent him climbing up the chassis of the car to the upturned side. He struggled to lift the door. All was dark inside. Then he remembered that the lights had been on—maybe there was a ceiling light in the car. His fingers felt inside for the switch. It snapped on and a light glowed crazily below him.

He had to think an instant to explain why this light wasn't overhead as it should be. Then he saw the twisted form of a man slumped against the lower side. Jon's lips seemed too stiff to move. It was Al Scotti. Blood trickled slowly from a wound on his forehead.

"Mr. Scotti!" The cry, the unnaturalness of the sound, startled Jon. He had a feeling that he hadn't cried out. The only answer he received was another moan.

Terror whipped at him now. He scrambled back off the machine, leaving the light on inside and ran stumbling, falling, crawling, getting up and plunging on toward the cabin. Halfway there, struggling to get his wind, he thought vaguely that whoever it was with Al must have gone for help. He finally staggered into the cabin and panted out the story.

"We'd better go see what we can do," said Jane instantly, and both she and Phyllis began struggling into their ski suits to go back with Jon.

No one was at the car when they returned. Whoever it was that had walked away before Jon got there hadn't come back. Jane sent Phyllis to the Summers' for help, then she and Jon climbed into the car and tried to lift Al Scotti into a comfortable position. They could hardly move his big body, made heavier by the dead weight of unconsciousness. He didn't even groan now. Jon's lips were dry with fear.

In a little while Phyllis returned, and Tom Summers with her. Joe Summers had gone to work at the foundry on the night shift. All four of them struggled and worked until they lifted Al out of the car to the road. From the little feeble cloud of breath rising from his lips into the glow of Tom's flashlight they could tell that he was still alive.

Tom pulled the rear cushion from the machine. They draped Al lengthwise on it and began the slow, plodding trip the quarter mile up the road to his home. Every few rods they had to stop and rest.

At last they stumbled with their burden upon the porch of the Scotti house. Maria came to the door. Her face went white at the sight of them. As they staggered

into the living room and Mrs. Scotti saw them, she
screamed and sank down heavily in a chair. They laid
Al on the floor and Mrs. Scotti slid forward out of her
chair, kneeling beside him sobbing, talking to him in
Italian. Tony and George stood looking on, their faces
white with terror.

Jane went to the telephone and called a doctor in
Wayne. Then she directed the rest of them to help lift
Al to the couch and try to make him as comfortable as
possible. Now Mrs. Scotti rolled to her feet and took
over, tears still streaming down her dark, heavy cheeks.
"Maria. Towels," she ordered. Then she went to the
kitchen for hot water from the teakettle on the stove, and
she began bathing Al's bloody face, her soft, cooing Italian voice murmuring to him the while.

Still he didn't regain consciousness. The doctor arrived, a big stocky man, puffing from his car through the
snow, cursing the highway superintendent for not plowing the road better. He examined Al, and his face grew
serious. It was a severe contusion, he explained to Jane.

"My husban', he be all righ'," pleaded Mrs. Scotti.
"Please, Mister Doctor."

Al began to stir. He regained consciousness but didn't
seem to recognize anyone, not even his wife or Maria.
Mrs. Scotti sobbed silently now on a low stool near his
head.

There was nothing more the doctor could do and,
promising to return in the morning, he headed back
toward Wayne. At last Jane and Phyllis and Jon and
Tom set out for home, with Mrs. Scotti's stammered
thanks sobbing after them, and Maria's silent figure
standing in the doorway after they'd gone.

Tom accompanied the Woodwards up to the picnic ground to make sure they got there all right in the storm. The pot-bellied stove had to be rekindled. They had forgotten supper—they hardly felt like eating. Jon couldn't forget the person who had left Al Scotti injured in the car and hadn't come back. He had a hard time sleeping after he went to bed. None of them slept much. The temperature went down below zero. In the morning the storm had stopped and the sun glared on the white world of snow.

At breakfast Jane said: "It was a good thing you found Al last night, Jon. He would have frozen to death lying there unconscious until someone discovered him today."

After breakfast Jon waded through the snow over to the Scottis' to see how Al was. Maria met him at the door, smiling faintly. Her father was awake, showing just vague recognition of his surroundings. Mrs. Scotti was still damp-eyed but busy about the place with fierce energy.

To Jon's query, could he do anything to help out? Maria replied: "Thanks. But I've done all the chores."

Tony and George were out scooping paths.

The doctor came and examined Al again. He explained that Al had received a hard blow, causing him to lose his memory. It would take time for him to regain it. He prescribed rest.

Jon took this report home, then began shoveling out the drive. Phyllis and Jane joined him. They had dug out halfway down the hill when they saw a trooper's car stop at the overturned machine on the road and the troopers examine it and drive away. Then a taxi stopped and let Bob out. He waded up to them through the snow, grinning broadly.

"Need any help, you folks?" he asked. He'd been able to get back from Buffalo sooner than he had expected. The grin left his face when they told him about Al's accident. "This shoveling can wait," he said grimly, and set out for the Scottis'.

Al's face lighted up at the sight of him, showing its first real gleam of recognition. Haltingly he tried to tell Bob about the accident. It hadn't been an accident at all. He'd picked up that same guy he'd picked up a month ago who wanted to get out to Byrd's. Just as they came around the long curve below Five Acre Hill, the fellow had reached over and jerked the steering wheel, sending the car into the ditch. They had only been jolted up. Then the guy had hit him with something—a blackjack, maybe, and left him there to freeze to death.

The report of a second person in the car tallied with Jon's story of hearing the car-door slam after the crash and seeing tracks leaving the scene of the accident. Bob called the sheriff and troopers and reported this to them. Sheriff Bailey, a cousin of Merrivale Byrd's, put on a great show of investigating the case. He questioned Jon and Tom. He called on Mr. Byrd and questioned him about this stranger.

Mr. Byrd denied knowing any such person, or that anyone had come to his place last night. He suggested sarcastically that Al Scotti had drunk too much red wine, had just run into the ditch and bumped his head. All this other story was just Scotti's imagination. He was still out of his head.

Bob returned to Five Acre Hill, quite sure that Sheriff

Bailey would discover no one or nothing that would in any way incriminate his cousin, Mr. Byrd. They finished scooping out the drive and drove back to New Delphi.

Wednesday night at supper Bob reported that Mike Brogan told him that the two troublemakers hadn't been seen about the plant since Sunday.

"That makes it look like there was something to Al's story," said Jon. "If Al had frozen to death nobody would have known the connection between those fellows and Byrd."

Bob nodded. "Guess it was lucky for Al and for all of us that you found him."

CHAPTER SEVENTEEN

THE GARDEN AGAIN

BOB'S troubles at Universal eased up a little now. Late March came again and the weather moderated; gullies ran with melting snow. The Woodwards felt spring in the air.

They studied seed and nursery catalogues. They discussed and argued about what they should plant. Bob ordered four apple trees, two cherry trees, a Bartlett and a Seckel pear, two plums and a quince. Jane wanted a hundred asparagus crowns and twenty raspberry bushes. "And we want a strawberry patch," she said. They ordered garden seeds.

Now when the family went out to Five Acre Hill on week-ends, they raked last year's growth from the terraces and planned where to put their permanent garden stuff. Bob and Jon bought a load of chicken manure from Tom Summers and spread it over the garden beds.

Cal Dawson came and plowed the part of the lower field that they hadn't seeded to clover. And for a relative of Merrivale Byrd's, he unbent enough to glance up the hill at the cabin and the new living room and remark: "You folks are goin' to have quite a place out here before long."

"When we get it finished, we hope it'll be," said Jon. He was surprised at this friendliness, just as he had been surprised when Dawson came over promptly to plow on the date he had promised. But Jon got an inkling of Dawson's change-of-heart when the old farmer remarked another time:

"Got three jobs of plowin' for them other folks." He waved a gnarled hand over the hill toward the Brogan, Walsh and Hartzinger places. "A few more new folks come out here and I'll have all I can do." He seemed quite happy about it.

Jon reported these remarks to his father, and Bob said: "He's just beginning to see what people moving out from town the way we have can mean to him. Before, he made a small living out of his own run-down farm and plowing for the Summers, and maybe a half dozen others around here. The rest of the time he had to depend upon his relative Byrd for a living. That always kept him under obligation to Byrd. Bring a few more people like us out here and he'll be independent." Bob chuckled. "And Merrivale Byrd isn't going to like that."

In April, other workers from Universal came out to look for acreage on the Summers' farm. They looked at other property for sale in the vicinity, some owned by Mr. Holden of the Wayne Lumber Company. Then one Sunday Tom Summers came whistling breezily over to the Woodwards' and announced that his father was selling four more plots.

"Wonderful," cried Bob, "wonderful. Eventually eight more votes against Byrd."

Phyllis and Jon recited in falsetto: "Mr. Byrd *isn't* going to *like* that."

They all laughed except Jane. She turned her glance out over the long valley and frowned faintly as if she saw something that displeased her. Later she said: "With more and more people moving out here and threatening Byrd's position, he's going to try all the harder to break you at Universal, Bob."

"But I can't help it if they come out here, Moms."

"Of course not, but you started it."

He stared thoughtfully in front of him.

Jane continued: "Two more months and Phyllis will be graduating. If you get pushed out of your job this summer, it'll be difficult for us to start her in college this fall."

Phyllis's eyes grew wide with anxiety, her cheeks twitched a little. "Dad, you just can't lose your job! What'll I do if I can't go to college this fall?"

"Aw, Phil, you'll go all right!" spoke up Jon, but his voice didn't sound too confident.

"Anyhow, we won't worry about it now," Bob said, and walked down to look at the terrace garden because there seemed to be no other way to break up the discussion.

During the Easter holiday Jon spaded over the terrace beds for the early garden: peas, onion sets, lettuce, spinach, beets, carrots. The corn ground of last season and part of last year's oat field were sowed to oats. Already the upper part of the field, which had been seeded to clover, was showing green.

Jon asked his father what he planned to do with that clover, but like the oats last year, Bob didn't know. He had just wanted to see the early green of a clover field, then the red of a clover field in blossom, like those he remembered on the home place back in Illinois.

This year he planned to pull up the sweetcorn in late August, after it was through producing, cover the ground with lime, and seed the area to alfalfa. "And what will you do with the alfalfa?" asked Jane.

Bob knew she was teasing, so he said: "Raise goats."

"We will not!" came her firm answer.

But Jon had begun to fancy the idea of raising goats. The gardening didn't take up all of his time. There was more brush to trim, more wood to cut and leaves to rake up and put into the compost pit to rot down for future fertilizer. He still found time to spend at the Scottis' talking with Maria and watching this spring's flock of kids playing in the yard.

The old goats, four white Saanen and five brown Toggenburg does, nibbled the greening grass below the barn, while their kids ran, jumped, butted, danced. Black, brown, tan and white, they whirled and twisted helter-skelter, as unpredictable as leaves in the wind. The look in their bulging, yellowish eyes seemed devilish, humorous and wild all at the same time.

"They're so crazy," laughed Maria as two kids smacked together head on, knocked themselves down, bounced up with surprised looks and galloped off in opposite directions.

"Look at those." Jon pointed at four going up the back side of a sloping stone, leaping off the front side and circling back to repeat the trick. "They're as funny as kittens."

Once Jon remarked: "What does goat's milk taste like?"

"Haven't you ever tasted goat's milk?" Maria's dark

eyes stared at him in amazement. It was difficult for her to imagine anyone's not having tasted it.

He shook his head and she added, "We'll correct that right now. Come along." At the kitchen door, she called: "Momma, Jon's never tasted goat's milk."

"Hah, you no taste!" cried Mrs. Scotti. "I fix." She lunged forward out of her chair and moved her plump body across the spick-and-span kitchen with surprising agility. Her soft hand snapped open the refrigerator and brought out a gray jug. When she held out a brimming glass to Jon, she said: "This-a make you grow—make-a you big man."

He drank it, tasting carefully each swallow. It seemed thinner than cow's milk, almost like cow's milk with the cream taken off. "That's all right." He handed back the empty glass. "Thanks."

"Si. Si. You like?" Mrs. Scotti beamed enthusiastically. "It's-a good. Goat's milk and vino, ah, that's-a good-a drink."

Maria and Jon returned to the yard laughing.

Jon reported tasting goat's milk to his family: "I can't see any difference from cow's milk." That assertion didn't seem quite right and he added: "Or not much difference, anyhow." He looked toward his father. "If we had a goat out here we wouldn't have to buy milk. Gee, they're fun to watch."

"Now *you're* starting it!" cried his mother at once. "We're not going to have any goat. Goat's milk doesn't taste like cow's milk; I know it doesn't."

"Mother, did you ever taste it?" asked Phyllis.

"No. No, I haven't. But we don't want one of those silly things around here."

Then on Easter afternoon when Jon stopped in to see Maria, he found her helping her father plant garlic in their garden. The big Italian roared at him: "Jon, you save-a my life. I freeze like a stone if-a you no find." His long face beamed upon Jon's slowly reddening cheeks.

"All time, I beat my head," continued Al. "What can I do for this-a boy. Maria, she help. I give you a goat. When you folks come out for summer, I give-a you a goat. A beautiful goat I give-a you. She make three quarts-a milk a day. See, that-a one." His cloddy finger pointed at a brown, bewhiskered Toggenburg, standing with her forefeet high on the trunk of a white birch, stretching her sharp nose upward to nibble the tender branch-ends above. "That's-a one; she's-a yours."

"Oh—ah, thanks, Mr. Scotti," stammered Jon, looking helplessly at Maria. But she was smiling happily. "I don't know if my folks'll let me take it."

"Sure! Sure!" roared Mr. Scotti confidently. "I speak-a the Boss. I fix everything smooth." He made a flat gesture with his hand.

All the way home, Jon was tugged back and forth by his thoughts: Gee, it'd be fun to have a goat, but, gee, Moms won't hear of me having one.

When he told about Al Scotti's offer his mother threw up her hands. "No, sir! We'll have no goats here!"

Jon again looked for support from his father. "Aw, gee, Moms, I'd like to raise goats."

"Since when have you taken a liking to animals?" she cried in exasperation. "It's always been Phyllis before. Get yourself rabbits or chickens or turkeys—anything but goats."

"But Al wants to give me a goat, Moms."

"Tell him to keep his old goat!"

"Moms, Al's just trying to make it up to Jon for finding him last winter. If we don't let him do something, he'll feel hurt." Then Bob added thoughtfully: "Besides, we haven't moved out here for the summer yet."

No more was said. The others knew that he was reminding them of the unstable circumstances of his job.

But the next week-end Jon and Bob began digging the basement and furnace room of the new house. It was the sound of hammering in the neighborhood which seemed to spur them on. The new families who had bought land of Joe Summers were putting up cabins. They had come over earlier to look at the Woodwards' cabin; they had taken Bob's specifications for material, and now they were building shacks similar to the Woodwards'.

A week later the pounding seemed to rise to a crescendo. The neighborhood echoed with its triumphant thunder. Jon and Bob finished the digging of the basement. When they stood back and studied the finished job, Bob said: "Next Saturday we can order cement and sand and pour the floor." His eyes were shining with excitement.

Jon felt the same bursting eagerness. The new house, like a plant in the spring, had started to grow again. But the next Saturday afternoon, after the sand and cement had been delivered, Jon went over to Scotti's to tell Maria that the next day they'd start building again. He was full of the idea. He boasted wildly: this year they'd get the rest of the new house built and maybe they'd live out here permanently then.

On the way home he heard the clop-clop of hoofs on

the black-top up ahead. He knew instantly the rider on the chestnut horse—Merrivale Byrd.

And Mr. Byrd recognized him too from a distance, and by the time they met, his face seemed almost black with rage. He didn't offer a greeting; he just snarled: "Your father seems to think he can fill up this country with squatters and get away with it. Well, he'll learn before long that he's going to pay plenty for his effrontery." Then, jabbing his spurs into the sweat-dark flanks of his horse, he galloped on up the road.

Jon felt himself grow hollow at this threat. All that evening he brooded over it, but said nothing to the rest of the family. Lying awake in bed, he wished something would happen to Merrivale Byrd to rid them of his menacing nearness. If there was some way to beat him. Wild ideas knocked about in his head, and his father's snoring in the cot across the room kept him awake a long time.

The next day they mixed cement and poured the floor of the furnace room and cellar space for the new house. They had to work fast and hard. The sun beat down fiercely. Their clothes were soon soaked with sweat. They enjoyed it. The pull and push of the hoes in the sand and cement, the slop of the thick greenish mixture on the floor, the spreading and smoothing of the surface with the straight-edge, gave them a feeling of strength compounded of enthusiasm and excitement as well as muscle.

But in the afternoon Jon could keep the secret of his meeting with Byrd no longer and told his father. Bob stopped his work, leaning on the mixing hoe. His glance shifted to the finished wall of the living room and a frown pinched his forehead. Jon saw anxiety in his father's blue eyes.

"I suppose," began Bob, resuming work, "Byrd sees the handwriting on the wall and he's out to get me because I started it. Everything's been going smoothly at the plant lately, but something may start happening any day. Besides, in another two months that big order'll be completed." He shrugged his strong shoulders. "There's no use borrowing trouble."

But by Wednesday of the following week, Jon saw the worry deepening in his father's eyes. When they went down to the basement workshop in the Delaware Street house to build screens for the living room of the new house, he asked: "What's the trouble, Dad? Is something happening at the plant?"

Bob gave him a searching look. "I didn't know I was showing it." Then he added: "Don't tell Phil or Moms. I had a conference with Hardy this afternoon, and he says they've started sniping again. Byrd has apparently appealed to Sullivan-Schuyler to do something, and the new line is that the big order is so near completion that I'm no longer needed."

"What're you going to do?" asked Jon anxiously.

"What can I do?" Bob went on marking a piece of screen frame for mortising. "Hardy says sit tight again."

Jon jabbed the wood chisel into the bench thoughtfully. "Maybe we ought to tell Mr. Holden out in Wayne."

"How can we?"

"Well, he's got some influence in Universal. He did something last summer."

Bob went on marking angrily. "I can't just go to him

and say, 'Mr. Holden, Universal's trying to bust me. Will you help me out?' "

Jon saw the angry pride in his father's face. That was his dad's old familiar characteristic blazing-up: too proud to curry favor with his superiors or to ask their support. It was a pride that didn't recognize intrigue and petty vengeful acts. If a man was a good worker, then he should be kept on; if he wasn't, then he should go. Favors and the expectation of personal consideration never entered Bob Woodward's picture of keeping a job. It was all a matter of worth.

Watching the angry flash of the pencil in his father's tight fingers, Jon had the feeling that there was something right, something big, about his dad's attitude. It was a matter of principle, yet if they lived up to that principle they might lose what they were trying desperately to win. He couldn't figure out what ought to be done about it.

The next evening Phyllis and Jane started talking about graduation clothes. Jon saw his father warn him with a glance, then join the conversation as if everything were certain for the future. From graduation clothes to a college bulletin which had come for Phyllis that day, the talk progressed and Jon watched his father acting as if all were well.

For a while he wondered if things might not have taken a turn for the better. Saturday morning, he asked: "Shall I order ten bags of cement and another load of sand when we go through Wayne?"

But Bob replied quickly: "Guess you'd better not." Then he seemed to hunt for some reasonable excuse. "We'd better plant corn this week-end."

CHAPTER EIGHTEEN

GRADUATION

THIS spring the seeds planted in the terraced garden, enriched by chicken manure, seemed to jump through the ground, the green sprouts flinging back the soil. But if the vegetables grew with vigor, so did the weeds, and Jon had to spend every Saturday hoeing and weeding the garden.

Phyllis helped him. She began it as part of a bargain: repayment for his spading of a flower garden plot above the limestone ledges. Then she went on helping him and Jon didn't remind her that she was overpaying. He wasn't too fond of cultivating the garden.

But Phyllis had discovered that she liked to weed and hoe. She had enough of Van Buren High and her classmates in five days of the week, and the rest of the time she wanted to be out in the woods and the garden.

Every Saturday morning on the way out to Five Acre Hill she asked her mother to let her out at the Summers'. She went to see the dozen hens Tom had kept for her all winter and the twenty-five new chicks he was starting for her this spring. Then she hurried on up to join her brother.

Once she said: "I'll be glad when school's out."

"Weed the carrots, will you, Phil?" Then he added: "Why?"

"Because then I can get my chickens over home here."

Five Acre Hill was "home" to all of them now, even Jane.

"Won't you be sorry when you finish high school?" he wanted to know.

She started talking: Sure, a little bit, but they'd be out here and that was more fun than high school, and this summer more of the new house would be finished—maybe all of it.

Jon felt a little twinge of pain at her optimism.

She chattered on: In the fall she'd go away to college. Maybe enough of the new house would be completed so that Mother and Dad and you (Jon) 'd be living out here. And when she came home at vacation time, she'd come right out here. That would be wonderful.

Her voice bubbled with enthusiasm as if she planned to go to college only to make the return to Five Acre Hill more enjoyable. Her face shone and her eyes sparkled. This summer she'd raise her chickens and flowers and she hoped Mother would let Jon take the goat Mr. Scotti wanted to give him. She thought goats were cute. And if it looked like they'd get enough of the new house done so that the family could move out here for good, then Jon could get a dog and she'd get a kitten. . . .

As she rattled on, Jon's face grew longer and longer. The secret he kept with his father weighed him down. He interrupted her: "But, Phil, supposin' you can't go to college. Suppose Dad loses his job—maybe we'll have to sell Five Acre Hill." His voice was pleading. He wanted to come right out and say, "Gee, Sis, don't go building up your dreams so big. Then there isn't so much chance of being disappointed."

"Oh, nothing like that's going to happen," she answered confidently.

He stopped his work and looked at her. In gay-print shorts and halter, her dark hair tucked up under a sun-helmet, she crouched over the carrot row, her slender strong arms and legs showing a dark tan.

"Aw, Sis, I don't think you ought to be so certain. Nothin' might work out, and you'd have an awful let-down."

"Oh, pooh! Universal can't get along without Dad. They found that out last year in spite of Mr. Sullivan-Schuyler."

Jon said no more and grimly resumed hoeing a pea row. Gee, how he wished they could go on building the new house, but he knew his dad didn't want to spend even the ten dollars a week allotted for Five Acre Hill in the precarious circumstances. He felt that his father was right.

But there were things he could do that didn't cost money. He laid a flagstone terrace in front of the big living room and a path across to the cabin. That was fun. Flat stones were plentiful. All he had to do was go to the ledge on the edge of the hill, pry them loose with the crowbar and carry them up.

Phyllis, and even Jane, helped him. It was fun for all of them. Then once, while Phyllis and he were working alone, she asked: "Why don't you and Dad do any more work on the new house? You haven't done anything for over a month."

"Well—" he began, then he finished quickly: "Dad wants to let the money accumulate a little before we start." He knew that wasn't the truth, but it seemed to satisfy his sister. "There's no hurry," he added.

And there were things his dad and he could do that didn't take money. On Sundays they peeled the bark from poles they had cut during the winter, creosoted them and started building the sun-deck railing. That was fun too.

The day they finished that job, the first Sunday in June, Jon noticed that his father was more than usually sober. Once, after Jon spoiled a cut, his father lashed at him:

"Watch what you're doing! You can saw straighter than that!" Then he seemed ashamed. "I guess we can make it fit after all. I didn't mean to snap your head off." He sank down suddenly on the end of the sawhorse and looked miserably at Jon. "They asked me for my resignation yesterday."

Jon felt the skin in his throat pulling at a swallow that wouldn't go down. Now what were they going to do? He couldn't let his dad see the look of fear in his eyes and let his glance shift over the finished railing of the sun-deck, down over the garden and the field below, the swimming pool gleaming off to the right. Five Acre Hill was just beginning to come along fine. Now this had to happen.

At last the swallow that choked him vanished and he asked in a weak voice. "Did you resign, Dad?"

"No. Not yet," replied Bob. "Hardy advised me to ignore it and make them discharge me. But if I do that, it'll be harder for me to get a job somewhere else."

After a silence, Jon said mournfully: "Phil won't get to go to college now."

"We mustn't let Moms and Phyllis know how things stand, son." He looked searchingly at the boy. "They're both getting fun out of Phil's graduation—we mustn't let this spoil it."

But the black outlook took the enthusiasm for any more work out of both of them. As soon as the railing job was done they quit work without a word. Jon wandered down the drive and turned up the road toward Scotti's.

Maria was picking strawberries. "Come help," she called.

He joined her and somehow he felt better just being near her. But his silence spurred her to talk—about school, the garden, the goats. Occasionally her dark eyes flashed to his serious face. "How's the new house coming, Jon?" Her tone was eager and full of genuine interest.

"Dad and I just finished the railing around the sundeck." He watched his fingers searching among the leaves of the plants for the clusters of red berries.

"You going to start building again next week?"

"Guess not." He hardly spoke above a whisper.

"What's the matter, Jon? Has something happened?"

For a moment he didn't reply, then he settled back on his heels. "Aw, gee, Maria, it looks like we're licked. I don't know what we're goin' to do." He confided the situation in her, adding hastily, "But don't let Phil and Moms know."

"I won't." Her fingers came up with a huge red berry.

She turned it over carefully, then handed it to him. "You haven't eaten any—try this one."

Jon looked at the egg-sized berry as if he were seeing something for the first time, then pinching off the stem, he popped it into his mouth.

That seemed to satisfy Maria. "Don't worry," she said, "something'll happen so's they can't get along without your dad."

Maria's confidence gave Jon a straw to cling to. He didn't for a moment expect her to save the situation, but her certainty that everything would be all right gave him courage.

The next week he watched his sister bustling through her last days of school. There were final dress fittings, invitations to commencement and engraved calling cards to select and order; there was endless talk. She got up in the morning excited and flushed and went to bed at night still flushed and happy. Jane looked after details and enjoyed it, while Jon and Bob stood in the background feigning enthusiasm to hide the unhappy truth held secret between them.

One evening at supper Bob remarked that they should consider renewing the lease on the Delaware Street house. Jane looked thoughtful, then replied: "Let's let that go until Phyllis is through school."

The subject was dropped. Phyllis started talking about college. She and her best girl-friend, Mary Frome, were planning to room together, and she wanted to invite Mary out to Five Acre Hill this summer. She chattered on and on, then she glanced at the clock, and rushed off to Van Buren High to a rehearsal of the Senior Class play.

After she'd gone, Jon and Bob sat silent, their faces

stiff. Jane got up from the table and began clearing away the dessert dishes. Bob shifted his position.

"Jon, maybe we ought to go down to the workshop and build some bookshelves for the new living room," he said.

Without even remarking, "We haven't anything to build them of," Jon followed his father down the basement stairs.

They leaned against the bench, and Bob said: "They asked me again if I'd made up my mind—they want my resignation."

Jon felt a lump in his throat; he couldn't reply.

After a pause, Bob went on: "I'm still ignoring it. I don't know if that's the right way to operate or not."

The silence grew between them; Jon just couldn't talk. It certainly looked as if they were sunk.

Bob picked up a pencil and began making lines on the bench. "I've been thinking," he said, "if we put a hydraulic ram in that tile line you put across to the swimming pool, we could force water up to the new house."

"How does a ram work, Dad?" The question came out in a rush. Jon knew as well as his father that talk about a hydraulic ram was just so much dreaming if Bob lost his job.

Bob went into an explanation of the workings of a ram, drawing a diagram on the bench. Jon listened, questioned, forced his attention, until they both became so immersed in it that reality was pushed out of their thoughts.

But Saturday morning when Jane drove Jon and Phyllis out to Five Acre Hill, Jon's face was set with grim resolution. He asked to be let off in Wayne. "I'll walk out later," he explained. "I want to look over some stuff in the lumberyard."

"You going to start work on the new house again?" asked Phyllis at once.

"I said I just wanted to look at some stuff." He spoke sharply, then he grinned an apology for being so curt.

But that wasn't what he intended to do. He went immediately to the lumber company office.

"Hello, Jon," said Mr. Smith briskly. "I've been look-ing for you to come in. About time you and your dad were doing some more building out there, isn't it?"

Jon swallowed, then asked huskily: "Would it be possible for me to see Mr. Holden?"

The manager grew serious at once. "He won't be in today, Jon. Won't I do?" He waved toward the chair opposite him. "Come on, sit down a moment. Spill what's on your mind, Jon. I'll pass it along to Mr. Holden."

Jon perched on the chair edge and began haltingly: "Dad wouldn't like it if he knew I was going to do this. He doesn't like to ask favors. You see, he thinks that fair treatment doesn't make favors necessary."

Mr. Smith frowned. "You're good customers, Jon. We'll give you plenty of credit if that's what you mean."

"Oh, it's not that!" cried Jon quickly. He chewed his lip a moment, then told about Universal's demanding his father's resignation. "I thought maybe Mr. Holden could do something—maybe like he did last summer. I hadn't ought to've asked—Dad won't like it."

"So that's it! Byrd's out to get your dad fired again." Mr. Smith sat up straight. "Well, you can depend on this, Jon. I'll tell Mr. Holden. We think you people are doing the right thing and we want to see you carry it through."

Jon left feeling better, but it was hard for him to work at Five Acre Hill. When Maria came over it was a fine excuse to stop, and they went up to the sun-deck above the new living room and stretched out lazily on deck-chairs.

"This is grand," she said. "Won't it be wonderful when you get the rest of the house built?" She saw the cloud on Jon's face and hurried on: "I told Dad about what they were trying to do to your father at Universal. Dad says that if your father resigns, the workers in his section will strike."

"Gee!" That was all Jon could get out, he found his lungs empty of breath. He wanted to say, "Gee, Maria, that's swell." But it suddenly struck him, "Was it?" Maybe if the workers threatened to strike, that would only aggravate the situation. The big shots wanting his father's scalp would use the strike as a weapon against him.

"Isn't that swell?" cried Maria eagerly, her dark eyes bright with excitement. "They're going to pass a resolution tonight after work. They're having a meeting."

"But your father may get into a lot of trouble," said Jon quickly. "Maybe he'll lose his job too."

Maria sobered. "That's what Momma says. But Dad says, 'So I lose-a my job and Boss he lose-a his job and we set down on farm. That's-a fine.' " She laughed gaily.

Jon's thoughts whirled. He stammered: "But Phyllis couldn't go to college. And—and you won't be able to go to art school. . . ."

"It hasn't happened yet, Jon." She waved a thin dark hand at him as if to sweep away foreboding, then she jumped up. "I'll be seeing you." She ran down the back steps from the sun-deck and hurried off toward home.

All the next day Jon squirmed on the twin points of what might happen as the result of his telling Maria and Mr. Smith about his father's predicament. He was glad when they had to leave for New Delphi early Sunday afternoon so that Phyllis could get ready for the baccalaureate sermon in the evening.

The next week came final examinations and the rush of Class Night, the Class Play and Commencement. Jon didn't have time to do much worrying. And Phyllis whirled through her final week at Van Buren High radiant and happy. She came home Thursday night after Commencement with moist eyes.

"Well, it's all over. I've had a wonderful time." She removed the mortarboard from her dark hair and slid out of her dark gown and laid it on the table beside her graduation presents. For a moment she examined the presents, flipping open a book, fingering the leather of a bag, then she turned the wrist-watch, gift from her parents, around on her slender wrist. Suddenly she looked at the others: "Mother, can we go out home tomorrow—can we move out for the summer? I want to get my chickens."

That made Bob chuckle. It was the first time Jon had heard his father give a really honest chuckle in weeks.

Ever since last Sunday Jon had been waiting for his father to say something about the situation at the plant. But Bob hadn't mentioned his job all week. Once he had brought up the subject of renewing the lease on the Delaware Street house, but again Jane had put him off.

Now Jane said: "Aren't you rushing things to get out to the country, Phyllis?"

"It'll be so dull here, Mother," said the girl. "Can't we go out tomorrow?"

"But we've got to think about moving our belongings out there." Jane's finger tapped nervously on the table.

"We don't have to take out any more than we did last year," came back Phyllis.

Jane looked up steadily. "I think we should give up this place and move out there permanently."

"Move out there permanently!"

"Give up this place!"

Bob, Jon and Phyllis sat stunned, forgetting to close their mouths in their astonishment.

CHAPTER NINETEEN

TO THE COUNTRY TO STAY

B
UT, Moms." Bob regained some of his composure. "Do you mean that we should give up this place and move to the country to stay? For good and all?"

"Why not?" Jane looked at the three astonished faces, thoroughly enjoying herself. "That was the idea back of getting a place in the country, wasn't it? We were to move out there to stay and be able to turn what we now pay in rent into the college educations for Phyllis and Jon."

"But, Moms." Bob tried again to get hold of the situation. "We haven't the new house built. We've only the living room and the cabin. You'll have to put up with too many inconveniences until we get the rest of the new house done."

"I put up with all those inconveniences last summer, didn't I? And I didn't mind." Her expression was determined. "You and Jon'll get the north section of the new house built before winter. That'll be enough to move into. Of course things'll be upset for a year or two, but I'm willing to face it. I rather like living in the country, you see."

"Oh, gee, Mother, that's swell," whispered Phyllis.

Jon saw the look of misery filling Bob's face. He felt like crying himself. Moms and Phil didn't know how

216

things stood. Here was Moms all set to go through with living in the country, and they couldn't do it. He watched his father slump forward, rest his elbows on his knees and begin talking to the rug.

"Moms, I didn't want to talk about this so soon. I'd hoped to keep it under my hat until Phyllis got the last bit of fun out of graduating, but I guess I'll have to break the news. I don't see how we can give up this place and move to the country, and it doesn't look as if we'd be able to build any on the new house this summer." He ran his fingers through his stiff hair with an angry gesture. "And it doesn't look as if Phil could start to college this fall either."

Jon heard his sister gasp. All she'd said about going to college and coming home to Five Acre Hill, while they worked in the garden, came back to him. He didn't dare look at her.

"Our neighbor, Mr. Byrd, again?" asked Jane calmly.

Both Jon and his father were startled by her calmness.

Bob nodded. "They asked for my resignation two weeks ago. The workers heard about it and protested, and Mr. Holden apparently heard too and he's worked against it. Anyhow the request's been dropped temporarily. But in another month the big order will be completed and"—again he ran his fingers through his hair—"I'm afraid I'm finished with it."

"Oh, Dad," Phyllis sobbed. Jon looked into his sister's glistening eyes, while she choked out: "Don't worry about not being able to send me to college." Her voice grew stronger. "I know shorthand and typewriting. I'll get a job." The sudden radiance coming into her face seemed to dry her eyes. "Maybe I can even help pay for the new house on Five Acre Hill."

Bob swallowed desperately. His face was a conflict between joy at her willingness to accept the situation and even to help out, and misery that he couldn't carry out his plans for her as he'd hoped. He started to say something but couldn't utter a sound. His chin dropped and he stared glumly at the rug.

It was Jane's calm voice that pulled them together. "I think you're all taking a very dim view of the situation. The uncertainty of your job, Bob, makes it all the more imperative that we move to the country for good. Suppose you lose your job at Universal? If we stay here, we'll have to pay out rent, and that'll add to our expenses. If we move to the country we'll save all that and you can look for a new job from Five Acre Hill almost as easily as from 1524 Delaware Street."

Jane smoothed her dress emphatically before going on: "As for Phyllis's going to college, we have enough saved to put her through two years. We can divide that amount and put her through one year. The rest we'll use to keep us at Five Acre Hill until you get a new job. It'll cost less living there."

"But what about Phil's second year?" asked Bob.

"We'll meet that problem when it comes. Maybe you'll have a new job and she can go on. Otherwise she'll just have to drop out."

"And what about Jon? He'll be ready to start to college a year from this fall?"

"Don't you worry about me, Dad," cried Jon, squaring his shoulders. "If there's no money to start me in college,

I'll hitch-hike out to the University of Illinois where you went and work my way through just like you did."

"You see," said Jane, "this whole thing doesn't rest all on your shoulders, Bob. We're one big fighting front." The smile on her face took on radiance from her shining eyes. "We pride ourselves on being a democratic family, so let's put this to a vote. Phyllis, how do you feel about giving up the house here and moving to Five Acre Hill for keeps?"

"I'm all for it, Mother," said the girl quickly.

"And you, Jon?"

"Aye!" His voice was loud and full of spirit. He remembered back to the vote his father had taken in the family on the issue of going out to look at Five Acre Hill.

Bob raised his head, smiling, but there were tears in his eyes. "I've a good stout family, haven't I?" he said, his heart full of pride.

"It's simple," said Jane. "We've got to see it through."

Taking a deep breath, Bob said: "I don't know how the landlord's going to react to our not giving him a month's notice that we aren't renewing the lease."

"I gave him notice the first of June," said Jane.

"Moms, you're swell! There's nothing can stop us."

"Well, we'd better get to bed now," she said to avoid further adulation. "We've a lot of work to get done tomorrow."

The next day Jane, Phyllis and Jon sorted out the furniture, clothing and other things which they wouldn't need in the country, and disposed of them. They had to reduce the stuff to be moved to the smallest possible amount because it would all have to be stored in the new living room for the present.

A moving truck was hired and Saturday morning Jane, Phyllis and Jon drove out to Five Acre Hill, and no tears were shed that they would never again return to 1524 Delaware Street.

Of course Phyllis stopped off at the Summers' and told Tom they were moving out, and before noon he brought her dozen hens over to her chicken run. He said he'd bring her twenty-five chicks over in the evening after they came in to roost and he could catch them.

The moment Jon saw Maria Scotti on the road he ran to tell her the news.

"That's swell," cried Maria, extending both her hands in greeting. "Year-around neighbors you'll be."

They did a ring-around-a-rosy in the road, both of them laughing happily. Then he grew sober: "We'll be kind of upset for a while—have to store all our stuff in the new living room. But if Dad can get his job straightened out, you'll see the rest of our house go up like a rocket plane."

"They've withdrawn the request for his resignation, haven't they?" Maria looked worried. "That's what Dad said."

"Yes." Jon slowly swung one of her hands. "But you see the big order is almost complete, and they're sure to try to get him once that's out of the way."

"Well, they'd better not!" Maria's dark eyes snapped.

When Jon started back up the hill, he asked: "Coming over for a swim this afternoon?" Maria nodded and hurried on along the road toward home.

All of them went swimming about five o'clock, even

Jane. They splashed and dove in the clear, cool water of the pool. Suddenly a yellow sports car flashed past above them on the road, its horn blaring. All stared in amazement at the yellow streak disappearing around the curve to the east.

"Tessy!" ejaculated Tom Summers. "Now summer can begin. Tod Sullivan-Schuyler is back."

They all laughed. But Jon grew sober quicker than the others.

"He's got a car of his own now," remarked Maria.

"Wasn't it a pretty one?" Phyllis was still looking down the road.

Jon saw the direction of her glance and frowned; Tom saw it too and said: "Yes, matches his character—yellow."

That evening when Bob got there, he said: "This is wonderful. I really feel like I'm coming home for the first time in twenty years."

"When all our furniture gets moved out here and piled in the new living room," retorted Jane, "you'll begin to think that home was never like this."

"Moms, you're not getting sick of your bargain already?" His face clouded with worry.

"Of course not, darling. I didn't propose moving out here with any idea of finding romance in it."

Then Phyllis came running around the cabin. "Look! Two eggs! And my hens have just been over here since morning."

"Well, well!" Her father examined them as if they were gems. "The farm's producing."

Phyllis and Jon ate those two eggs for Sunday breakfast. They ate on the terrace in front of the cabin and were just finishing the meal when George Scotti came over the rise in front of the new house leading two goats. "Look, callers," snickered Phyllis.

The others stared and Jane's face grew serious.

The boy came down the flagstone path toward them half timidly. The old bewhiskered Toggenburg he led walked close beside him, eyeing the family in front of the cabin curiously, while the younger goat tagged behind, pulling on its rope, trying to snatch a mouthful of leaves. George went straight to Jon, his dark eyes giving the others a frightened look; then he stammered:

"Pop—says these are for you. She—" he waved a small hand toward the old goat—"she give good milk." He pulled the leash of the young goat. "She bambino—make a good goat for milk someday." He thrust the rope ends toward Jon.

Mumbling a thank-you without knowing it, Jon automatically grasped the leads, and George Scotti scampered back up the path like a scared rabbit. The goats looked after him, nickering, pulling on their ropes to follow.

"But—but you can't accept them," choked out Jane.

"Aren't they nice?" Phyllis came around the table to pet the big goat's slender, soft nose. "You nice old thing!"

Bob strangled a chuckle. "Looks like Jon's already accepted them, Moms."

"You'll have to take them right back!" cried Jane indignantly. "I don't want such—such—such animals around."

That old Toggenburg looked at her with bulging yellow eyes. "Baaa!" she said.

Bob couldn't hold in any longer. "There, Moms, there's your answer." He let out a whoop.

"I tell you I won't have them around!" Jane's face flamed an angry red. "I'll move back to New Delphi if you keep them. Jon, you've simply got to give them back."

"But, Moms." Jon looked hurt. "They'll give us milk."

Bob was still rocking with laughter. "We've got livestock. Chickens and goats. We'll get eggs and milk. We're all set!" He slapped his hand down on his thigh.

Jane began to see humor in the situation, but she insisted: "I don't want them. I won't drink the milk."

"Jon and I'll drink it," spoke up Phyllis.

"No," Jane said stubbornly. "I'm putting my foot down on goats."

"Not too hard, Moms," said Bob, and went off in another roar of laughter. Then he sobered: "Come, Moms, shall we put it to a vote? To keep the goats or not to keep them?"

"All right," said Jane, knowing she'd lose. "But where'll you put them?"

Jon sought for an answer. "In—in that old shack down below the ledge." He waved toward the stone shanty Tom Summers had built. "It'll need fixing up, but it'll work."

"And we'll stake 'em in the clover," added Bob. "I knew we seeded that clover for some reason. Moms, it's a cinch."

Jane accepted defeat with a loud sniff and got up to clear away the breakfast dishes. Then she screamed: "Jon! Pull it away! That—that beast is eating the tablecloth!"

Jon jerked at the young goat, but it hung onto the

corner of the cloth. Only Bob's quick clutching of the cover saved all the dishes from being pulled onto the terrace.

"See! That's what happens!" cried Jane. "Look what it did to my good tablecloth."

"Guess we'd better get them out of here quietly," said Bob, forcing a straight face, "before Moms is driven to do something desperate."

They led the animals down to the clover field and staked them out, then went to repair the stone shanty. It required a new roof, and the rough window openings had to be framed in and covered with chicken wire. "This'll do for the summer," said Bob. "We'll have to fix it up better for the winter."

That afternoon Jon went over to thank Al Scotti for his gift. "Don't-a mench. You save-a my life. I have too much-a goat anyhow." The big Italian laughed jovially.

Maria asked: "Can you milk her?"

"Oh, sure," said Jon quickly, then added: "At least Dad can. He used to milk cows when he was a boy."

But that evening Maria came over at milking time. "I thought maybe you'd need help," she explained.

"Thanks, but I used to milk." Bob looked a little put out that his prowess seemed under doubt.

They brought the goats in from the clover field, the old goat's udder swinging full and hard between her legs. Bob tied her to a small tree and confidently set the small pail down at her right side. Jon and Maria looked on.

Jon sensed that his father had become suddenly uncertain. After all this wasn't a cow. He couldn't just sit on a stool, grip the pail between his knees, thrust his head against the animal's flank and begin milking. Bob scratched his head, looked sidewise at the silent Maria, then dropped on his knees and grasped the goat's two teats. "So goatie, so!"

The animal's hind leg came up like a stick and hit him in the chest and she bucked and bounced around the tree.

"You darned beast!" he said furiously.

"Baaa!" replied the goat. "Baa-uh-aa-aa."

Bob walked forward on his knees after the animal and tried again. Again the goat bucked, kicked, twisted and nickered. At last Bob glanced sheepishly at Maria.

"How do you do it, Maria? I don't seem to understand her psychology."

Jon snickered and got a black look from his father.

"Guess she's used to me milking her," said Maria. She stepped forward, picked up the pail and approached the goat. "Stand! Violet! Stand now!"

"Maa," said the old goat feebly.

Then Maria knelt at the rear of the animal, pushed its bony legs apart, and pulling the two teats of the udder between them began milking with swift, rhythmic movements into the pail.

"Oh." Bob shook his head. "So that's the way it's done. Well, I guess you'll have to teach Jon."

"Sure. I will." She smiled around at the two of them. "I'll come over in the morning." In a little while she stood up and handed the two-thirds-full pail to Bob.

They climbed back up the hill to the cabin.

"Look, Moms!" cried Bob. "Milk—almost two quarts."

"Did you milk it?" came Jane's skeptical question.

"Well—" Bob flushed.

"Jon, did you milk it?"

"Maria did," admitted Jon.

Jane laughed jeeringly. "Maria, aren't men a helpless lot? Can't even milk a little goat."

Maria laughed with her.

"Well, Moms, next time you try it," dared Bob.

"Maybe I will." She gave him a haughty toss of her head.

Just then Phyllis returned home from the Summers', cuddling an orange ball of fuzz, a kitten. "Tom gave it to me. Isn't it sweet?" She held it against her cheek a moment, then set it down on the terrace.

"Phyllis Woodward!" cried her mother. "Haven't we enough animals here without your adding a cat?"

"But he's so cunnin'," explained the girl.

Already Jon and Maria were crouching down trying to get the kitten to play. Then Bob knelt and wagged a finger. "Piss-wiss-wiss," he said, and the kitten scampered toward him. "You're a little rascal," said Bob, lifting it up in one of his big hands.

"I give up," stormed Jane. "I give up! Turn the place over to chickens and goats and cats!"

"I'm going to get a dog," said Jon.

"Ooh!" Jane threw up her hands and went into the cabin to prepare the Sunday evening meal.

Monday the moving truck brought the furniture from 1524 Delaware Street, and the haulers unloaded it in the new living room. There wasn't much space to spare, and Jane and Phyllis and Jon stared at it a bit ruefully.

"I guess we've moved to the country to stay, all right," sighed Jane.

Jon squared his shoulders. "Looks to me like Dad and I'll have to get more house built pretty soon."

CHAPTER TWENTY

JOB IN THE BALANCE

JON and his father could survey Five Acre Hill now with a certain amount of satisfaction. The goats browsed and nickered in the clover; the chickens cackled in the chicken run. Their sweet corn was almost knee-high, the oats starting to head up. This year the garden, enriched by chicken manure, was really producing. They were eating spinach, salad, radishes and scallions; the peas were blossoming.

But their looks of satisfaction vanished when their eyes rested upon the new house, the living room filled with their belongings from New Delphi. One evening, a few days later, Jon said: "Don't you think we might build a little more, Dad? Go on with the basement and cellar?"

Bob shook his head gloomily: "A showdown's awfully close at the plant. We may need our money for other things."

A few days later Maria asked Jon: "When are you and your father starting work on the house again?"

"We can't right now," he explained. "Dad says we can't start anything until his job at the plant is settled."

They were picking cherries. Maria went on pulling the red fruit from the branches, but her expression had turned grave. She didn't pursue the subject of the Woodwards' new house. This summer Jon was helping pick the Scottis' cherries on shares.

"Moms is going to can up our share," he said proudly.

Maria, practical and country-wise, asked: "How will you keep them? You need a cellar."

Jon couldn't answer that one, and later Maria mentioned the subject casually to Jane. It worried Jane. Last year they'd taken the canned stuff up to the basement of their house in New Delphi. But that wasn't possible this year.

They were all sitting on the terrace of the cabin after a swim and Maria suggested, with a tentative gesture at the bristling forms for the basement walls, untouched since the last crisis at the plant, "Maybe Mr. Woodward and Jon could finish that part. You could keep stuff there."

"Sure. We might do that," agreed Jon eagerly.

That evening Jane passed the suggestion along to Bob. He shook his head, but she insisted: "It's a necessary expense. If we're in for some rough going, Bob, I've got to can up all the food possible and we must have a place to keep it."

Bob was thoughtful. Jon watched his face intently, hopefully, and at last his father said: "I guess that makes sense all right. We'd better finish the basement part. After all, it won't cost so much."

The next day Jon ordered more cement and sand and wheeled up stones. Before going for his swim, he mixed a batch of sand and cement dry, and in the evening after Bob got home from work, the job was resumed.

They made good progress. The area was only ten-by-

sixteen, and Jon laid up wall during the day, with Jane's and Phyllis's help. By the following Sunday night, the walls were up and ready for the first floor. Jon and his father poured that on the Fourth of July.

It was an everyday occurrence now to see Tod Sullivan-Schuyler flash past in his yellow sports car. Then one

afternoon the yellow streak swung up the drive to Five
Acre Hill. Young Sullivan-Schuyler pulled to a stop at
the corner of the flagstone terrace in front of the new
living room.

Jane and Phyllis were sitting here in the shade, enjoying the view down the valley. They stared in astonishment at their visitor as he stepped arrogantly out of his
machine.

"Good afternoon, ladies." He offered them a short
bow. "I just dropped in to pay my respects to the Squire's
neighbors."

"That was very thoughtful of you," replied Jane with
twinkling eyes.

Tod Sullivan-Schuyler didn't seem to know quite how
to take that remark, but he maintained his supercilious
tone: "Yes, indeed. Besides, Miss Phyllis has the out-
standing feminine charm in this rural area."

"A fine compliment. Thank you," said Jane.

Phyllis hadn't said a word. Her fingers worried the
magazine she'd been reading, while her eyes watched
the posturing of young Sullivan-Schuyler. As he strutted
her cheeks reddened as if she felt shame for him.

Just then Jon, who had been pointing up the wall of
the new basement section, found an opportunity to
break off his job and came around the corner of the
house to the terrace. He was stripped to the waist, looking brown and strong. At the sight of Tod his eyes
smoldered in his sweat-streaked face.

"Hi, Tessy."

Young Sullivan-Schuyler gave him a haughty look,
then addressed Jane: "That drudgery-besmirched juve-

nile should be taught better manners. His opprobrious greetings are not decorous, to say the least."

Jane's lips twitched, but she managed to say evenly: "Outrageous, isn't it?"

"Yes, indeed." Again Tod Sullivan-Schuyler didn't seem to know quite how to take this.

Jon stood on the edge of the terrace, his fists clenched, his face grim, while Phyllis looked more pained and unhappy.

Tod pulled his act together and changed the subject: "I understand that you people have moved out to this agrarian spot permanently."

"Yes," admitted Jane. "We've come to stay."

"It'll be a shame if you have to fold your tents and quietly steal away," said Tod with a mocking twist to his lips.

"Oh, I don't think we'll be moving," replied Jane, but for just an instant the look of amusement left her face.

Then as if he'd completed his duty, young Sullivan-Schuyler bowed: "I must trip along. Good afternoon." He swaggered to his yellow roadster and roared away down the drive.

Jane burst out laughing. "He reminds me of Major Hoople in the comics," she said, and continued laughing.

But neither Jon nor Phyllis joined her.

"He wouldn't be so bad if he didn't talk like a sap all the time." Phyllis spoke up with sudden warmth. She tried to fix her attention upon her magazine again, but couldn't.

And Jon asked pointedly: "What'd he mean by it

being a shame if we had to fold our tents and the rest of that baloney?"

"Oh, he was just talking," Jane said.

But that evening they learned what young Sullivan-Schuyler meant. Bob came home sober and thoroughly dejected.

"I'm on the spot this time," he admitted. "They've gotten smart. They're not asking for my resignation; they're not even attempting to fire me. This time they're offering to transfer me to the Buffalo plant."

"Why, you can't transfer," cried Jane.

Jon and Phyllis just sat stunned.

"Of course not, unless we give up Five Acre Hill." Bob's eyes were dark with anger. "But that's what Byrd's after. And of course if I refuse to be transferred, they can fire me with what is called a 'clear conscience' by the Management."

"Oh, Dad," wailed Phyllis, twisting her handkerchief.

Jon stormed: "One of these times I'm going to punch that rat Tessy Sullivan-Schuyler right on his big nose."

"No, you're not, Jon," said Jane firmly. "It may be too late to save the situation on this front. But Tod's a spoiled boy who is mighty lonely. All his big words are put on to hide his unhappiness. I believe if someone were really nice to him once he'd change. It may be too late for a changed young Sullivan-Schuyler to be of any help about Bob's job, but we can at least try being nice to him."

"Aw, Moms, be nice to that drip!" Jon was horrified.

But Phyllis looked at her mother with understanding.

Jane continued: "Anyhow, Bob, I think you should

refuse to be transferred. We are simply not going to give up Five Acre Hill. If you lose your job, we'll just have to accept the situation until you find another."

"I hoped you'd say that, Moms," whispered Bob.

However, Jon wasn't willing to take things as they came. He blurted the situation out to Maria at his first opportunity. "I'd like to show those guys in Universal!" he cried. "Someday I'll get even with old man Byrd too! And I'm going to punch Tessy in the snoot before the summer's over."

Maria seemed to grasp how things stood quickly. "I'll tell Dad the trick they're pulling this time," she said. "The workers'll strike if they try to transfer your father."

Jon grasped her hand and shook it enthusiastically.

The next afternoon Jane got the whole group, the three Scottis, the four Summers and Phyllis and Jon, on the terrace in front of the new house and talked to them about being nice to young Sullivan-Schuyler.

"All you youngsters have been brought up in normal families," she explained. "It's hard for you to understand a boy like Tod. He's always had all the money he wanted. His parents have given him money to make up for their lack of love and attention. It's made Tod into a horrid person, but if we're nice to him we might win him over to our side. So don't call him Tessy and mimic his big words and ridicule him. Try treating him as you treat each other."

"But, Moms—" protested Jon.

Tom interrupted: "Well, we can try it, Mrs. Woodward."

Only Phyllis seemed ready to accept the idea with

understanding. The others were willing to change their attitudes toward young Sullivan-Schuyler because Jane asked them to.

The next time they were all in swimming and the yellow sports roadster flashed around the curve from the direction of Wayne, Phyllis waved. Tod brought the machine to an abrupt stop on the black-top with a screaming of brakes, swinging in across the road to the left side above the swimming pool.

Jon dove into the water, his teeth gritting. But Tom had seen Phyllis wave and he called up to young Sullivan-Schuyler: "Hello, Tod. How about coming in for a dip?"

Tod seemed nonplused by this cordial greeting, then he replied: "Sorry, the H_2O appears to be a bit thick." He didn't take his eyes off Phyllis who sat on a flat stone at the edge of the pool, swishing her feet in the water. "Miss Woodward," he said imperiously, "how about going for a bit of a ride? I'll wait while you change to something suitable."

"Thank you," replied Phyllis smoothly, "but not today."

Jon saw Tom Summers' face darken, then brighten at Phyllis's refusal.

"You're missing a real treat," purred Tod Sullivan-Schuyler. "Well, I must limp along." The yellow car started with a jack rabbit leap in second gear and disappeared up the road.

"I don't care what Moms says," stormed Jon. "That guy's a rat, and being nice to him won't change him."

"He didn't act nearly so phony today," defended Phyllis quickly. "Did he, Tom?"

Tom reddened, his forehead wrinkling a little as he said: "I expect we ought to give him the benefit of the doubt."

That evening Bob reported that the news that the company proposed to transfer him was being circulated among the workers at the plant. Already there was agitation for a strike if it was carried out. "The dopes," growled Bob. "They'll only get themselves into a lot of trouble."

But Jon's face grew bright at his father's report. Later he walked over to see Maria. His spirits were high: leave it to Al Scotti and the workers, they'd make the Management drop his dad's transfer.

Maria and her father were trimming back the grapes.

"We stop-a everything if they move Boss," said Al Scotti, brandishing the clippers. "We tie plant in a knot. Only Boss we want and nobody different."

"They're going to have a mass meeting at the plant Saturday night," Maria told Jon later. "They're going to decide what to do then."

All this made Jon feel cocky: they'd show 'em! He didn't feel that it was necessary to be nice to Tessy. Every afternoon now when they were swimming, Tod stopped in his yellow sports car and asked Phyllis to go for a ride. Phyllis always refused, but in a nice way. Tom was friendly, but Jon could see that he was forcing it. Jon and Maria never spoke to young Sullivan-Schuyler. They weren't going to be openly nasty to him because

Jane had asked them not to be, but they didn't see any sense in going out of their way to be nice either.

And Jane had cautioned Phyllis: "You can be nice to Tod, but I don't want you to go riding with him. He's too reckless a driver."

"I won't, Mother," Phyllis agreed.

That was the way things stood on the home-front as the week came to an end.

By seven o'clock Saturday night Bob wasn't home. "I guess we might as well eat supper," Jane said with a worried frown. "I don't see what's keeping him. Did he say anything to either of you about being held up tonight?"

Jon and Phyllis shook their heads.

Could there have been an accident? They finished supper and washed the dishes. It was after nine o'clock and almost dark when Bob came up the drive. He joined them on the terrace and sat down without saying a word.

"What made you so late?" Jane asked.

He shifted in his chair. "The workers had a mass meeting," he said slowly. "They're threatening to strike if I'm transferred. Al Scotti and Mike Brogan are behind it." He leaned back with a tired sigh.

"I went to the meeting and argued with them. I told them I wasn't being dismissed from the company, just moved, that was all, and the company had a right to do that. I pointed out that a strike would hold up production, and the country needs production badly. But the crazy dopes wouldn't listen. Mike Brogan got up and said: 'If the board of directors isn't worrying about production, then why should we?'"

"What're they going to do?" interrupted Jane tensely.

Bob sat there for a moment in silence. Phyllis's kitten climbed up on his knee and he began to pet it. The noise of its loud purring seemed to startle him.

"Finally I told them that if they struck, I'd just have to resign. Nothing at all would be gained by striking. Then Al Scotti said: 'We all know what's-a behind this, Boss. You resign and we strike anyway.' I've been arguing until I'm all in. I argued with Mike and Al all the way home. Those guys are as stubborn as mules. The only thing I accomplished at the meeting was to get them to put off making a decision. It's a case completely outside normal labor relations. If they strike, even their union heads'll declare it unauthorized. But apparently that isn't going to stop them."

Jon slumped down in his chair. He heard his sister quietly blow her nose in the darkness. It sure looked like they were sunk this time! It sure did!

CHAPTER TWENTY-ONE

ACCIDENT

THE new week began with the pressure of waiting increasing. Jon talked with Maria: "Maybe Dad's right. Striking won't help. It's this transfer offer that's got us licked."

"They're goin' to strike!" she said fiercely, then she looked away, eyes glistening. "It's a mean trick, that's all it is—a mean trick. And Dad says they're goin' to strike no matter what your dad does."

As if by mutual agreement now, both of them tried to be nice to Tod Sullivan-Schuyler when he stopped while they were swimming. Jon even managed a nod and forced a grin. Maria waved to him along with Phyllis.

They hadn't any clear-cut idea of what this would accomplish. When alone, Jon toyed with the idea of somehow getting friendly with young Sullivan-Schuyler and appealing to him to use his influence to let his dad stay at the New Delphi plant. But that was only a dream to Jon; he could never have swallowed his pride to do it.

Once he even thought that maybe if Phyllis accepted young Sullivan-Schuyler's invitation to go riding with him that might save their dad's job. He felt disgusted with himself after thinking it, and his sister's continued refusal to ride with Tod made him proud of her.

But young Sullivan-Schuyler persisted: "Young lady, I shall importune you until you capitulate."

"Thanks, Tod," she replied, always smiling, "but I really prefer swimming. Come on in for a dip?"

Each time she refused Tom Summers seemed to heave a sigh of relief, and his show of friendliness toward Tod became less forced. "Sure, come on in."

"Thank you," answered Tod with tilted chin. And every time Phyllis turned down his invitation, his face seemed to grow more sullen. He was accustomed to getting what he wanted, but this time he was completely frustrated. His fury increased daily.

On Wednesday afternoon Jon began cutting the ripe oats. The sun beat down hot and the rust on the grain made him itch. Phyllis and Maria went huckleberry-picking in the swamp behind Scotti's. They hadn't returned by four-thirty and Jon decided to take his swim anyhow. Tom Summers came whistling along, already in his bathing suit.

"Where's Phil?" he wanted to know at once.

"She and Maria went to pick huckleberries."

They went down to the pool, dove in and splashed and swam about in the cool water. They hardly said a word to each other, as if they had quarreled, and all the time they kept glancing up the road expectantly. At last Jon blurted out: "I've been nice to Tessy just about as long as I can stand it."

Tom stopped swimming and stood up, his head and shoulders out of the water. "Same here," he admitted grimly. "He's a skunk and that's all there is to it."

They heard voices and saw Maria and Phyllis coming

along the road. Maria had stopped at home and was already in her bathing suit; Phyllis carried her pail as if it were heavy.

"Get any huckleberries?" called Jon.

"Loads." Phyllis held up her bucket of fruit.

The girls were standing above them now on the edge of the road. They all heard the car coming and around the curve from the east roared the yellow roadster of Tod Sullivan-Schuyler. He pulled up with a screech of brakes beside the girls.

He had eyes only for Phyllis. "Not yet immersing your sylph-like figure in the mundane H_2O, I see."

"We've been huckleberrying," said Phyllis. "The bushes were loaded." Her glance shifted to Maria. "We're going again tomorrow afternoon. Want to come along, Tod?"

"Tomorrow is an aeon away. How about taking a ride with me right now?"

"I'm too hot. I want to take a swim and cool off."

Young Sullivan-Schuyler's chin trembled. "Young lady, stop dallying! This time we're going for a ride." He flung open the car door in front of her.

Phyllis didn't budge, but the smile vanished from her face. "No, Tod. I said I wanted to go for a swim and cool off."

The trembling of his chin ceased abruptly. For an instant his eyes shifted to Maria, who was halfway down the bank going over to the swimming pool. They came back to Phyllis hard and determined.

"Young lady, it's time you were taught that a Sullivan-Schuyler brooks refusal for only so long, then he acts."

His long arm flashed out and caught her wrist.

"Stop, Tod!" Phyllis pulled to get away. "I said I didn't want to go for a ride."

Her pail of huckleberries fell to the road and spilled a purple splotch on the gravel shoulder. She tried to claw loose from his grasp, but he pulled her toward the open door of the machine. "Stop it, Tod!" she panted, slapping at him. She fought fiercely, pulling, struggling.

Tom Summers scrambled up out of the swimming pool, and Jon swam frantically toward the nearest bank. Young Sullivan-Schuyler had pulled the struggling girl into the car. He took his feet off the clutch and brake and pushed down on the gas; the car, in second gear, leaped forward, throwing Phyllis back against the seat. The moment he let go her wrist and grasped the wheel to straighten up the car on the road, she flung back the unlatched door and jumped clear of the machine.

Jon, Tom and Maria saw her hit the side of the road, stand erect for the fraction of a second, then one of her legs twisted crazily and she pitched headfirst down the bank into the ditch. Maria screamed. Tom leaped over the wall along the road and reached Phyllis first. Jon followed close behind him. Her leg bent unnaturally under her and she didn't move; her eyes were closed.

"We've got to get her out of this ditch," said Tom.

Jon, pale, his sunburned brown hands trembling, helped lift her. "She's hurt bad." His eyes were wide with fear. "We've got to get her to a hospital."

He stood up and, cupping his hands, yelled at the top of his lungs: "MOMS! MOMS! Bring the car! Phyllis has been hurt!" He yelled that over and over until he saw his mother hurrying to their machine parked near the new living room.

When he looked around, young Sullivan-Schuyler had backed his roadster up even with them and stood beside it, white-faced, staring down at the unconscious girl. Maria had dropped on her knees beside Phyllis. Her two brothers came running up. After a quick look at Phyllis, Maria's dark eyes flashed at Tod, then she swung on her brothers: "Tony! Go home and tell Momma to call the troopers. Run! Run!" Her voice rose to a scream.

Tony turned and sprinted up the road. Tod Sullivan-Schuyler understood what that meant; his hand on the yellow fender of his sports car began jerking violently. He edged around the front to get in under the wheel and get away from here.

Jon saw what he was doing and leaped after him. "Where're you goin', you?" His voice was husky, his fists were hard, his face stiff with fury. He grabbed young Sullivan-Schuyler before he got the door closed and dragged him back to the road, ripping his tan sports shirt.

Tom yelled: "He's too big a lug for you to handle!"

But the warning was too late. Tod swung a hard blow to Jon's chin and sent him staggering across the road.

Tom came around the car like a whirlwind, grabbed the escaping Sullivan-Schuyler by the shoulder, and spun him around to land a crushing blow on his long chin. "This is somethin' I've been waiting for, Tessy!" he yelled.

Reeling back on the road, Tod threw up his guard— he knew how to fight, how to defend himself. But Tom was all around him, swinging with fury. Tod's nose was bleeding. A blow in the plexis doubled him up. He tried to parry the punches; he tried to get close in and clench, but a right hook caught him on the chin with the sound of a baseball bat slugging a ball, and he stretched out on the black-top, his heels flying up and down again with a sharp thud.

Jon had got dizzily to his feet. His gaze rested an instant on the unconscious Tessy; then both Tom and he looked up to see Jane backing the car toward them down the road.

"What happened?" she asked, climbing quickly out of the machine.

Tom panted out the information. "We've got to get Phil to the hospital."

They lifted her gently to the back seat of the Woodwards' car; then Jon climbed in with her, and Jane drove. Tom and Maria stayed behind. Young Sullivan-Schuyler had begun to roll back and forth on the road, slowly regaining consciousness.

Jon and his mother stayed at the hospital, waiting for a report from the emergency room. An hour and a half later Phyllis was in a ward, resting comfortably. Her ankle had been broken and she was badly bruised from the fall. They left her smiling faintly: "I'll be all right, Mother."

When they got home, Bob was there. "How's Phil?" he asked at once. They told him.

Tom Summers, Maria Scotti, the yellow car, and Tod Sullivan-Schuyler were gone.

"Young Sullivan-Schuyler's in jail," Bob explained. "I got here the same time as the troopers and when Tom told me what had happened I had Tessy charged with malicious mischief."

"I hope he gets the works," gloated Jon.

"He can't get much." Bob shook his head. "With Phil hurt no worse than she is—and I'm mighty glad it was no worse." He took a deep breath. "Anyhow, his uncle'll probably have him out on bail before morning. Tod's a minor, so we'll have to bring suit against him and his parents."

Then it occurred to Jane. "You're home early, aren't you, Bob?"

He slumped down in his chair. "I resigned my job." His glance shifted to the partly cut field of oats below them. Jon and Jane were silent—they'd been expecting this—there was nothing to say. At last Bob added: "Guess we can finish cutting the oats tomorrow, can't we, Jon?"

The next morning Maria Scotti came over to report that Tod Sullivan-Schuyler was out on bail, and Merrivale Byrd was indignant about the whole affair.

Later when she was alone with Jon, she said: "Dad says they're goin' to strike at the plant. They're goin' out and stayin' out until your father comes back."

All Jon could reply was: "Guess it's too late now. We're licked."

In the afternoon they brought Phyllis home from the hospital. She ached all over and her ankle pained her. Bob and Jon moved all their furniture to one end of the big living room and fixed up their best bed so that she could rest in it and look out of the front window down the long valley.

Bob reported that a hearing on the case against young Sullivan-Schuyler and his parents was set for the following afternoon. "Merrivale Byrd is already trying to whitewash the whole thing," he added.

That evening after supper Jon, Jane and Bob sat on the terrace in front of the living room where they could talk to Phyllis through the open window. "Beginning next week," Bob remarked, "I'd better start looking for another job."

They were all silent. Suddenly a big car turned in at their drive and came slowly up the hill. The liveried chauffeur swung it to a stop near the terrace and got out to open the rear door for a tall, dignified man, who hesitated, looked at the silent, unmoving Woodwards, then advanced toward them.

"My name's Sullivan-Schuyler," he said.

"Good evening." Bob gestured coldly toward another deck chair.

Their visitor looked embarrassed and sat down. A slightly gray and unhappy look tightened his wrinkled features. "I came over to talk about my son's responsibility for seriously injuring your daughter," he continued.

"Yes," said Bob. The others remained frigidly silent.

The unhappy look on Mr. Sullivan-Schuyler's face increased. "I'm quite aware that Tod's a bit of a problem," he admitted. "Not all the boy's fault, you know. I'd like to get him off; so, frankly, I've come with a proposition. I'll take care of all expenses and pay your daughter twenty-five hundred dollars damages."

The Woodwards all seemed to hold their breaths. And into the silence came the sharp creaking of crickets. At last Bob said: "It's all up to Phyllis. Phil, did you hear?" He glanced toward the window of the living room.

"Yes, I heard," came her low voice.

Mr. Sullivan-Schuyler looked a little startled.

"Well, what do you say, Phil?" asked her father.

"No," she answered in the same low voice.

Mr. Sullivan-Schuyler studied his polished toes. "Tod's spoiled and arrogant, but he didn't intend to injure your—ah—Phyllis." He lifted his glance, pleading at the screen. "Going through with the suit against us won't make Tod change his ways." A faint smile hovered around his lips. "I think the Summers boy did him more good by knocking him out."

Phyllis asked through the window: "Did Tom hit him—Tod, I mean?" This time her voice seemed eager.

"Yes," replied Bob. "You were unconscious, but they had quite a scrap."

Mr. Sullivan-Schuyler unbent to chuckle. "Young Summers hung some pretty good ones on my son."

The atmosphere warmed a little, but no one said anything until Phyllis asked: "But what about your job, Dad?"

"That has nothing to do with this," said Bob quickly.

"But it has!" Her voice came through the window strong now. "It has, Dad!"

Bob didn't argue with her.

Then Jane spoke up angrily: "I don't think this affair can be just whooshed away with money, Mr. Sullivan-Schuyler. Mr. Byrd is saying that our daughter tricked your son, leading him on. That's slander!"

Her eyes blazed at their visitor. "I talked to all the youngsters who came here and suggested that they ought to try being nice to Tod. I realized that he was a spoiled child who was really lonely and defensive at heart. He didn't have much chance for improvement associating with his uncle."

She let that soak in before continuing: "Mr. Byrd,

through you, has been trying to break up our settling here and I felt that there was no reason to add to his vindictive attitude by continuing to make your son an enemy. But there was no idea of leading him on and Phyllis refused repeatedly to ride in his car when he asked her day after day. The charge that she led him on is a lie, and if necessary it should be thoroughly aired in the courts. It can be proved a lie; then we'll take care of Mr. Byrd."

Mr. Sullivan-Schuyler took a deep breath after this heated attack. "Well, Mrs. Woodward, to be quite frank, I know that Tod was entirely to blame. As for this other angle, I think it is all rather stupid and unfortunate. I can see now where I made a mistake agreeing to Merrivale's wishes to use my influence to have Mr. Woodward removed from Universal."

He paused and laced his fingers together. "Suppose I leave the other proposition I made stand and assure you that your resignation will not be accepted, Mr. Woodward, and that your transfer will be withdrawn."

There followed an abrupt, thick silence, then Bob said in a strained voice: "It's up to you, Phyllis."

"I'll accept that," came the strong voice through the screen.

Mr. Sullivan-Schuyler stood up. "I'll see that you have the money and an agreement in writing before the hearing opens tomorrow." He looked around, adding: "You've a nice place here."

Then he walked to his car and the chauffeur drove him away, leaving the Woodwards gaping after him.

CHAPTER TWENTY-TWO

SWIM SHIFT

BOB'S job was secure now. Universal refused to accept his resignation and gave him an extra two weeks' vacation in recognition of his production accomplishments for the past year. Almost immediately the house on Five Acre Hill began to grow.

Every morning Jon and his father climbed out of bed, groaning with stiff muscles. They were at work by seven o'clock. As they worked, their eyes shone with a hardness, a determination, a concentration that was a little frightening to Jane and Phyllis. And they tumbled into their cots at nine o'clock at night completely exhausted.

They were building now what they called "the second level" of the house. Already finished was the living room and the cellar-basement off the right-rear corner. The "second level" was to extend from the top of the cellar-basement across the back side of the living room.

First they had to wall in a narrow tunnel between the living room and the bank upon which this "second level" was to be built. Bob planned this passage to conceal the heating ducts from the furnace in the cellar-basement. It took them two days to construct this passage.

By the end of another two days they had poured the floor and foundation of the "second level." This extended from the top of the cellar-basement across the rear of the living room to what would eventually be the garage unit, and involved the laying of pipe and drain-lines to the bathroom. They were ready now to start the walls.

One whole day was given over to hauling stones. They borrowed the Summers' trailer and pulled up load after load to the high ground. In the evening Bob announced: "Tomorrow we start the walls." The next day the forms were built.

All this took continuous figuring and planning. Jane laughed to see Bob and Jon come over to the cabin for lunch or dinner. They'd walk a few steps along the flag-stone path, then turn and stare back at the growing house. Bob would point out something to Jon or Jon to his father. They'd pause to discuss it. Then they'd turn around and walk a few steps toward the cabin, stop again, and turn back for another look.

Jane would call: "Can't you break away from that job?"

They'd glance toward her, startled, grin sheepishly, and come on to their meal.

"They eat, talk and sleep that house," Jane complained.

Jane made a point of bringing over a lunch mid-morning and mid-afternoon and insisting that Bob and Jon stop their work to eat it. But she had other things to do beside cooking meals. The beans were ready for can-ning and the corn soon would be.

Phyllis was carried up to a chair on the sun-deck where she could watch Jon and her father at work, and she helped her mother snap the beans into lengths for canning. Later she shucked the corn and stripped the silk from the yellow ears. Her mother processed and canned the vegetables in the cabin, and when the jars were cool, Jon and Bob carried them back to the cellar, on their way to the job, and lined them up on the shelves.

The cellar was the first thing Phyllis wanted to see when she got her crutches and could swing about the place. "I want to see all we've done, Mother," she said, her eyes sparkling.

Once she said: "I almost wish I weren't going to college this fall. It'd be so much fun just to be here and watch the house grow and eat the stuff we've canned."

And there was tomato juice to make and tomatoes to put up and cucumbers to pickle. The fruit season was approaching: peaches, plums and pears. Activity on Five Acre Hill mounted to a crescendo. But occasionally one or another took time out to express satisfaction at their accomplishment.

Jane could say proudly: "We've canned forty quarts of tomatoes." When Jon and Bob pulled the forms from the kitchen walls, Jon said: "Gee, Dad, it's really beginning to look like a house."

But there was no longer time for any afternoon swim. Tom Summers and Maria Scotti came over regularly to the pool and stopped up later to talk with Phyllis and see how the new house was coming. But with Jane busy canning and Phyllis only able to get around on crutches, they didn't help with the house building as they had the year before.

One afternoon when Tom came up, he said: "Saw Tessy yesterday—walking. Haven't seen him in his car since the accident."

"How'd he act?" asked Phyllis quickly.

"Didn't say a word—just walked right past me."

Phyllis was seated near the rear of the sun-deck where she could watch Jon and her father work. Tom looked on for a little while, then climbed down to the new floor and began helping Jon mix cement. He glanced up at Phyllis and winked.

"Guess I'll have to show them how it's done."

"Guess you will!" snorted Jon.

"I did all right last year," came back Tom defiantly.

"You don't have to help us." Bob looked down from the scaffold with a worried frown. "After all, it's our job."

"But it's fun." Tom glanced at Phyllis for approval.

The next afternoon Tom came up and began helping instead of going swimming. Later Maria stopped in.

"Tessy went past this afternoon, walking," she reported. "He actually spoke to me."

"Weren't you flattered?" asked Jon from the scaffold.

She made a face at him, then climbed down from the sun-deck and added her help to Tom's. The following day at the usual swimming time she came over dressed in slacks and began piling stones on the bed of the scaffold within Jon's reach.

"No fun swimming with just the kids," she explained.

The sound of the children splashing and yelling down at the pool came up to them. But the kids stopped swimming earlier than usual this afternoon and wandered up to the new house, first to watch the work, then to carry stones.

A let-up came in vegetable canning and Jane joined them. She and Maria carried water for the cement.

Once Bob looked down from the scaffold at the swarming crowd below and remarked: "Looks like we have quite a crew on our job."

Phyllis complained: "You're having all the fun. If my leg was just well, I'd help too."

"We'll make you timekeeper," laughed her father.

But she couldn't sit still and watch. She pulled herself up on her crutches and swung back and forth across the sun-deck. Once she came to the rear to announce: "I just saw Tessy going along the road. I thought he waved, but maybe I was mistaken."

The others didn't seem to hear her. They were discussing Supervisor Byrd and the coming election. He was going to have a fight, Tom said.

"I hope he loses!" growled Jon.

"Who's running against him?" asked Bob.

"John Lang," spoke up Maria. "Mr. Holden's backing him. He's a war veteran."

"There should be quite a block of new voters out here this fall if they are induced to register," said Jane.

"Dad says that we've got to see that everyone who can vote does his duty at the polls this fall," stated Tom firmly.

"Have a lot of shots for one Byrd, eh?" remarked Bob with exaggerated soberness, and everyone whooped their laughter.

The walls of the new house seemed to go up twice as fast during that hour-and-a-half period every afternoon. Jon and Bob built wall from the scaffolding, while Tom, Jane and Maria kept them supplied with cement and stones. The younger children scampered around, helping, adding to the general confusion.

One afternoon when Maria started down to the pool for water for the cement she came face to face with Tod Sullivan-Schuyler at the corner of the living room. No one had noticed him come up the drive. His gray flannels were neatly pressed and his two-toned shoes spotless. He carried a box of candy under his arm.

Maria was too surprised to speak and Tod swallowed several times before he could say: "I'd like to see Miss Woodward."

"She—she's up on the sun-deck," stammered Maria, and hurried past him as if she were scared. Halfway down the hill she looked back and saw young Sullivan-Schuyler picking his way around the upper side of the new house to where all the activity was going on. Pails clattering, she ran the rest of the way to the pool. She wanted to get back and see what happened.

Tod Sullivan-Schuyler climbed around and over piles of stone, timbers, boards and sand to the open end of the house unit under construction. Before he was aware of it he came upon the busy workers.

George Scotti noticed him first and just stared. Jane saw the boy staring and turned to see what he was bug-eyed about. She blinked in amazement, then read the embarrassed, miserable look on young Sullivan-Schuyler's face.

"Why, hello there, Tod," she exclaimed.

All work came to an abrupt halt. Jon stared down open-mouthed from the scaffold. Tom Summers jerked his head up and his hands tightened on the handle of the cement hoe. Even Bob was surprised and held his trowel heaped with cement, forgetting what he had been about to do. But he was the first to recover.

"Hello, Tod. How're you?"

"Very well, sir, thank you." Tod spoke formally, but there was no evidence of affectation in his tone. He wet his lips. "I—uh—came to see—Miss Phyllis."

"Right through there." Bob pointed to the doorway opening upon the sun-deck; then he leaned over the unfinished wall and called: "You've got a caller, Phil."

Tod walked up the three steps to the sun-deck. Phyllis was as astonished as the others to see him. She had been reclining lazily in a deck chair, her injured leg stretched out on the support. At the sight of him she sat up, wide-eyed.

"Good afternoon." Tod managed a feeble smile and again seemed to lose his voice. "Uh—may I? Will you accept this box of sweets?" He laughed nervously. "Box of candy, I mean." He handed it to her.

"Oh, thank you." She held the box uncertainly for a moment, then began to unwrap it, fingers trembling.

Only Bob had resumed work. He poked energetically with his trowel. The others seemed frozen, but they were all trying desperately to hear what was said on the sun-deck.

Tod looked around helplessly and began: "Kind of dull—you know—nobody swimming down in the pool. . . ." He sat uncertainly on the edge of a chair, elbows on his knees.

The cover to the candy box finally came off from Phyllis's trembling efforts. "My, aren't they lovely!" She offered the assortment of chocolates to him, and he took a piece. "May I offer some to the others?" she asked.

"By all means." Then he added: "Sure, go ahead."

She pushed herself up, grasping her crutches. Tod

sprang up, arms outstretched, to assist her, but she swung expertly across the sun-deck, holding one crutch by the pressure of her elbow while her hand carried the box of chocolates.

"Do you working people want some candy?" she called when she reached the doorway to the room under construction. "Tod's brought me some chocolates."

They all stared up at her, but didn't move. Tom's face grew darker and Jon glowered fiercely. The younger children looked scared, but they licked their lips. Tod stood behind Phyllis in the doorway, his face flushed, his hands fidgeting with the edge of his tweed coat. No one came to get a piece of candy. Phyllis swung down the rough steps to the floor. She approached her mother first and offered her the candy.

"Thank you." Jane removed a glove and took a piece. "This was really nice of you, Tod," she added, smiling at the embarrassed boy.

Tod only grew more crimson and didn't reply. He slouched down the steps after Phyllis and nervously picked up a cement hoe to cover his confusion.

Phyllis offered Tom a piece of candy, but Tom's hand jerked back as if it would burn him. "They're good, Tom," she said, her eyes pleading with him. He took a piece. Then she offered the box up to her father on the scaffold.

"Guess I could use a little extra energy right now," Bob said with a chuckle.

Jon took a piece reluctantly, giving the embarrassed Tod a black look. The younger children needed no persuasion from Phyllis for them to accept the candy.

By the time everyone had taken a piece, Tod began to

control his embarrassment. He laid down the cement hoe gingerly. "I don't want to interrupt your work," he said. "I guess I'd better run along."

"Oh, you're not interrupting us," said Jane quickly.

Phyllis turned to protest his going, but her throat felt tight and she couldn't get words out.

"I'd like to come sometime and watch," said Tod, "if —if you—" He stalled.

"Sure, any time," said Bob genially.

Tod turned and disappeared around the house, leaving them staring after him in amazement.

It was Jon who found his tongue first. "This candy 'll probably make us sick."

"Now, Jon," said his mother sternly. "Bury the hatchet. You've no need to hold onto your grudge."

Just then Maria arrived with her pails of water. She stared at them, out of breath from hurrying, then panted: "What—what happened?"

Jane explained. Phyllis offered Maria some candy, adding: "Tod said it was dull now that no one went swimming in the pool in the afternoons."

"Do you think he'll really come around again?" Tom wondered aloud.

"I think so," said Jane. "He's lonesome."

"Well, if he does," groused Jon, "we'll put him to work."

"Jon!" warned his mother.

The work gradually got under way again.

Sure enough, the next afternoon Tod Sullivan-Schuyler appeared at the job. Phyllis was standing in the doorway to the sun-deck when he arrived, watching the others work.

"Good afternoon," he greeted. He smiled nervously, uncertain of his welcome.

Jane and Bob greeted him cordially; Tom, Jon and Maria just nodded. Phyllis said: "Come on up to the sun-deck, Tod."

"I'd like to watch them do this," he said, the smile on his face growing more firm.

A slight frown crossed Phyllis's face. The work continued, but everyone seemed a little self-conscious. Tod moved closer to where the cement was being mixed and watched the process carefully. Tom and Maria ignored him, and Jane acted as if he'd always been one of the gang. Jon and his father worked on steadily laying wall from the scaffold, but Jon's face wore a heavy scowl. Phyllis came down the three steps from the sun-deck and joined the group.

At last Tod seemed to have watched long enough. He picked up an extra hoe and began pawing at the sand and cement with tentative, exploratory, curious strokes. "How do you do this?" he asked hesitantly.

"You just mix it all up," said Tom haughtily.

"Tom's an expert cement-mixer," spoke up Phyllis quickly, and smiled appealingly at Tom.

Tom demonstrated how to hoe the sand and cement together. "Like this," he said, working with long, sure strokes.

Tod began to imitate him, learning rapidly.

"Now we make a hole in the center," Tom explained, trying to be very academic with his demonstration. He hoed the loose mixture from the center to the outside, walking around the pile until a crater rose up on the floor. "Now, Maria, water!"

Maria poured a full pail into the crater. Some of it splashed, splattering olive-green drops on Tod Sullivan-Schuyler's clean flannels. Maria gulped and stared, horrified.

"Think nothing of it, my girl." Tod gave an indolent wave of his hand and some of his old glibness returned to his tone. Then he caught himself and added: "It doesn't matter. They're an old pair anyhow."

To hide more embarrassment, he peeled off his sports coat and began mixing the water with the sand and cement in earnest. Before the batch was thoroughly wetted down, Tod and Tom were trying to outdo each other at the job. Now everyone present seemed to realize that the stiffness among them was gradually vanishing. The usual talk and kidding started up again.

Phyllis sat down on a pile of lumber, her crutches propped beside her and complained: "This is what always happens. People come to visit me and before I know it, they've left me alone and are helping to build the house."

"You're our decoy, Phil," laughed Bob. "You'd better get back up on the sun-deck and start enticing more help up here."

They all laughed at this remark, even Tod.

The fresh batch of cement was scooped to the box on the scaffold and Tod said eagerly: "Let me do the next, will you?"

Tom and the others looked a bit startled.

Jane, who acted as foreman of the ground crew, said:

"All right, Tod, you mix the cement. Tom and I will get more stones up on the scaffold."

Maria went down to the pool for more water.

Everyone worked energetically. Occasionally Tod asked: "How'm I doin', Tom?"

Every time Tod spoke, Tom and all the others seemed surprised at his normal speech. Jon, up on the scaffold, glanced down several times to make sure he'd heard right. Finally the dry mix was completed, then water was added until a proper paste consistency was achieved, then Tod attempted to scoop it up to the box on the staging. Handling that soft, runny stuff on the scoop wasn't so easy. Once he tipped the edge of the shovel too steeply and the full load slid back over the top of the scoop, splattering down the length of his neat flannels.

"Oh!" screamed Phyllis and Jane in horror.

Tod, Tom, Jon, and Bob all stared at the ruined trousers. Then Tod laughed as if it were a good joke. "Guess they're no worse than the pair you fixed for me last summer, eh, Jon?" He grinned at Jon on the staging. "Remember that handful of mud you tossed for me to catch?" He went on laughing.

Jon's face reddened. He tapped his trowel against the scaffold. "That was a dirty trick I pulled on you," he admitted.

Tod gave him a deprecating wave of the hand. "Think nothing of it. I had it coming to me, old boy. If you recall, I had been behaving a bit aloof."

All of them realized that he was mimicking himself and they burst out laughing.

"Guess you're a bit of all right, old chap," came back

Bob, and the laughter grew louder, and Tod seemed to enjoy the joke on himself as much as any of them.

When six o'clock came and the helpers began to break away to go home, Tod was still with them. He was tired, his hands blistered, his clothes a sight. But he said: "Do you mind if I join you tomorrow? This is fun, working on the swim shift."

"Swim shift!" All of them stared at him.

"Sure. You used to go swimming at this time," he explained, "so this is sort of the swim shift, isn't it?"

Thereafter this period from four-thirty to six was called the swim shift. It was the high point of the day's work and Tod Sullivan-Schuyler was never an absentee.

One week before the end of Bob's vacation the walls were roughed up and he said: "We'll get the roof on before I go back to Universal."

"Looks like our house will be pretty well grown by fall," remarked Jon.

"Do you think it'll ripen before frost?" Jane asked, laughing.

That afternoon the doctor removed the cast from Phyllis's ankle, and she began to learn to walk again. And Jane said to Jon and Bob: "You needn't expect much more help from me. I'll have my hands full getting Phyllis ready for college."

CHAPTER TWENTY-THREE

JON MAKES A SPEECH

BOB and Jon got the roof on the new unit of the house the last week of Bob's vacation. This time they used a Celotex shingle that required no sheeting under it. The sound of their hammering thundered over Five Acre Hill, and every afternoon the swim shift showed up to help.

One day Tom asked Jon where he was going to high school—New Delphi or Wayne? Jon hadn't made up his mind. "I don't know yet."

"We've got a good school in Wayne," said Tom.

On another afternoon, Tod Sullivan-Schuyler remarked to Bob: "Mr. Woodward, Uncle Merri was hinting around the other day, wondering if he could get your support for him in his campaign for Supervisor this November."

Bob bristled and Jane stiffened, and all of them wondered if Tod's change had been engineered to this end.

"Don't shoot!" said Tod. "Unc put on a fine act when he learned I was coming over here to help you. But later he got the idea of making political capital out of it."

"Are you serious, Tod?" Bob asked, with eyebrows pinched.

"Yes, sir. I'm not kidding."

"Well, we've come to like you, Tod, but your uncle

has made it plain that he's not a fit person for public office."

Tod chuckled. "I told him you folks felt that way and he didn't like it much, so I promised to use my influence." He laughed and the others joined. "Unc's not so bad when you get him away from politics and the idea that he's one of America's first families."

"I hope we can beat him at the election," spoke up Jon. "I don't care if he is your uncle."

"Personally, I think it'd do the old boy good," replied Tod, "but don't quote me."

They all laughed heartily.

Then Tom started talking for Jon's benefit. "There's going to be a good political fight this fall. And we have fun at school. Mr. Carsen, the superintendent, let us campaign in school just as if we were old enough to vote. We have party rallies and speeches and the Monday before election we vote."

Jon took all that in and after supper that night he announced that he wanted to go to high school in Wayne.

He started a week later, riding on the school bus with Maria and Tom and the other children. That was different from going to school in New Delphi, and he liked it.

There were still two weeks before Phyllis had to leave for college. She was able to get around now without her crutches. Tod Sullivan-Schuyler was going to college too and likewise had two weeks of vacation still. For one of those two weeks, he came over every afternoon and chatted with Phyllis and Jane.

Tom Summers heaved a sigh the following Sunday when Tod announced that he was leaving in the morning to get ready to go to Yale. "See you next summer," he said to all of them, but especially, it seemed to Tom, to Phyllis. They all waved "good-by" as he went swinging down the drive to the road.

Again this fall Jon went out for football. The coach in Wayne High School started him playing tackle, the same position he had played last year in Van Buren High, but after a few afternoons of playing, he was moved into the backfield, playing halfback opposite Tom Summers. But football practice after school took Jon away from work on the new house.

Bob continued to work in the evenings after he got home from Universal, and the two of them worked on Sundays. It continued to grow and "ripen," as Jane put it. They got the windows in and began finishing off the rooms inside, putting in partitions and window and door frames.

By the end of September, however, it was too dark for Bob to work after he got home from New Delphi. One evening he remarked: "If we just had the place wired for electricity I could work in the evenings, dark or not."

"Well, why don't you have the place wired?" asked Jane.

"Just the little matter of our ten dollars a week, Moms," he replied.

Jane didn't answer for several minutes, then she said: "Now that Phyllis is settled at college and we're not paying rent here as we had to in New Delphi, I don't see why we can't put more money into Five Acre Hill."

"But, Moms, we came out here under the stipulation that we'd put no more than ten dollars a week into the place." Bob winked at Jon and Jon's eyes grew bright with amusement.

"Well, I think I'd like to move over to the new house from the cabin before winter sets in," said Jane.

"Guess we'd better put it to a vote." Bob pinched a grin. "How do you feel about it, Jon?"

"It's okay with me, Dad."

"Stop being so legal!" Jane twitched her shoulders, provoked at their teasing.

After that, things began to happen at the new house. Bob wired it and signed the contract for the electric company to bring the power up from the road. Fixtures arrived for the kitchen and bathroom. Bob even bought a furnace, and it was set up in the basement and connected to hot-air ducts.

"We're not going to get everything done before it gets cold," Bob said, so they concentrated on the kitchen. It was finished and Jane painted the walls. Then the one bedroom and the dining room were finished and painted.

Now Jane and Bob moved over to the new house, leaving the cabin to Jon and the surplus furniture. As soon as the electricity was turned on Bob worked after supper and Jon helped him after finishing his school homework. They attached the bathroom fixtures and laid a linoleum tile floor. By the end of October the new house had become quite livable.

Meanwhile Jon was having an exciting time at school. Wayne had a good football team—Tom Summers and Jon Woodward made a fine pair of halfbacks. So far the team had won every game.

The local election campaign grew hotter by the day,

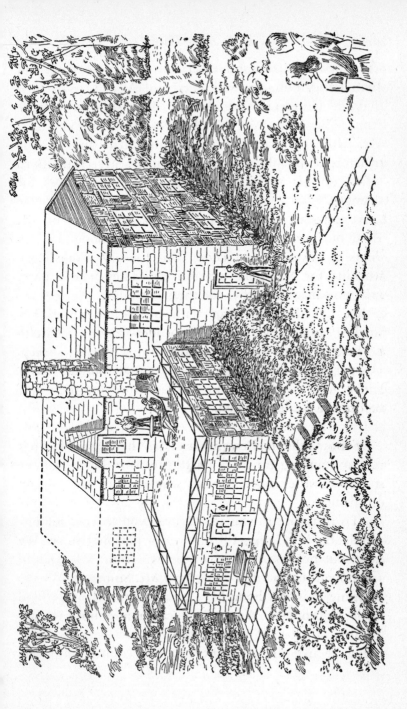

with the principal contest between Merrivale Byrd and John Lang. Bob, Joe Summers, and Al Scotti saw to it that the newcomers into Wayne Township were registered. They talked up John Lang who was supported by Mr. Holden, owner of the lumberyard, and by the progressive people of the community. Merrivale Byrd relied on his political machine and his relatives for strength.

At the start of the campaign, the supporters of Mr. Byrd outnumbered those of Mr. Lang among the students in Wayne High School. But Jon and Tom began working for Mr. Lang aggressively. They held a party rally and made speeches for their candidate.

Jon talked things over with his father while they worked on the new house. He got ideas for the debate to be held the day before election, and wrote his speech. His party had selected him, as a popular football player and a good speaker, to say the last word for their side before the students voted.

"Fellow schoolmates and friends," he began. He felt uneasy standing up there on the rostrum before all the students in the school; his hair seemed to be standing up on his neck.

"To illustrate to you why I urge you to vote for our candidate, Mr. Lang, I'll tell you a personal story. We came out here more than a year ago from New Delphi and bought five acres of land from Mr. Summers. We are building it into a home. We have cleared the land and made it produce. We built a cabin and now we are building a house. This has been fun—it's been exciting. We were like the forefathers of our country, pioneers coming to new land and building homes. But we were twentieth-century pioneers.

"With us came money—a little, to be sure—but before I finish I will show you how that little brought by one family can be multiplied into much by many families."

Jon's hand shot out, finger pointing: "Harry Dawson, your father plowed our field for us." His finger swung across the room: "Mary Parsens, your father delivered many loads of material for us from the lumberyard." His finger jabbed again. "Sylvia Larsen, we have bought many groceries at your father's store." Jon paused. His fingers fumbled with his notes.

"Now don't get the idea that I think we did you a favor. Favors don't enter this picture. We did what we did in buying our five acres and building our home because it was fun—the most fun anybody can have. But in having fun we brought work to your father, Harry, and your father, Mary, and business to your father's store, Sylvia."

Jon took a deep breath. "Since we moved here, fifteen other families have moved out here from New Delphi. The fathers in the families still work in the city and on their free days they are building their homes here. None of them have moved here permanently like we have, but they will in a few years, and there'll be still more to come. Their coming has meant more work for Wayne Township residents and more business for Wayne's business people.

"There's enough land not being lived on in Wayne Township to take a thousand families." Again he pointed: "That will mean more plowing to do than your father can get done, Harry, and more material to haul than your father can haul from the lumberyard, Mary, and your father, Sylvia, will have to get a bigger store.

"All of these families will have fun—they'll have more fun than they've ever had in their lives, like we've had during this past year. They'll be happy. And, most important, they'll be building homes for America, the greatest constructive thing anyone can do for our country."

Jon paused and got a pattering of applause. He took a deep breath and continued: "Now Mr. Byrd, the incumbent supervisor, opposed our coming to Wayne Township. I won't bother to tell you the many ways he tried to force us to give up our project. He was violently against our coming, and he is against the coming of more families. He is against the welcoming of more work and wealth into Wayne Township—work and wealth which will benefit all of us.

"Our candidate, Mr. Lang, stands for increasing the wealth of Wayne Township. He's for a community of happy, prosperous American homes.

"Judge for yourself, then. Will you re-elect a man who tries to keep wealth and happiness from coming to Wayne Township, or will you elect a man who stands to do everything in his power to bring that wealth and happiness here? My friends, vote for Mr. John Lang!"

He sat down and the auditorium shook with applause.

Russel Collins, a freckled-faced boy, made the speech for Mr. Byrd. He attacked the foreigners coming to Wayne Township; he warned against the trickery of the city slickers settling among them.

Someone in the audience yelled: "How about city

slicker Woodward playin' football? Why don't *you* play football?"

Mr. Carsen, the superintendent, intervened for order.

Russ Collins went on to praise Mr. Byrd for lowering taxes and maintaining an efficient county management.

During the three-minute rebuttal, Jon pointed out that all present were foreigners or descendants of foreigners, that only the Indians had a right to the real name of Americans, hence Mr. Byrd's supporter was attacking his own candidate and himself as well as everybody present. On the subject of taxes, he said: "It is simple mathematics. Perhaps Mr. Byrd has kept taxes low. But if a thousand families are encouraged to come to Wayne Township, they will improve the township, they will increase the amount collected in taxes, which will reduce the taxes on individuals even lower than they now are."

After the debate the students voted.

When Jon went to his seat in the study hall, Maria Scotti whispered to him as he passed: "That was a swell speech, Jon." He noticed the closed shorthand book before her on the desk. Tom Summers waved to him across the hall.

At noon the vote of the school was announced and Mr. Lang won by fifty-three votes. Jon reported the vote at home.

"I hope it's like that tomorrow," said his father.

On Election Day all the fifteen new families who had bought property in Wayne Township and had built cabins here, came down and voted. Bob and Jane went to the polls and cast their vote; then Bob hurried back home to work on the house.

Jon got a surprise that day. Maria Scotti had taken his speech down in shorthand and typed it out. Tom showed the transcript to Mr. Lang, who had it printed Monday afternoon and distributed to everyone in the township.

Election night the Woodwards stayed up late, listening to returns reported over the radio. They didn't expect to hear how the local contest came out until the following day, but at eleven o'clock a loud knock on the front door preceded Tom Summers' violent entrance.

"Mr. Lang won!" he shouted. "Nine hundred majority!"

Bob and Jon both whooped, and Jane said: "Well, I guess that's giving Mr. Byrd the bird."

Jon went to bed proud and happy. They had won out. And he could look ahead with a feeling of satisfaction that the new house would be in pretty good order when Phyllis came home for Thanksgiving.

CHAPTER TWENTY-FOUR

SECOND THANKSGIVING

THE day before Thanksgiving Jon and Jane deco-
rated the new house with ground pine and red
winter berries. It was planned that they would eat before the big fireplace in the living room, and the dining
room was turned into a bedroom for Phyllis.

She arrived Wednesday evening, quite the young lady
now, pleased with Jon's "Gee, you look pretty, Phil."

"Howdy, politician," she replied.

Thanksgiving dinner the next day was more orderly
and to Jane's liking than it had been the year before, but
the family's exuberance was undimmed and their appetites were as hearty as ever. Jane folded her arms and
smiled with satisfaction. Certainly her efforts were ap-
preciated.

Late in the afternoon Tom Summers came over. He
didn't seem to know quite what to say to Phyllis at first;
then she started talking biology, amoebas and worms,
and he lost all his shyness abruptly.

Jon got up in disgust at such conversation and went
up the road to Scotti's. "Come on over, Maria," he said,
and she walked back with him.

They found that Phyllis had turned on the radio and
she and Tom were dancing. Even Jane and Bob danced.
Once when Jon and Maria stopped dancing and stood by

the open window to get some fresh air, Jon said: "Next year I'll be away to college."

"So will I," replied Maria.

"But we'll be home for Thanksgiving." He studied her face against the heavy drapes of the window. "By next fall Dad and I will almost have our house finished."

"Won't that be wonderful!" She smiled at him suddenly, her dark eyes bright.

He looked out of the window. "And someday I want to build a house for myself just like Dad and I built this one."

"I want to help build my own home," Maria said. "I want to help with my own hands the way your mother helped you and your dad." Her glance turned back to the increasing brightness of the moon in the early evening.

The music stopped, the announcer brought in a diffent program, and Phyllis snapped off the radio. Then she said: "I almost forgot, I got a letter from Tod last week. He says his uncle is going into the real estate business since he lost the election—he's going to sell his estate. And Tod said he hopes to be here next summer to work on the swim shift to finish the house. He says he never had so much fun before."

"Hooray for Tod," yelled Jon. "He's an all-right guy after all."

But Tom frowned and remained silent. Noticing, Phyllis whispered: "Tod's going to study law, Tom. I don't think that law and my interest in biology would mix well, do you?"

A big grin spread over his lean face.

Then Jane came down from the kitchen proudly

carrying the punch bowl and cups. They all gathered around and lifted full cups while Bob proposed a toast.

"Here's to Five Acre Hill. It's our home. We've built it ourselves. It isn't finished. But a home should never be completely finished, because the fun of a home is in the building. But if I'm never able to do anything else for America I shall be content with the thought that I've done one of the most important things any man can do for his country and that is to build a home." He looked at the four youngsters. "I hope that all of you will be able to do the same within the next two decades."

They drank deep.

Jon said: "Dad, shall we break the cups?"

"Heavens, no!" said his mother. "I'm not going up to the kitchen for more, and there's still punch to drink."

Their laughter filled the large living room, burst through the open windows and rang over the land of Five Acre Hill.